BLACKSTONE AND THE TIGER

Recent Titles by Sally Spencer from Severn House

THE DARK LADY
DEAD ON CUE
DEATH OF A CAVE DWELLER
DEATH OF AN INNOCENT
A DEATH LEFT HANGING
THE ENEMY WITHIN
GOLDEN MILE TO MURDER
MURDER AT SWANN'S LAKE
THE PARADISE JOB
THE RED HERRING
THE SALTON KILLINGS

writing as Alan Rustage

The Inspector Blackstone Series

RENDEZVOUS WITH DEATH

BLACKSTONE AND THE TIGER

BLACKSTONE
AND THE TIGER

Sally Spencer

writing as

Alan Rustage

This first world edition published in Great Britain 2003 by
SEVERN HOUSE PUBLISHERS LTD of
9–15 High Street, Sutton, Surrey SM1 1DF.
This first world edition published in the USA 2004 by
SEVERN HOUSE PUBLISHERS INC of
595 Madison Avenue, New York, N.Y. 10022.

British Library Cataloguing in Publication Data

Rustage, Alan, 1949-
  Blackstone and the tiger
  1. Kidnapping - England - London - Fiction
  2. London (England) - Social life and customs - 19th century - Fiction
  3. Detective and mystery stories
  I. Title II. Spencer, Sally, 1949-
  823.9'14 [F]

ISBN 0-7278-5933-1

Except where actual historical events and characters are being
described for the storyline of this novel, all situations in this
publication are fictitious and any resemblance to living persons
is purely coincidental.

Typeset by Palimpsest Book Production Ltd.,
Polmont, Stirlingshire, Scotland.
Printed and bound in Great Britain by
MPG Books Ltd., Bodmin, Cornwall.

Chandrapore, Northern India, 1897

From his balcony, the Maharaja could see both the gardens which surrounded his palace and the town which lay beyond. It was a view much admired by the representatives of the British Raj, but even their appreciation – as they devoured it with their greedy, acquisitive eyes – had not succeeded in souring the pleasure he took from it himself.

A unit of his army was being drilled in the *maidan* – the town square. He watched it for a few moments with the trained eye of an ex-soldier, then nodded his head in approval. His men were good – much better than the soldiers from any of the neighbouring princely states. Which was not to say, of course, that they would be any match for the British Army. No, should they choose to, the British could sweep through Chandrapore in a matter of days.

The Maharaja had once seen a tightrope walker in a travelling circus, and it struck him now that his task involved as much of a balancing act as that performed by the man on the high wire. His army was just one case in point. If it had been any weaker, the British would have considered the state such easy pickings that they would have been unable to resist the temptation to overrun it. If, on the other hand, it had been any *stronger*, they might have perceived it as a threat which must be dealt with before it grew any more out of hand. By keeping it at just the size it was, he offered a warning – without making that warning into a threat.

His uncle would never have been capable of such a delicate balance, he thought. If his uncle had still been

1

ruler, Chandrapore would have become a part of British India long ago.

His mind drifted back to the outbreak of the Second Afghan War, when he himself had been a colonel in the Chandrapore State Army.

'We must help the British to fight the Afghans,' his weak-spirited uncle had told him. 'We must show them we are their true friends by offering them the use of our troops.'

The offer had been duly made, and the Viceroy had accepted it. The Colonel had suspected that the acceptance had more to do with tact and diplomacy than actual military necessity – for just as an adult will agree to let a child help him in a task rather than hurt that child's feelings, so the Viceroy had welcomed assistance from Chandrapore. Not that the Colonel had been against the plan himself. He was a soldier, and is such, welcomed the possibility of active service. So he ha ' taken his contingent of infantrymen, cavalry, camels and elephants up to the frontier, where it had fought side by side with the British Army.

He had acquitted himself well in the war, and had been invited to train with the Honourable Artillery Company on English soil.

'You must go,' his uncle had said. 'There is no question of it. It would be an insult to the Viceroy if we refused.'

The old maharaja had never seemed to realize that he was a monarch in his own right – never fully appreciated the fact that he was the heir (albeit an unworthy one) to a long and distinguished line of warriors and statesmen. The rulers of the state had always borne the title of Tiger of Chandrapore, but in his uncle's case the *Worm of Chandrapore* would have been a more appropriate one. Why, the man had been so afraid of the British that there was no act of subservience that was beyond him. Yet, once more, since the uncle's plans concurred with the nephew's own wishes, the Colonel had held his peace and gone to England.

It had been while under training with the Honourable Artillery Company that he started to plot his *coup d'état.*

It would be a gamble, certainly, he argued with himself. The British did not like to see any change of Indian rulers in which they had played no part. On the other hand, if he could convince them that a change of government meant no threat to the British position, the Viceroy might just be willing to let it slide.

Fortunately, no such gamble had been necessary. The spine had not been the only part of his body in which the old maharaja lacked power, and he had died leaving only daughters behind him. That did not give the Colonel all he might have wished for, of course, because it was his father, not he himself, who ascended to his uncle's throne. Thoughts of patricide naturally began to enter the Colonel's mind, but before these thoughts had time to develop, his father had had the good grace to contract a fever and die. And thus it was that the Colonel was a colonel no longer, but the Maharaja of Chandrapore.

'Father! Father!' shouted an excited voice behind him.

The Maharaja turned to face the new arrival. Though the boy was only six, it was already obvious that he would grow to be a tall, well-built man. And a beautiful one, the Maharaja thought. His hair, now hidden by an elaborate gold turban, was thick, shiny and jet-black. He had huge dark eyes, like those of his dead mother, and a smooth skin which was more olive than brown. Whenever he appeared in public, the people gasped at the sight of him. He was, indeed, a golden child.

'Is it true, Father?' the boy asked.

'Is what true?' the Maharaja asked, sweeping the boy up into his arms.

'Is it true that we are going to England?'

'Yes, it is. But how did you find out?'

The boy looked down at his hands, as if he had suddenly realized that perhaps he had said too much. 'One of the palace monkeys told me.'

His father laughed. 'Perhaps that is true,' he conceded, 'but I'll warrant that this particular monkey had a chamberlain's chain of office around his neck. Tell me, my boy, does the news please you?'

'Oh yes, Father. It pleases me greatly.'

'Then perhaps you will tell me where England is.'

'Isn't it near to Bombay?' the boy asked hopefully.

The Maharaja laughed delightedly. 'No, it is much further away than Bombay. It is far across the ocean.'

'Like Ceylon?' the boy asked.

'Even further. Did the chattering monkey who revealed this news to you before I had chance to do so myself happen to tell you *why* we are going?'

'Yes, we are going to see Queen Victoria. But why do you not just order her to come and see us?'

The Maharaja smiled at his son's naivety, though the edges of that smile were somewhat tempered by his own resentment. How could he explain to the boy that a maharaja had absolute power over life and death in his own state, and yet was expected to bow his head to a foreign queen? Could Balachandra even begin to understand that while his father was a king to his subjects, he was only a prince in the eyes of the British, since the only monarch they recognized in India was their own?

'If I ordered her to come here instead of us going there, it would be she who had the holiday, not us,' the Maharaja said to his son. 'Is that fair?'

'No, it isn't,' the boy agreed. He paused for a moment. 'Father . . .'

'Yes, my son?'

'Is to see Queen Victoria our *only* reason for going?'

'What other reason could there be?'

'I hoped . . . I hoped . . .'

'Yes?'

'I hoped you might be looking for a new wife.'

'For a new mother for you, you mean.'

'Yes,' the boy confessed. 'For a new mother for me.'

The Maharaja felt a stabbing pain in his heart. Balachandra had never known the mother who had died giving him birth, yet despite the scores of retainers who constantly fussed over him, he still felt the need for her.

'We will find you a new mother soon,' the Maharaja

promised, 'but she will come from India, not England.' He placed his son back on the floor and patted his head. 'I am happy that you came to see me, but I have many serious matters still to think about, and so now you must go away again.'

'Of course, Father,' the small boy said dutifully.

The Maharaja watched as the boy crossed the room and disappeared into the corridor. There had been a time when he had had ambitions for himself, but that was no longer the case. If he had hopes of expanding Chandrapore at the expense of his neighbours, if he wished to see the British leave and the Maharaja of Chandrapore become emperor of all India – and both these things were very much in his mind – then these dreams were not for his own benefit, but for his son's. Balachandra was the very centre of his being. He loved the child with all his heart.

The Maharaja looked down on to the gardens. In the orchard, the honeybees were busily engaged in collecting nectar from the blossom. In the water garden, two servants were clearing away weed which threatened to clog the stream. And in the rose garden, the young Prince Nagesh, the Maharaja's cousin, sat on a carved bench and gazed at the distant horizon as if he could see his future written there.

Nagesh seemed aware that he was being watched. Indeed, there were times when it appeared as if he deliberately chose to position himself in a place where his cousin could not fail to notice him.

'Here I am, Mahavir!' he seemed to be saying, by his very presence. 'Look at me! See how regal I am. My father was younger than yours, which is why you are maharaja and I am not. But do not worry – my time will come.'

'Never!' the Maharaja said aloud to the challenge which had never actually been put into words. 'Never will I allow that to happen. My throne is for Balachandra. It is his right.'

He wished that he could have Nagesh killed. But he knew that, as powerful as he was, such a bold act would be a step too far. Nagesh had his supporters in the court – men who

5

would probably not risk their own necks in an attempt to put him on the throne but would willingly face the possibility of death to avenge his murder. And so, for a while longer at least, Nagesh must be allowed to continue living.

Another man had now joined Nagesh on the bench – a spindly man with thick wire glasses. No sooner had he sat down than the two of them fell into earnest conversation, so intense they could almost have been plotting.

But whatever Nagesh might think, there was no plot being hatched there, the Maharaja told himself. Sapan Aggarwal was not only his secretary, he was his *man*. Aggarwal recognized that, but for the Maharaja's generosity, he would still be bent over a desk in a dusty Bombay office. He saw clearly where his future lay, and when his master had asked him to pretend to make friends with Nagesh – the better to establish what thoughts were going through the ambitious prince's mind – he had readily agreed.

The spindly secretary was gesturing towards the town. Perhaps he was suggesting to Nagesh that, but for an accident of birth, all this could have been his. But the prince had better be careful how he answered such statements, especially when there were more witnesses around. Were he to utter anything which might be construed as treasonable, then even those courtiers who supported him would not dare to object when he was executed.

The Maharaja turned away from the garden and walked over to his desk. There was a pile of papers there relating to his journey to England, and when Aggarwal finally returned from his task as *agent provocateur* to Nagesh's conspirator, the final details would need to be confirmed.

It was vital that the trip went well, the Maharaja told himself. It did not so much matter what was said while he was there – the vital thing was what was *understood*. The British government must learn to appreciate the fact that the political stability of Chandrapore depended on his continuing rule. They must come to believe that the queen had no more loyal ally than he – and perhaps she didn't, for there was not a prince in the whole of India who would not stab the British in the back if he thought he could get away with it. And, most important of all, there must be an acknowledgement that Balachandra was the rightful heir to the throne of Chandrapore – and that the British would back his claim, with bayonets if needed.

The Maharaja picked up a cigar with one hand and a silver bell with the other. Then, after a second's thought, he replaced the bell on the desk. He didn't want the arrival of servants to interrupt his train of thought at that moment, and in order to avoid such an inconvenience, he was perfectly willing to perform the onerous task of lighting his cigar himself.

He inhaled the smoke, and relished the soothing effect it had on him. There was no need to worry about the expedition to England, he thought. His secretary, the ever-efficient Aggarwal, had the whole matter in hand. Even the dispatch of the beast, with which he intended to create a huge sensation on the streets of London, was well underway. It would all run as smoothly as clockwork.

And having thus assured himself that nothing could possibly go wrong, the Maharaja turned his thoughts to further triumphs he could as yet see only hazily in the even more distant future.

The Maharaja was not unique in such musings. It was a common trait of great men to plan ahead in such a manner. No doubt Julius Caesar and Abraham Lincoln had done exactly the same thing.

One

London, August 1898

Sam Blackstone, one-time orphan, sometime soldier and currently a detective inspector in the London Metropolitan Police, placed his fingers firmly in his ears and awaited the worst.

The worst came, a few seconds later. The horrendous clang of a thirteen and a half ton bell being struck by a four hundred and fifty pound mechanical hammer made his eardrums screech with protest, despite the protection his fingers had given them. The rest of his body, too, protested at the experience – trembling as the shock waves passed though it, and continuing to tremble even after they had gone.

Showing no sense of mercy or compassion, the great bell just above his head reverberated a second time, and while this should have been easier to assimilate now the novelty had gone, the ears and legs quickly informed the Inspector of the contrary.

Blackstone removed his fingers from his ears. His head seemed to be ringing at least as loudly as Big Ben had done, but he supposed that he should be grateful the kidnappers had set the exchange to take place at two o'clock, rather than at midday.

The Inspector walked to the edge of the parapet of the bell tower, and focused his field glasses on Westminster Bridge. It was said that if London was the heart of the British Empire, then it was the horses which kept that heart beating at such a rate. And looking down, Blackstone had no doubt that was true.

9

There were dozens of horses on the bridge at that moment. Teams of four pulled the double-decker omnibuses by which the less affluent members of the public travelled around the city. Single horses sat between the shafts of the hansom cabs which the more prosperous used as their means of transportation. Then there were the goods vehicles – the furniture and livestock vans which needed at least six horses to move them; the chimney sweep's van which, though loaded down with sacks of soot, made do with one old nag.

The pavements, too, were choked, but with bustling pedestrians – workmen and clerks, beggars and flower sellers. At that time of the afternoon, the traffic flowing across the bridge was almost as deep and relentless as the river which flowed under it, the Inspector thought – and the kidnappers would have been well aware of that.

Blackstone fixed his glasses on the almost portly young man standing at the midpoint of the bridge. The man was wearing a top hat and slightly worn, slightly old-fashioned frock coat. In his hand, he was carrying a bulging leather attaché case.

The Inspector chuckled at the memory of his sergeant's disappointed expression when he had been presented with what was to be the first frock coat ever to have graced his back.

'Couldn't we have laid our hands on something a bit smarter?' Patterson had asked.

'Yes, we could have,' Blackstone had replied. 'And if the object of this exercise had been to impress some young women of your acquaintance, no expense would have been spared in making you look the perfect ladies' man. But that's not our aim, is it, Sergeant?'

'No, sir.'

'So what *are* you supposed to look like?'

'A tight-fisted northern industrialist who'd rather limp than pay a doctor's bill.'

'Exactly. And may I just say that in that coat, you'll fit the description to a T.'

And he did, Blackstone thought. Anyone who took the time

to study him at close quarters would soon see that he was far too fresh-faced to be Obadiah Ramsbottom, but based on their previous form, the kidnappers were unlikely to linger.

Blackstone shifted his gaze from Patterson to the blind clog dancer, otherwise known as Detective Constable Dove. The constable wasn't doing a bad job at all, he thought. Dove was clumsy – but not *too* clumsy. And he had certainly assumed the air of a man who knew that a few coins, thrown in pity, were all that stood between him and starvation.

He moved the glasses again, and briefly studied the costermonger who appeared to be taking a rest from the heavy work of pushing his barrow up and down the streets. Very convincing, as was the flower girl, despite her distinctly masculine build.

Everything – and everyone – was in place. The trap was set, and now all that remained was to wait for the prey to fall into it.

Two

The first kidnapping had occurred several weeks earlier, in mid-June. The victim was Vanessa Elizabeth Todd, the eleven-year-old daughter of a prosperous merchant banker and the eldest of his six children. She'd disappeared on a family expedition to London Zoo.

'Vanessa went off to buy a bag of buns so that the other children could feed them to the animals,' the tearful governess who'd been in charge of the expedition had explained. 'She's normally a very responsible girl. But she . . . she just didn't come back.'

'You searched the zoo thoroughly?' Blackstone asked.

'No, I . . . not personally. I stayed with the other children. But the coachman, Thomas, and James, who's the second footman, were both with us, and they . . . and they . . .'

'They searched?'

'Yes.'

Which was a bit like closing the stable door after the giraffes had bolted, Blackstone had thought.

But he hadn't said it out loud. Either the woman was the best actress since Lily Langtry – in which case it would have been a pointless statement to make – or, more likely, she was telling the truth – so reminding her of her failure would have been unnecessarily cruel.

The servants, too, seemed so open and honest that Blackstone would have ruled them out of his inquiry even if he hadn't received the report on the mysterious woman – heavily veiled – who'd been seen leaving the zoo with a girl who matched Vanessa Todd's description.

The girl had seemed to show some reluctance to leave, but the woman had been most insistent. It couldn't have sounded more like a kidnapping if there'd been a town crier walking ahead of them to proclaim the abduction.

A ransom note arrived, just as Blackstone had expected it would. In what was a barely legible scrawl, it told Mr Todd that if he ever wanted to see his darling daughter again, he would place one hundred pounds in an attaché case and take it to Victoria Station.

'We think that you should pay it,' Blackstone had told the girl's concerned father. 'A hundred pounds is by no means a *small* amount of money, but I imagine you can easily afford to raise it. And once the kidnappers have their ransom, they'll release your daughter.'

'But what if they don't do that? Might they not . . .' the merchant banker gulped as he struggled to maintain his stiff-upper-lip, '. . . might they not just kill her?'

'Why *should* they? They'll have the money. You will have fulfilled your part of the contract. What possible reason could they have to run the risk of being hanged?'

'They may ask for a further ransom,' the merchant banker had pointed out.

'They won't.'

'But how can you know that?'

'This is a very amateur gang,' Blackstone had assured him.

'They demanded a hundred pounds, which – it is true – is probably a fortune to them. But if they'd truly known their business, they'd have studied your background and asked for much more. And *being* amateur, they'll also be nervous, which means they'll release your daughter as soon as they possibly can. You'll get her back – as well as most of your money. And I'll get my criminals.'

'How?'

'Because they *are* so amateur. Once they have the hard cash in their hands, they won't be able to resist spending it. And in the world they move in, a man with a guinea in his pocket is headline news. It won't be long before one of my informers leads me to the gang.'

'You make it sound so easy.'

'It is so easy,' Blackstone had replied – almost regretfully, for he enjoyed the art of detecting. 'Trust me, and I'll return your daughter to you.'

The merchant banker handed the ransom over to a nondescript little man on Victoria Station. The detectives posted to follow the kidnapper soon lost him in the crowd, just as Blackstone had known they would. The girl was found – dazed but unharmed – by a uniformed constable on Mile End Road, less than an hour later.

Then Blackstone sat back and waited. Sooner or later, he'd told himself, he would receive the information that a normally down-at-heel criminal was splashing around money at the dogs or at the Whitechapel Wonderland. All he had to do was be patient.

He *was* patient – but he waited in vain for the lead he was expecting.

13

Three

Nothing out of the ordinary seemed to be happening on Westminster Bridge, though sufficient time had passed for the chiming in Blackstone's ears to have disappeared almost completely.

Patterson still stood there clutching his attaché case to him as if it contained something of value, the clog dancer continued to dance, and the flower girl with the broad shoulders glared discouragingly at anyone who looked as if he might be intending to buy a bunch of violets or a single red rose.

Blackstone checked his watch. Five minutes past two. Were the kidnappers merely late, or were they not planning to turn up at all?

On the bridge, Sergeant Patterson found himself thinking, none too warmly, about Obadiah Ramsbottom.

'A thousand pound?' the northern manufacturer had exclaimed, when he had received a ransom note written in the same hand as the one which had been sent to Mr Todd. '*A thousand pound!* That's outrageous! I could build meself a whole new mill for a thousand pound!'

'We're concerned with your son's safety here,' Sam Blackstone had reminded him quietly.

'That's as mebee. But we know value of our brass up north, an' a thousand pound is still a lot of money. Besides, I pay me taxes – an' a damn sight too many of them in my opinion. I expect the police to protect me from scoundrels like these. It's time you started earnin' them fancy wages of yours, Inspector.'

Blackstone, who pledged half his wage to Doctor Barnardo's orphanages and could barely get by on what was left, permitted himself a thin smile. 'My sergeant will take your place on the bridge, if you wish. Now, if you could just see your way clear to advancing us the ransom money—'

'I'll do no such thing,' Ramsbottom had replied firmly. 'Use torn-up newspaper to pad out your bag with.'

And, since there seemed to be no point in pushing the matter any further, that was exactly what they had done.

'A mean soulless man, that Obadiah Ramsbottom,' Blackstone had said when the manufacturer had left them.

'A mean, soulless man indeed,' Patterson thought, as he stood on the bridge waiting for the kidnappers to show their hand.

From his vantage point in the bell tower, Blackstone watched as the hansom cab travelling towards the Embankment suddenly swerved across the road, on collision course with the side of the other hansom going in the opposite direction.

The driver of the rogue cab lashed at his horse and reined in frantically, but it was too late. Though the horse did not smash into the other vehicle, the cab it was pulling most certainly did.

Blackstone sighed. 'That's just what we needed,' he said aloud, though there was no one in the tower to hear him.

The second cab rocked unsteadily, then toppled over. The driver went sprawling. His horse, still between the shafts, reared hysterically. More horses panicked, and several of them followed the example of the hansom hack and reared. A coal wagon spilled its load. Another wagon, piled high with empty fish boxes, swayed dangerously from side to side.

'What a bloody fiasco!' Blackstone groaned.

When Patterson saw the whiskered gentleman attempting to clamber out of the capsized hansom, his first instinct was to rush forward and assist him. Then he reminded himself that whatever else was happening on the bridge, he had a more important job to do.

The driver of the hansom seemed to share none of Patterson's concern for his passenger. Having once clambered

15

to his feet and dusted himself down, he made a beeline for the cab which had been the cause of his misfortune.

The two cabbies – one still mounted behind his hansom, the other standing in the road – squared their shoulders in anticipation of the conflict they both knew would come.

'You've got no right to be put in charge of an 'orse, Ben Brightwell!' said the one standing on the bridge. 'No right at all.'

'Weren't my fault,' said the other. 'The 'orse went a bit off course, but you could 'ave avoided it, Jonty Andrews, if yer'd had anyfink at all about yer.'

The man who had thus been established in the mind of the growing crowd as 'Jonty' made a rush at his rival's hansom. The rival – Ben – reached for his whip, but left it a second too long – for while his fingers were still groping for the handle, Jonty had taken a firm grip of his left leg and was in the process of pulling him to the ground.

Once again, Patterson had to restrain his urge to intervene.

One of the cabbies caught the other a heavy blow on the chin. The man's head rocked, but a second later he had launched a worthy counter-attack at his opponent's ample guts. A circle of onlookers quickly gathered around them, and even from a distance, Blackstone could tell that they were cheering and some of them had started making bets.

The Inspector scanned the area beyond the fight. And as he had already begun to suspect – not to say feared – he saw that a second drama was in progress.

A woman was at the centre of this new disturbance. Literally at the centre! She stood alone, gazing into the faces of the crowd which formed a semicircle around her. Then she pointed. It was clear what she was saying. Her pocket had been picked, and she had spotted the guilty man. The man in question raised his hands as if to call on heaven to proclaim his innocence, but several other people, ignoring his appeal to the deity, had already started to manhandle him.

Very convenient, Blackstone thought grimly. Too bloody convenient!

He swept the scene with his field glasses, like a hawk searching out prey. Despite all the temptations to break rank, his men still held their positions, and he was proud of them for that. But at the same moment he was starting to gain a better appreciation of the planning which had gone into the kidnappers' operation – and he had no doubt that there would be at least one more challenge to test the resolve of his detectives.

The test came an instant later. The explosions were so loud that the sound of them carried even to the bell tower, bringing with them memories of rifle fire in the hills of Afghanistan. But it was not rifles which were being shot now. Such an extreme was unnecessary. Simple firecrackers – easier to conceal, much simpler to deploy – were doing an excellent job of wreaking all the havoc that the kidnappers could ever have desired.

On the bridge women screamed and old soldiers instinctively flung themselves to the ground. The horses, already in a state of nervousness, reacted to this fresh horror with total panic.

'Hold your positions,' Blackstone urged his men, though he knew they had no chance of hearing him. 'Hold your bloody positions!'

The blind clog dancer broke cover first, grabbing the reins of a rearing horse which threatened to trample a small child. The costermonger and florist followed, stepping in to restore order just as they had been trained to. Which left Patterson alone – unwatched and unguarded.

Blackstone pounded his forehead with his fist. He wished there was something he could do to assist his sergeant – but even if God suddenly granted him wings, he would still arrive on the scene too late to do anything.

The two men were easy enough for him to spot. Both wore cloth caps and mufflers which effectively hid most of their faces, both moved in with the lithe assurance of professional thugs.

The thugs had known there'd have to be two of them on this particular job, Blackstone thought bitterly. They'd considered every eventuality – including the fact that the man carrying the ransom might be wearing a top hat.

The Inspector watched helplessly as the men took up their positions – ground his teeth in frustration as one of them lifted Patterson's hat clear of his head and the other struck the sergeant's now-exposed skull with a blackjack.

Patterson swayed, a look of total incomprehension filling his face. The thug who had removed his hat quickly discarded it and made a grab for the attaché case. The sergeant offered no resistance. He was out for the count, and by the time his legs obeyed the message from his brain and crumpled beneath him, the two thugs were already making their way towards the southern end of the bridge.

Four

B lackstone gazed pensively from his office window down on to the busy Thames below. Less than a decade earlier, the Metropolitan Police had worked from a cramped building which had taken its name from its location – Scotland Yard, a mean square so close to Charing Cross Station that the air around it was thick with cinder dust. And look what they had now, he thought. *New* Scotland Yard stood proudly on the banks of the Thames, its lower floors built of finest Portland stone, its corner turrets proclaiming to the world that here was an organization to be taken seriously. Thirty-one superintendents were based in this new Yard, as well as 598 inspectors, 1831 sergeants and 12,738 constables. It was the epitome of modern policing, and it should have struck fear into the heart of each and every criminal. The only problem, he concluded, was that as the Force got bigger, the crooks seemed to be getting smarter.

'It was a nice touch, that,' he said grudgingly, as he turned away from the window. 'A very nice touch indeed.'

Patterson, who was sitting in a chair facing Blackstone's

18

desk, rubbed the back of his head. It had only recently ceased to ache – and now was starting to itch. 'What was a nice touch?' he asked.

'That bit of play-acting the two cab drivers put on for you. "Look where you're goin', Ben!" "It was all your fault, Jonty!" Once they'd started addressing each other by name, who'd ever have imagined they weren't exactly what they seemed to be?'

Patterson groaned. 'Certainly not me,' he admitted ruefully. 'There's no possibility they really *were* cab drivers, is there?' he added hopefully.

'Not a snowball's chance in hell,' Blackstone assured him. 'While you've been sitting back like an injured puppy, letting the doctor fuss and minister over you, I've been working. To be more specific, I've been reading reports from the two cabbies who had their hansoms stolen from them not half an hour before the fracas on Westminster Bridge.'

'The same two cabs?'

'No doubt about it. Their licence numbers were a perfect match with the ones involved in the so-called collision.'

'So who else do you think was in on it?' Patterson asked. 'The woman who claimed that she'd been robbed?'

'Yes, but that's only the start. There were the two who attacked you, and at least another two whose job it was to throw firecrackers under the horses' hooves. How many are we up to so far?'

'Seven.'

'Plus a couple more men held in reserve.'

'Held in reserve for what?'

'To create even more diversions, should it have proved to be necessary – which it didn't!'

Patterson rubbed the back of his head again. 'Don't blame the rest of the boys. They had no idea anything like that was going to happen. I was in charge, and if anybody's responsible, it's me.'

Blackstone shook his head. 'Don't blame yourself, either,'

he said. 'You couldn't have known what was coming. You were like a lamb led to the slaughter.'

The pocket watch which Obadiah Ramsbottom had checked three times in the last five minutes was the only thing that his father – poor bugger – had had to leave him in his will. It was a battered timepiece, which hadn't looked like much even when it was new, but it was accurate enough and there was no point in spending good money on replacing it.

'A quarter to three!' Ramsbottom fumed. 'We should have heard from that Inspector Blackstone by now. By hell, I thought the police in Preston were a bloody useless lot, but the ones I've seen down here make all our local bobbies seem like George Stephenson.'

'You should have paid the ransom, Obadiah,' his down-trodden wife sniffed tearfully. 'I always said you should have paid the ransom.'

'Nay, lass, that would have made no sense at all,' Ramsbottom replied. 'These criminals are just like mill workers – give 'em an inch, and they'll want a bloody mile.'

'At least if you'd paid the money we'd have had our Wilfred back by now,' Jessica Ramsbottom sobbed.

'We'll get our Wilfred back soon enough,' her husband assured her, with all the conviction of a man who had never been contradicted since the day his bank balance had grown to ten thousand pounds. 'Aye, we'll get 'im back an' it won't cost us no thousand quid, neither. Not if that Blackstone feller plays his cards proper.'

'I'm . . . I'm not so sure about that.'

'Well, I am. I know the common man better than he knows himself. An' the one thing he respects above all else is bein' showed a firm hand.'

'But suppose these criminals *aren't* "common men".'

'What else would they be? Do you think it's likely Lord Salisbury took the day off from the House of Lords to kidnap our lad?'

Accepting that further argument was pointless, Jessica Ramsbottom hung her head. She wished they'd never come to London; wished they'd never booked in at this posh hotel from which – somewhere between the family suite and the dining room – her son had been snatched.

'Aye, we'll have him back with us soon enough,' her husband repeated, checking his father's watch again.

There was a knock on the door.

'That'll be the police with our Wilfred, now,' Ramsbottom said. 'Well, answer the door, girl!' he called to his maid – the daughter of an impoverished relative.

It was not the police who had come calling. Instead, it was a hotel servant, carrying a gift-wrapped parcel.

'This has just been delivered for you, sir,' the man said.

'An' what is it, exactly?'

The servant looked down at the parcel. 'From its shape I'd say that it's a hat box – so I assume that it's a hat.'

'I've ordered no hat,' Ramsbottom told him. 'Are you sure it's intended for me?'

'It says "Mr Ramsbottom" on the label. And you're the only Mr Ramsbottom staying in the hotel.'

Ramsbottom sighed. 'I suppose you'll be expectin' a tip for bringin' it, will you?'

'It is customary, sir.'

'Customary my bare backside,' the cotton magnate said. 'Things have come to a pretty pass indeed when folk want payin' for carryin' a box up a few flights of stairs.'

But even as he spoke, he was feeling in his pocket for the smallest coin he could find.

The hotel servant took the tip almost as graciously as he would have done if he had considered it adequate, and departed.

Ramsbottom took the parcel over to the table.

'It's very heavy for a hat,' he commented. Then he noticed the stain which was beginning to form at the base of the package, and added, 'An' as far as I know, hats don't leak.'

A sudden look of horror came to his face. He ripped away the wrapping paper, lifted the top of the hatbox, and gazed inside.

'Oh my God!' he moaned.

He had been right when he'd assured his wife that the kidnappers would return his son – but only *partly* right.

'I been reading the kidnappers all wrong,' Blackstone confessed to Patterson, half an hour later. 'I assumed that they only asked for a hundred pounds when they took Vanessa Todd because they didn't know what they *could* have got. But I see now that wasn't the reason at all.'

'So what *was* the reason?'

'They wanted the police to be involved in the case, but they didn't want us to be *too deeply* involved. By setting the ransom at a hundred, they purchased just the amount of police interest they required.'

'Required for what?'

'For their rehearsal of the real crime.'

Patterson rubbed the back of his head again. Like a victorious army on the rampage, the itching seemed to be spreading out.

'So you're saying that Vanessa Todd's kidnapping was nothing more than a try-out for the kidnapping of Wilfred Ramsbottom?' he asked.

'No,' Blackstone said. 'I'm not.'

'Then you've lost me again.'

'Vanessa Todd's kidnapping was like the first read-through of the script,' explained Blackstone, who had recently acquired a passion for the theatre. 'Wilfred Ramsbottom's was more like a full dress rehearsal for the actors. That's why they upped the ante. By asking for a thousand pounds, they were ensuring that we'd become actively involved – because they wanted to see what we could do when we were really trying.'

'So why did they cut Wilfred's head off and send it to his parents in a hat box?' Patterson asked. 'That won't get them any money, will it?'

'No, but they didn't actually *want* any money this time. I suspect that they'd have been very disappointed if Obadiah Ramsbottom *had* decided to pay up. They may even have chosen him precisely *because* they'd figured he wasn't the sort of bloke to hand over his cash.'

'You're saying they planned to cut poor Wilfred's head off right from the start?'

'I'm saying they always hoped they'd have a *reason* to decapitate him. And we gave them a good one, didn't we – an attaché case stuffed with last night's newspaper.'

'So – if I'm following you correctly – they did it to show that they mean business?'

'That's precisely why they did it.'

'And they weren't interested in the thousand pound at all?'

'Correct.'

'Which means that when they stop rehearsing – when they put on a proper performance – they'll be demanding a bigger ransom?'

'A *much* bigger ransom.'

'Which, if you take things to their natural conclusion, means that they're planning to kidnap someone very important.'

'Oh yes! Someone very important indeed,' Blackstone agreed gravely.

Five

Reginald Dilkes, as several of his more embittered colleagues were always willing to point out, had a great talent for self-satisfaction. Indeed, they would further claim, he had turned it into almost an art form. Such attacks did not bother Dilkes. He had, in his own unbiased opinion, good reason to be proud of himself. His column – 'The Eyes and Ears of London' – was the most thumbed page of the *Evening Chronicle*. Minor peers fawned on him outrageously, and even lesser royals thought twice before they were rude to him. It was years since he'd actually been asked to pay his bill in any of the fairly fashionable restaurants, and one of the better seats at the theatre was always his for the asking. There was no doubt, in other words, that he was a force to be reckoned with.

His original purpose in going to Claridge's Hotel that afternoon had been to interview a visiting American railroad millionaire, but he had approached his task without much enthusiasm. The problem, as he saw it, was that ever since the industrial boom on the other side of the Atlantic, American millionaires had become so commonplace that they were starting to lose their public appeal. The tall, bearded nigger – on the other hand – was a novelty which might well tickle his jaded readers' fancy.

The 'nigger' in question was sitting at the other end of the lobby, on a carved teak chair which could almost have been called a throne, and had certainly not been supplied by the hotel. He was dressed in flowing silk robes covered in elaborate embroidery. In front of him was a polished brass table (again undoubtedly alien to Claridge's). A delicate china teapot rested on the table, and though the man was far from alone – several other men sat cross-legged on the floor at his feet – there was only one cup.

Dilkes made his way across the room to where the exotic foreign party was situated. There shouldn't be any difficulty in getting an interview, he told himself. The niggers would probably be glad to have somebody speak to them almost as if they were equals.

Two of the men sitting cross-legged on the floor watched the journalist's progress with keen interest, and when the man's intended destination became apparent, they rose slinkily to their feet.

Dilkes noted their action with some approval. It was quite right that the two niggers should rise at his approach, he thought. True, the rest of the party were still seated, but the moment they too saw him, they'd probably jump to their feet smartly enough.

He drew level with the group, but no one else stood. Uppity lot, he thought – but he considered himself something of a liberal, and was quite willing to make allowances for the fact that they were too ignorant to know the proper way to behave in the presence of a white man.

Dilkes looked down at the man sitting on the chair. 'You don't happen to speak any English, do you, old chap?' he asked.

The two standing Indians now moved with astounding speed, and before he had time to appreciate what was really happening, the journalist found himself sandwiched between them. Not only that, but they had taken a firm grip of his arms and he felt a slight pricking in his side which he could only assume came from the point of a dagger.

'Here, what's going on?' he demanded.

One of the men sitting cross-legged on the floor looked up. He was, Dilkes saw, wearing steel-framed glasses and a look of disdain. 'Is there some purpose to your invasion of our privacy?' he asked.

'Eh?'

'Who are you, and what do you want?'

If the journalist had not been being held so tightly, he would probably have shrugged. As it was, he said, 'My name's Reginald Dilkes. I'm a famous newspaper reporter. I wanted a word with your mate here.'

'My mate?' the man with steel glasses repeated. 'Are you perhaps referring to His Majesty, the Maharaja of Chandrapore?'

'If that's who he is.'

'I am his personal secretary. Please enlighten me – why should you *wish* to speak to "my mate" here?'

'Tell your blokes to let go of me, before I call the management!' Dilkes said, starting to realize how humiliating his position might seem to others, and feeling an anger building up inside him.

'It would be a mistake to call anyone,' the secretary said.

'You can't threaten me!' Dilkes blustered.

'Nor am I trying to do so. I am merely pointing out that if you were to call the management, you would be the one to be thrown out on to the street.'

'Me? Thrown out?'

'Undoubtedly. And to avoid such an unpleasant occurrence, I will give you one more opportunity to answer my question. Why do you wish to talk to the Maharaja?'

There was a confidence and certainty in the other man's tone which unnerved Dilkes. He still couldn't see the manager taking a nigger's side rather than his, but perhaps it would be better not to put the matter to a test.

'Like I said, I'm a journalist,' Dilkes told the secretary. 'I work for the *Evening Chronicle*. I wanted to do an interview on your mate. I thought my readers might find it interesting.'

The secretary looked up at the Maharaja. The Maharaja nodded.

'His Majesty is willing to grant you an audience,' the man in steel-framed glasses said. 'But there are certain conditions attached to such an audience. You must not look him directly in the eye, and you must address him at all times as "Your Majesty".'

Bloody cheek! Dilkes thought. Still, he'd already gone through the humiliation of being manhandled by these niggers – he might at least get a good story out of it.

'All right,' he agreed. 'But tell these two hooligans of yours to let go of me first.'

The secretary nodded. The two guards released their grip and melted away into the background.

Dilkes cleared his throat. 'Why, precisely, are you in London?' he asked the Maharaja.

'Why, precisely, are you in London, *Your Majesty*?' the secretary corrected him.

'Why are you in London, *Your Majesty*?' Dilkes agreed reluctantly.

'Are you happy to continue this audience in English?' the Maharaja asked, in a rich deep voice. 'Or would you feel more comfortable if we converted to French?'

The question was even a bigger loss of face than the manhandling had been. Dilkes looked down at the floor. 'I don't speak French,' he admitted.

'I don't speak French, *Your Majesty*!' the secretary said.

Dilkes glanced quickly around him to see if there was anyone in the lobby he knew. There was not.

'Your Majesty,' he added.

'Very well, we will proceed in English,' the Maharaja said. 'I am here for two purposes. The first is to shop.'

'Shop for what . . . Your Majesty?'

'For motor cars.'

'Motor cars?'

'That is what I said. Mr Benz of Germany makes a very fine one called the Viktoria. I intend to buy a dozen of them.'

Dilkes gulped. 'A dozen?' he repeated. 'But won't that be very expensive . . . Your Majesty? Where do you think you'll get the money from?'

'You are being impertinent!' the secretary growled.

'That is quite all right, Aggarwal,' the Maharaja said. 'Tell me, Mr Dilkes, what do you know about Chandrapore?'

The journalist sniffed. 'Not a lot.'

'Do you, in fact, know *anything* about it at all?'

'I know it's in India.'

'But not in *British* India.'

'What do you mean?'

The Maharaja shook his head, almost pityingly. 'It doesn't matter,' he said. 'Do you have any idea of the size of my state?'

The nigger was trying to make a monkey out of him, Dilkes thought. Well, the bugger wasn't going to get away with it.

'I believe Chandrapore is about the same size as Devon,' he said, trying to sound authoritative.

The Maharaja smiled. 'Devon, England?' he asked.

'Of course Devon, England!'

'Then you have clearly been misinformed. Chandrapore is, in fact, slightly larger than the entire British Isles.'

'You're joking!' Dilkes said.

The Maharaja looked down at his attendants. 'Are they laughing?' he asked.

'Well, no.'

'If I had been making a joke – even an extremely weak

27

one – they would have been roaring their heads off. What is the population of the British Isles, Mr Dilkes?'

'I'm not sure I could say exactly.'

'It is roughly twenty-eight million people. Chandrapore has only twenty million – but that is still more than enough loyal subjects, I think you will agree, to raise the money for their beloved Maharaja to buy a dozen motor cars for his personal use.'

'I . . . I suppose so,' the bemused Dilkes agreed.

'You asked me my other reason for being here,' the Maharaja continued. 'It is to pay a visit on my fellow monarch.'

'Your fellow monarch?'

'Queen Victoria.'

'Your *fellow* monarch?'

'I am invited to the India Office for tea tomorrow. My dear sister Victoria has agreed to send an honour guard from one of her finer regiments to accompany us. I do not care one way or the other about such things, but no doubt it will create an interesting diversion for the common people to gaze on.'

'The common people!' Dilkes said, almost exploding in his indignation. 'Are you talking about English men and English women as *common* people?'

'And English children, too, I should imagine.' The Maharaja waved his hand airily. 'You may go now.'

The time had come to stand up for himself and for his country, Dilkes decided. Somebody had to tell this jumped-up nigger that having all the money in the world still didn't make him anything like the equal of the lowliest Englishman. Yes, he needed putting in his place. And the man who put him there might as well be Reginald Dilkes, the Ears and Eyes of London.

The words were already forming in his mouth when he saw that the two ruffians who had manhandled him earlier were back in position, and had their hands resting lightly on their jewelled – but probably still lethal – daggers. The Maharaja had turned away from him – had already, it seemed, forgotten that he ever existed – but Dilkes felt the

28

secretary's eyes burning into his forehead, and knew what he had to do.

'Please convey to His Majesty my thanks for his granting me an audience,' he said, almost choking on the words. 'It was very gracious of him indeed.'

The secretary gave the journalist a supercilious smile. 'It was merely a case of *noblesse oblige*,' he said, 'but since you speak no French I suppose you have no idea what that means.'

Six

There were few streets in London in which the air was as damp as it was on Burr Street. A slight breeze from almost any direction carried on it moisture from either the docks or the Thames, and even in the driest of summers the window frames and doors – and perhaps even the people – continued the process of slowly rotting away. It was a desperate street in which hard times would be replaced – but not for long – by times which were not *quite* so hard. People died young there, and any man living on it who reached the age of forty could consider himself fortunate indeed.

As Blackstone walked down Burr Street that late evening, he was aware of all the eyes which followed his progress. Eyes from behind tattered curtains, eyes from deep in dark alleys. Eyes in front and eyes behind. Maybe a dozen pairs of them in total – and all of them hostile.

Perhaps he should have put on a fiendishly clever disguise, he mused fancifully. Sherlock Holmes, whom his creator Conan Doyle described as being as tall and thin as Blackstone was himself, certainly would have worn one. Holmes, in this situation, would have contrived to appear a much shorter man, possibly with a hair-lip and crossed eyes.

And he'd have looked such a sitting duck that he'd not

have got more than a hundred yards without having his wallet removed and his throat cut! Blackstone thought.

So it was better from his point of view – far better – that the watching eyes knew exactly whom they were looking at. They wouldn't see him as a soft target, and the only people likely to attack him were any of the three or four dozen criminals in London who felt they had a compelling reason to kill him.

He chuckled again at the thought of Sherlock Holmes in disguise. He enjoyed the Holmes stories himself. *More* than *enjoyed* them – he had learned a great deal about deductive reasoning from reading them. Conan Doyle was, in his opinion, a great writer, and would probably have made a pretty fair detective himself.

It was only when that same writer described London and the people who inhabited it that he moved on to much shakier ground. The city was a far more complex place than Doyle made it seem. There were an infinite number of divisions and boundaries which were never shown on any map. Simply crossing from one street to the next could take the traveller into another world – one which was governed by an entirely different set of rules to those operating in the apparently identical street he had just left.

In a way, Blackstone supposed, Conan Doyle was forced into such simplifications by the very nature of his work. The diversity of the capital city could not be encompassed in a single short story, or even in a very long novel. Still, in some ways the stories contained the essential truth, for though no one criminal had the power of Conan Doyle's Professor Moriarty – the Napoleon of Crime – there were plenty of lesser 'Napoleons' running their operations in the darker parts of the metropolis. Indeed, the main point of this expedition into the docklands was to contact one of these minor dictators.

The Wellington Arms loomed up ahead of him. The pub was so close to the Thames that Blackstone could hear the river lapping against steps where the watermen's boats lay moored. Most men *walked* down the steps to those boats, but he knew of at least three who had been dragged down by their heels, and had not objected – even as their heads banged on each and every step – because they were long past objecting to anything. It was thoughts of that nature which made Blackstone glad he had his pistol with him.

The Inspector glanced quickly around to see if any of his closest enemies were lurking in the shadows, then pushed open the door which led into the public bar of the Wellington.

The place was full, as it always was at that time of night. Watermen and costermongers stood drinking pints, sailors on shore leave knocked back whiskies as if their throats were on fire. There were leather tanners and dock workers, warehouse men and low-class prostitutes. They were so tightly packed together that it was a wonder they could even breathe – yet despite the cramped conditions they all took the greatest care not to infringe on the area of clear space which surrounded the table in the corner of the room.

The man who was sitting alone at the table was in his mid-thirties. His hair was the colour of straw, and as wispy as a neglected thatch. His eyes were of the palest blue. Though there was a knife scar running down his left cheek, he did not look like he was much of a fighter. Nor were appearances deceptive – Tommy Keogh had not got where he was by being handy in a fight – he had done so by persuading others it was to their advantage to do his fighting for him.

Blackstone fought his way through the crush, and made his way over to the table. Behind him, the bar had fallen silent. Some of these watchers did not know who he was, and marvelled at his temerity. And even those who did recognize him thought he was pushing his luck.

Tommy Keogh watched the policeman's approach impassively. He gestured that Blackstone should take a seat, then raised his head and gazed with his pale blue eyes into the silence.

'What's the matter?' he demanded. 'This is a pub, ain't it? Yer 'ere to enjoy yerselves, ain't yer?'

He paused, awaiting a response.

'Yes, Tommy,' some brave soul mumbled, and then the whole bar was agreeing that, 'Yes, Tommy,' it was.

31

'Then bloody well get on with it,' Keogh ordered.

The bar had been noisy before, but now the noise level was even louder, as all the customers strove to prove that if Tommy wanted them to enjoy themselves they would – whether they wanted to or not.

Keogh took a sip from the glass of vintage brandy which stood on the table. 'What brings you down on to my patch unannounced, Inspector Blackstone?' he asked, the pale eyes giving nothing away.

'What do *you* think brings me down?' Blackstone countered.

Keogh ran his hand through his thin thatch of hair. 'The kidnappings?' he asked.

'The kidnappings,' Blackstone agreed.

'Don't know nuffink about them. I've 'ad a few people seen to in me time, but it's just not me style to cut up kids – not even rich ones.'

'So whose style is it?'

Keogh scratched his head again. 'Now there, I've got to admit, yer've got me.'

'Are you telling me that you don't know?'

'Exac'ly.'

'But would you give me the information even if you *did* know?'

The other man favoured him with a thin smile. 'Like I said, it's not my style to go cuttin' up kiddies. But I'm not about to shop anybody who does. It's a tough world, Mr Blackstone, and we all have to do whatever we can to earn a crust.'

'Live and let live?'

'Yers, in a manner of speakin'.'

'It's a pity the kidnappers don't have the same philosophy,' Blackstone said, with a tinge of regret in his voice.

'What do yer mean?'

'You get away with a lot of the things you do because we haven't got the manpower to stop you,' Blackstone said. 'Take last Thursday, for example.'

'What about it?'

'There was a ship called the SS *Baltimore* moored in the

Thames just opposite Billingsgate Fish Market. It had armed guards posted on the deck all night, because part of the cargo was antiques destined for America.' Blackstone paused. 'I'm not boring you, am I, Tommy?'

'No. Not yet.'

'About an hour before the fish market opened for business, a ketch appeared on the river, apparently intending to unload its catch. There was a man standing on the deck, and he asked the guards on the *Baltimore* if they fancied buying some fresh fish from him. Said he could let them have it for a very reasonable price. That was clever, wasn't it?'

'I dunno what yer talkin' about.'

Blackstone smiled. 'We always think we can peg people, don't we? So if somebody seems a little bit dishonest, that's what we think he is – *a little* bit dishonest. The guards on the ship thought the man on the ketch was trying to make himself a few bob by selling things that didn't exactly belong to him, and they saw no harm in going along with it. After all, it seemed like a good deal, in which everybody benefited – except the man whose fish they were. The guards told the ketch to come alongside – and the moment it was close enough, two more men suddenly appeared on the deck, both armed with pistols. The guards were disarmed, the antiques were stolen. It was a clever plan, Tommy. One of your best.'

''Ang on, 'ang on,' Keogh interrupted. 'I got an alibi. I was in Sarfend when that robbery happened.'

'I'm sure you were,' Blackstone agreed. 'But what about Tufty Squires and Harry the Hook? Where were they?'

'Dunno. Not me business.'

Blackstone laughed. 'The robbery had your trademark stamped right through it,' he said. 'And because the goods were stolen from a ship, we could call it piracy if we had a mind to. You could hang for that, Tommy.'

'Not me!'

'You,' Blackstone contradicted him. 'If we really made the effort, we could pin it on you. The problem is, we don't have the manpower for a job like that – at the moment!'

'What do yer mean? At the moment?'

'There are some crimes that *have* to be solved, because everybody wants them to be,' Blackstone explained. 'The general public couldn't give a sheep's fart about the fact that some rich Yank has lost all his antiques. But kidnapping and murder? Well, that's an entirely different matter. Parliament will be screaming for results, and so will the newspapers. Especially after the next one.'

'The next what?'

'The next kidnapping. There's a definite progressive pattern to this case, don't you think?'

'Yer speakin' in riddles.'

'No, I'm not. Look at it this way, Tommy. The first victim came from a moderately prosperous family, the second from a family which you'd have to describe as quite rich. The third's going to have a *very* rich dad indeed. And once he's been snatched, they'll bring in policemen from everywhere – Bristol, Glasgow, Manchester, Cardiff . . . Perhaps they'll even ask for help from the French and the Americans. The whole of London will be saturated with coppers. Nobody will be able to commit any crimes. Worse – from your point of view – in their attempts to find leads in the kidnapping, they may well uncover some clues that can be used to solve old crimes. Do you understand what I'm saying?'

Keogh nodded gravely. 'It's very worryin' when a man can't go about the business of honest, decent thievery wivout havin' to look over his shoulder every coupla minutes.'

'So you'll help me? You'll find out who's behind these kidnappings?'

'I'll try me best,' Keogh promised. He squared his shoulders. 'After all, as a loyal subject of Her Majesty, the Queen, it's me duty.'

'You're a true patriot, Tommy,' Blackstone said, one half of his forked tongue firmly in each cheek.

Seven

It was the early afternoon of the day following the one in which Obadiah Ramsbottom's refusal to pay the ransom had cost his son, Wilfred, his head. The Maharaja of Chandrapore was sitting in the salon of his suite at Claridge's, waiting for the start of the most important few hours of his visit to England.

'It is true that Victoria has agreed to meet me this afternoon,' the Maharaja said to his trusted secretary, the only other person in the room. 'But where has her government decreed that this meeting should take place? In the India Office! If I had been a European monarch – a *white* monarch – she would have received me at one of her palaces.'

It was no more than a realistic assessment of the situation. However much he talked to others of the queen being his equal, the Maharaja was too much of a political animal to believe it himself – or to imagine Aggarwal believed that he believed it. Yet even though he accepted things as they were – for only a fool railed against that which he could not change – it still rankled a little.

'And though she will incline her head to me,' the Maharaja continued, 'I will be expected to bow deeply to her. She may treat me as if I were a distant cousin, but in her eyes I am never more than a cousin who comes from a vastly inferior line of the family.'

'The sign of a great man is not that he is the most powerful man in the world,' Aggarwal said. 'It is that he sees the strengths and weaknesses of others, and knows how to use them to his own advantage. In that respect, Your Majesty, you tower above both the English queen and the rest of the so-called Indian princes.'

That was no more than a fair comment, at least as far as his brother monarchs were concerned, the Maharaja thought.

How they boasted! How they deluded themselves about their own strength!

'Why do the British not annex my state as they have annexed so many others?' they would ask. 'Because they are afraid of me!'

Almost as afraid as a tiger is of a monkey, the Maharaja would think to himself.

The greater did not normally crush the lesser until given a reason. The tiger had better things to feast on than monkey flesh, and it was only if the monkey persisted in throwing nuts at it that it would take any action.

Of course the British were willing to allow the princes to act independently – as long as that independence had its roots in an unquestioning allegiance to the British crown. And of course the princes were allowed to cheat the British collector of some of the tribute money – as long as he did not try to hold back *too* much. Aggarwal was right – the great man saw the truth and seized what advantage he could. Thus, if he were to be no more than one of the dogs at Victoria's feet, he would make sure he was the dog she most cherished and most indulged.

'How the other princes brag when they return from London,' he said, inviting his secretary, on this occasion, to laugh at his fellow rulers.

Aggarwal dutifully complied. 'How they compete with each other to demonstrate the honour the English queen has seen fit to show them,' he said.

'"I was given an escort of fifty soldiers",' the Maharaja said, in a squeaky voice which was a perfect imitation of the ruler of a neighbouring state. '"I was given an escort of a hundred",' he continued, in the deeper voice of another prince. 'But you are right, Aggarwal. The glory is not theirs. It is showered on them as I shower coins on my poorer subjects.'

Aggarwal risked a chuckle which had not been directly elicited. 'How envious they will be when they hear how you chose to arrive at the India Office,' he said. 'What a masterstroke. What genius!'

The Maharaja nodded, to show he accepted the compliment as no more than his due. It was true that the original plan had not been his at all. It had not even come from an Indian, but instead had been proposed by one of the cursed white invaders. Nevertheless, it would have withered on the bud if he had not decided to cultivate it. And that was the measure of true genius – to know what to nurture and what to consign to the rubbish heap.

'The Maharaja of Jalandhar arrived at the India Office in the biggest motor car he could find,' he said. 'Hoshiarpur thought he had got one over on Jalandhar when he travelled in a gold coach. Both those are as nothing when compared with what I am about to do!' A sudden, troubling thought came into his mind. 'What if the British cavalry horses are frightened when confronted by the might of India?' he asked worriedly

'The horses are well trained,' Aggarwal said.

'But perhaps not well trained enough. If they panic and destroy my triumphal parade, I will hold you and your idea responsible.'

There was barely a flicker in Aggarwal's eye as he noted that the whole project had suddenly become *his* idea.

'Your Majesty cannot be held responsible for the actions of the queen's horses,' he said. 'If they scatter, any shame that is to be had will fall on the queen's army. Dhiren, I assure Your Majesty, will not falter.'

'No,' the Maharaja agreed. 'He is a good beast – a reliable beast. That was part of my calculation when I came up with the plan.'

Aggarwal nodded. To be the secretary of a maharaja, he thought, it was necessary to be as cunning as a snake and as swift as a mongoose. And that was only on days when nothing went wrong.

'Go over to the window,' the Maharaja said. 'See what is happening on the street.'

Aggarwal did as he had been instructed. 'A crowd has gathered,' he said. 'They have no idea what is about to happen, but because the street had been closed off to traffic they know that *something* is.'

37

A sudden roar went up from the crowd below.

'Dhiren is coming?' the Maharaja asked.

'Dhiren is coming,' Aggarwal agreed.

Eight

The two men – the tall, thin, almost biblical-looking inspector and his shorter, slightly plump sergeant – left the Embankment and made their way up Whitehall.

They were not going anywhere in particular – they were just walking. Blackstone, even though he was authorized to take hansom cabs, liked to walk. It was a habit he'd grown into when he was a lowly detective constable, he'd once explained to his sergeant, and now he found that it helped him to think. Patterson did not share his boss's enthusiasm. In his opinion, there was no point in *being* an inspector if you didn't take advantage of the perks of the job. And whilst pounding the pavements might be good for the brain, it was hellish hard on the feet.

'I can't fathom it,' Blackstone said. 'I can't fathom it at all. I've put the screws on some of the biggest villains in London for information. It shouldn't have been too difficult for them to find out what we need to know. Bloody hell, there's not a pocket picked without their permission, or a house broken into without one of them first giving the nod. And what have they come up with? Sweet Fanny Adams!'

'Perhaps they really *don't* know anything,' Patterson suggested.

'Well *of course* they don't know anything. In their own interest, they'd tell me if they did. The question is, *why* don't they know anything?'

'The obvious conclusion is that it's a new gang which has started up,' Patterson said.

Blackstone shook his head. 'These things have to evolve.

You don't get to be as good as they are without serving a long apprenticeship.'

'I'm not sure—' Patterson began.

'Well, I am,' Blackstone said firmly. 'Think about any business! Think about Harrods! It's a big store, these days, but it wasn't always. It started as a corner shop on the Brompton Road. The owners learned their craft and made their mistakes when it didn't really matter. Then, when they were ready – when they'd honed their skills – they expanded. The question is, where did this gang learn its trade? How did it evolve into the well-oiled machine we saw in operation on Westminster Bridge yesterday? How could any of it have happened without the criminal fraternity noticing?'

There was no satisfactory answer Patterson could come up with, and so he said nothing. The two men walked on in silence, Blackstone thinking about the evolution of criminal gangs and Patterson wondering why his boss – who had much older feet than he had – seemed not to share his preoccupation with acquiring corns.

Perhaps he could talk Blackstone into taking a cab back to Scotland Yard, Patterson thought as they passed Horse Guards. And then, looking around him, he realized that even if he could persuade his boss, there was not a cab to be had. In fact, even in the short time it had taken them to walk from Parliament Square, the volume of traffic seemed to have thinned out considerably. Now why on earth should that be, he wondered?

The explanation was not long in coming. There were half a dozen policemen stationed at the top end of Whitehall, and they were diverting all wheeled traffic away from the street.

'Looks as if somebody important is coming this way,' Patterson said.

'What?' Blackstone asked.

'They're stopping the traffic. Must be some sort of procession.'

'There's *always* some sort of procession in this city,' Blackstone said grumpily. 'Is it any wonder crime's going up, when we have to spend half our time babying dukes and earls and foreign princes.'

They walked a short distance along Pall Mall, then turned on to Regent Street.

'No traffic here, either,' Patterson said. 'This must be on the procession's route.'

Blackstone did not reply. He was so absorbed in his own thoughts that it was questionable if he even heard.

'What next?' he said, almost under his breath.

'Pardon, sir?'

'We've had the daughter of a moderately rich Londoner kidnapped, and then the son of quite a rich northerner. What next? The Crown Prince of Sweden?'

'I don't think the Swedish royal family is in London at the moment, sir,' said Patterson, who knew about these things.

There was a sound of horses' hooves in the distance, then the procession about which Patterson had been speculating appeared at the end of the street.

For a moment, the sergeant's mouth flapped open and he was unable to speak. Then the words came to him.

'Bugger me sideways!' he gasped.

The procession was certainly an impressive sight. Leading it were mounted cavalry. And not just any cavalry, but the Royal Horse Guards – one of the most prestigious regiments in the whole British army. Their breastplates shone in the sunlight, the red plumes from their helmets swayed gently as they rode in perfect, disciplined formation. But though the cavalry would have attracted a crowd in their own right on most occasions, they were nothing but a poor sideshow now. Because behind them – unbelievably – was a gigantic Indian elephant.

In front of the huge grey beast danced musicians, playing on their pipes and drums. On either side of it walked beautiful young brown-skinned maidens, scattering rose petals from silver baskets into the bedazzled crowd which lined the route. And flanking the women were the bodyguards – tall, proud men with turbans and beards, each dressed in an immaculate

40

scarlet uniform, each with a ceremonial musket held firmly in his steady hands.

Yet however colourful the view at street level, it was the massive presence of the elephant which dominated the whole scene. It moved forward slowly but impressively – as large as a double-decker bus, as solid as a granite mountain. It was draped in a huge embroidered silk cloth which was worth more than an entire street in the East End.

On the beast's neck sat its mahout, a small brown man wearing only a loincloth. And resting on the elephant's powerful back was a howdah – or canopied seat – which was held in place by a thick strap running under the beast's belly.

The spectators were too entranced by the elephant itself to notice the howdah at first, but once they had seen it, it became the focus of their attention. And with good reason! It was a wonder to behold – a delicate work of art elaborately carved from ivory and teak and encrusted with a hundred large jewels.

It would have seemed almost vandalism to sit on this treasure, were it not for the fact that the two persons doing so – a man and a boy – looked created for just that purpose. Their jackets and trousers glowed as if they had been spun from the purest gold, the slippers on their feet of a delicacy which could hardly be imagined. They belonged in the howdah because they, too, were works of art.

Perhaps a minute had passed since they had first caught sight of the procession, and neither the Inspector nor the sergeant had moved a single step in that time. In Patterson's case, it had been an all-embracing awe which had brought him to a halt, and he had assumed – without even really thinking about it – that the same was true of Blackstone. But the Inspector was not a man to keep silent on an occasion like this – or indeed, on any occasion – and Patterson soon found himself wondering whether, perhaps, something was not quite as it should have been.

The sergeant forced himself to look from the spectacle to his boss. Blackstone was standing perfectly still, his left hand stroking his chin thoughtfully, his eyes almost closed.

'Is there a problem, sir?' Patterson asked.

Blackstone said nothing.

'I asked if there was a problem, sir,' Patterson repeated, speaking louder this time.

Blackstone's hand fell away from his chin, flopped down to his side and hung there loosely. His eyes, now fully opened, were filled with horror, and as he fixed his gaze on the elephant and the howdah, his whole body tensed.

'Sir?' Patterson said helplessly. 'Sir?'

It was plain that Blackstone was still not aware of his presence. The Inspector, in fact, was travelling in a world of 'maybes' which he was almost convinced would soon become a world of terrible reality.

'No!' he said, in a voice which was almost a croak. 'No, it couldn't be that. It couldn't possibly be that!'

Nine

The Maharaja looked down at the mesmerized mob below the swaying elephant, then turned towards the six-year-old boy sitting beside him. Everything he did, he did with thoughts of this child in mind. Balachandra – the young moon. A gift from the heavens. The most precious thing in the whole world.

'What do you make of all this, my son?' he asked.

The boy thought for a moment. 'The peasants seem very pale and also very stupid,' he said.

'Why do you say they are stupid?'

'Because of the way they gaze at Dhiren. Anyone would think they had never seen an elephant before.'

'Perhaps they haven't,' the Maharaja said. 'Outside the zoos, there are no elephants in England.'

'What is a zoo?' the boy asked. 'And if they have no elephants, how do they lift tree trunks?'

The Maharaja laughed indulgently. 'You have a great deal

yet to learn of India, but so much more of the world outside it. But there is no urgency. When the time finally comes for you to take my place, you will be ready.'

The creature in the back of the van was struggling hard to work out what was wrong. It was no easy task, for while his brain had proved more than adequate for dealing with his natural surroundings, he had been denied those surroundings for some considerable time now.

He was an animal driven by instinct, who killed his victims without compunction. He had expected the same fate to befall him once he had been captured, but instead his enemies had chosen to keep him alive. He did not understand this at all. For the defeated, death was as natural as the rain and the wind. What had happened to him since he had been taken most definitely was not.

There was space in the van – more space than he had been granted on the bullock cart, or in the train, or on the ship. Yet he felt no desire to explore his space, nor even mark it out as his own. He felt too drowsy for that. He did not know why this should be. A creature of the jungle, he understood traps and spears and even guns, but until this point in his life, drugs had never been a problem.

Though he considered the assignment he and his men had been given to be unnecessary, Sergeant Robert Simcox had carried out the early parts of it with the same thoroughness and diligence which had earned him his sergeant's stripes five years earlier.

'You are not to hold back the crowd,' he had instructed the constables under his command, 'but if any person steps into the path of the procession, you are to apprehend them.'

As if there really was any chance of them needing to actually do that! As if any of the people lining the street would block the progress of the Royal Horse Guards! And if they were unwilling to get in the way of horses, what were the chances they would put themselves in the path of an elephant? Still, he had been given his orders and he would both relay them to his men and see that those men carried them out to the letter.

The procession had already reached the top of the street. Simcox was on the point of giving his deployment a final inspection when, over the heads of the small crowd gathered on the edge of the pavement, he noticed that two police vans – or Black Marias, as they had become popularly known – were completely blocking the entrance to Charles II Street.

His first reaction was one of annoyance. He was supposed to be in charge of the operation, but how could he hope to be effective when his superiors had neglected to inform him of exactly what was going on?

Then annoyance gave way to curiosity. What purpose did the van drivers think they were serving? He was not expecting to make any arrests, and even if he did collar a couple of troublemakers, he wouldn't need *two* Black Marias to convey them to the police station. Then again, what was the idea of parking the vans in such a position in the first place? Two together served no purpose at all, unless to bar the road. And why should anyone wish to do that?

The procession was getting closer, but Sergeant Simcox decided he still had time to sort out the situation with the Black Marias before it actually arrived. With this purpose in mind, he marched briskly towards the two vehicles.

'Clear a way,' he said to the spectators on the pavement.

The men and women grumbled amongst themselves, but the sergeant was the law, and so they pushed and edged against each other until they had created a small thoroughfare along which he could pass.

Simcox examined the Black Marias. They did not *completely* block access to Charles II Street, as he had thought earlier. In fact, there was a small gap between one of the vehicles and the wall, just wide enough for a man – even a slightly heavy police sergeant – to squeeze through.

The procession had already passed by the spot at which Calvert and Ruddick were posted, but the two constables still had a job to do.

'It's not just a matter of clearin' all the traffic in front, you've got to stop it comin' up from behind,' Sergeant Simcox had told them.

'An' why's that, Sarge?' Calvert had asked.

'Because processions go slow, and other things go as fast as they can,' the sergeant had explained patiently. 'Do you really think the Horse Guards want to be overtaken by a wagon carryin' a heap of shit? An' how d'you think the poor bloody elephant will feel if it has one of them new-fangled automobiles right up its arse?'

Calvert had grinned. 'Point taken, Sarge.'

'Give it half an hour,' Simcox had instructed. 'Then you can start lettin' things through again.'

It was only a couple of minutes after the sergeant had left to inspect the rest of his men that the Indians arrived on the scene. There were five of them. Four were wearing a uniform similar to the men who had walked beside the elephant. The fifth – who was clearly the leader – was dressed in a flowing white jacket of the finest linen, and held in his hands the biggest rifle the two constables had ever seen.

As the five men passed through the barrier, Ruddick stepped in front of them to block their passage.

'Now then, what's this all about?' he asked.

'We are part of His Majesty's entourage,' the man in the impressive white jacket said. 'It is our duty and honour to protect his sacred person.'

'Then you're a bit late,' Ruddick told him. 'He's already gone.'

The Indian gave the constable a superior smile. 'There are those who protect His Majesty from the front and those who protect him from the rear,' he explained. 'Our task is to prevent surprise attacks from behind.'

'Is that why you're carryin' that bloody big gun?' Calvert asked.

'Exactly,' the Indian agreed.

'Well, given who you are, I suppose there's no harm in lettin' you go on your way,' Ruddick said.

'We have no wish to do that,' the Indian replied. 'We are perfectly content to wait here.'

'I don't see the point of that,' Ruddick admitted.

The Indian smiled again. 'You will,' he promised. 'Given time, *everything* will be made clear.'

Sucking in his stomach, Sergeant Simcox edged past the van which was blocking the entrance to Charles II Street. Once he was the other side of it, he became even more mystified. There should have been a horse between the shafts of each van, but there was not. Furthermore, there was no sign of any police constables in attendance. In fact, the only soul in sight was a young man in a shabby suit who had his cap pulled down well over his eyes and a muffler covering the lower part of his face.

'What's happenin' here?' the sergeant demanded.

The man with the muffler merely shrugged.

'Let's have a bit of respect for the law, shall we?' Simcox said. 'When a policeman asks you a question, he expects an answer. Usin' words!'

The sound of horses' hooves, interwoven with the beat of drums and shrill chant of the pipes, was growing ever closer. Though Simcox was still not alarmed, he was developing a sense of some urgency. His business was with the procession, he reminded himself. By the time it passed by this spot, he should be back at his post.

The other man had still not said a word, but Simcox got the distinct impression that behind his muffler, he was grinning.

'I'll give you one last chance to be civil, an' then I'm takin' you in,' the sergeant said. 'Don't bother to ask what the charge is. I haven't thought of one yet – but by the time I get you back to the station, I'll have come up with plenty to book you for.'

The man in the muffler reached into his jacket. When he brought it out again, he was holding something in his hand. It took Sergeant Simcox no more than a split second to identify the thing he was holding as a knife – but that was a split second too long.

The other man was an expert with his weapon, and no sooner was it free of his jacket than it was flying through the air. Simcox opened his mouth to tell the man he could not do that – but he plainly could, and even before the sergeant had got the first word out, he felt the blade embed itself in his chest.

He tried to raise his hands to pull the knife out, but somehow he did not have the strength. Though he didn't want to do it, he felt himself sinking to his knees. He attempted to speak – not to issue a command or an instruction, but only to ask why this should have happened. He got no further than a bubble of blood, and then he keeled over completely.

The man in the muffler walked over to where his victim had fallen, bent down and pulled out the knife. The blade was bloody, and he wiped it clean on the sergeant's uniform jacket before returning it to its sheath.

The procession was almost on him now. The man in the muffler had one more task to perform, and then he was done.

Ten

It seemed to the creature in the back of the Black Maria that two things were happening simultaneously. The first was that the back doors of the van were swinging open to reveal a harsh daylight which hurt his eyes. The second was that something sharp and moderately painful was poking him in the haunches.

His previous experience of the natural order of things told him that he should be curious about the former of these events and angry at the presumptuousness of the latter. But he was too tired for such displays of passion and interest, and contented himself with a lazy roar.

That should have done the trick. Back on his home ground, even a subdued roar would have been enough to have all other living things scattering in a panic. But it did not seem to work here, in his prison which no longer imprisoned him, because no sooner had the roar died away than he was being poked again.

His dull brain worked at the problem. Whatever was causing him pain could not apparently be persuaded to go away. Nor, since he seemed unable to identify his enemy, could he attack it. Clearly, then, there was no alternative but to remove himself from the source of his irritation.

He climbed to his leaden legs, and padded over to the now-open doors. His vision was blurred, and his hearing dulled, but even so he could detect sudden movement to both his left and right and register the screams which were going on all around him.

He did not notice that the floor of the van was higher than the ground outside. That would not have mattered under normal circumstances, because once he felt himself falling, he would have compensated for it. But these were *not* normal circumstances. The drugs had dulled his reactions, and instead of landing lightly on his feet, he crashed to the ground in an ungainly heap.

The screaming continued all around him, and now he could smell animals other than the human ones which had inhabited his world ever since his capture. He climbed awkwardly to his feet again. His vision was still not what it might have been, but even so he had no difficulty in identifying the four-legged creatures only a few feet away from him as juicy, hysterical horses. But better was yet to come. Immediately behind the horses stood a huge grey mountain which had begun to trumpet in alarm. Even in his doped condition, he knew he was not back in the jungle which was his home, but at least elements of his home seemed to have travelled to this strange place with him. On legs which were far from steady, he began an irregular progress towards the elephant.

When the people closest to the Black Marias heard the doors start to open, they turned their heads to see what was going on. And that was when they caught their first sight of the Bengal tiger.

Panic followed immediately. Those who could ran to the left or the right. Those who found these escape routes blocked stepped out into the road in front of the horses, their instincts telling them that it was better to be trampled to death than eaten alive.

The horses had been trained to endure the noise and chaos of battle conditions, and the sudden appearance of a small mob of frightened people was no more than a minor irritation to them. The tiger was another matter. Though they had never encountered any such beast before, they recognized the scent which filled their nostrils was that of a cold-blooded killer. A wave of fear washed over them, sweeping away all they had ever learned of discipline and order. They whinnied and reared. They fought the bits pulling cruelly against the delicate tissues of their mouths and spurs digging forcefully into their flanks. Mere physical pain had ceased to bother them. It was pure terror which was driving them now.

The ponderous elephant took longer than the highly strung horses to understand what was going on, but when it did, the effect on it was no less dramatic. Its trunk, which had been rolled a moment earlier, was suddenly extended and it was trumpeting a cry which might have been defiance or panic – and was probably a little of both.

The elephant's mahout, sensing the danger, attempted to remind the huge beast of its training by prodding it with his bullhook. It was a waste of effort. The elephant barely even noticed the painful pricking through its thick skin, for, like the horses, its whole consciousness was focused on the tiger.

The elephant suddenly reared. The mahout, caught off guard, tried to grab hold of one of the beast's large ears, but before he could establish a grip he found himself sliding down the neck and then falling to the ground. On the back of the elephant, the howdah swayed dangerously, but as long as the strap which ran under the beast's belly held, it was likely to remain in place.

A few of the Horse Guards had managed to regain control of their mounts, but many were doing no more than clinging on, while others had not even managed that basic feat and were lying dazed and shaken on the ground. The tiger continued his erratic progress into the street, though he was so bemused that he was either unaware of, or indifferent to, the consternation he was causing. The musicians and flower girls had already fled with the spectators, but the Maharaja's bodyguards had dropped down on to one knee and were already sighting their ceremonial – though still lethal – muskets on the Bengal killer.

The elephant now had all its feet back on the ground once more, but was resisting the attempts of its mahout to climb back on to its head. The howdah continued to rock dangerously, though the strap which ran under the elephant's belly still held. Inside the howdah, the Maharaja hugged his son tightly to him and tried to guess what chances the frail young body would have of surviving if they both jumped for it.

The bodyguards fired their muskets. One of the balls flew wild and struck a Horse Guard who was just climbing to his feet, but the others thudded into the body of the tiger.

The great striped beast roared in anger, and looked around in a desperate attempt to locate this new source of danger. But even as he was preparing to fight back as he always fought back, there must have been a part of him which recognized that it was already too late – that the wounds he had received were mortal. With one last, half-hearted snarl, he collapsed into a heap and died.

The danger had passed, but the elephant did not know that. It was no easy thing for a creature of its size to manoeuvre around so it was facing in the opposite direction, but what it lacked in gracefulness, it made up for in fearful speed.

As the huge animal turned, the mahout clutched desperately and ineffectually at one of its thick rear legs. He knew he was in great danger of being trampled to death, but he was more willing to risk that than face his master's displeasure.

Most of the crowd and Indian retinue had fled by now,

either north towards Piccadilly or south towards Pall Mall. The Maharaja's bodyguards, their daggers in their hands, cautiously approached the tiger, which, though dead, still twitched as its muscles contracted. On the other side of the Black Marias, in Charles II Street, Sergeant Simcox gave one last cough and then died.

The elephant had completed its turn and, trumpeting loudly, stampeded back up the street, scattering the fleeing spectators. The bodyguards, realizing that their attentions had been diverted by circumstances to the wrong animal, turned to give chase on foot.

So much had happened. So many people had seen so many terrible things which they would remember vividly until their dying days. And less than thirty seconds had passed.

Blackstone had begun to run towards the parade the moment he'd realized what might possibly occur.

'I should have thought this through,' he rebuked himself, as he gasped for breath and drew ever closer to the developing disaster. 'I should have seen this was too good an opportunity for them to miss!'

But even he – who had seen so many incredible things both in London and Afghanistan, who knew enough of the fiendishness of the human mind to be prepared to expect almost anything – could never have predicted the tiger.

He would have reached the level of Charles II Street much quicker if he'd had a clearer path, but he and Patterson were the only ones travelling in that direction, and to get there it was necessary to avoid panicked people and hysterical horses. Even so, he would have felt a quiet pride at the speed at which he had covered the route, had it not been for the fact that by the time he reached the dead tiger, the elephant had already begun its dash for safety.

Since the road had been closed to all other traffic, there was nothing to obstruct or slow down the elephant – at least nothing effective, for people bounced off its legs without it even noticing them.

The Maharaja, still clutching his son and whispering words of comfort, kept his eyes on the road ahead in the vain hope of seeing something which might save them. And suddenly – against all odds – there *was* something!

Standing squarely in the middle of the street ahead of them was a man dressed in the fashion of a nobleman from the Maharaja's own kingdom. And in his hands he was holding a rifle – a big one, like the ones the Maharaja had used himself when shooting elephants.

If he shot the elephant in just the right way, the Maharaja calculated, the creature would not drop immediately but would first slow down and then sink to its knees. And then he and his son could either jump to safety or else be thrown clear. It was a dangerous option, but less dangerous than all the others which seemed to open to him, and if he used his own body as a cushion for the boy's, it was more than possible they would escape with no more than a few bruises.

The man in the road ahead had raised the elephant gun to his shoulder.

'Shoot!' the Maharaja screamed, although he knew that the man probably couldn't hear him. 'Shoot, I say! Save my son, and I will reward you beyond your wildest dreams!'

There was an explosion which seemed so loud to the Maharaja's ears that he could almost have been in the gun barrel it came from. And then, beneath him, the elephant shuddered.

Eleven

Blackstone would later estimate that it had taken him less than two minutes to cover the ground from the point at which he had first noticed the procession to the entrance to Jermyn Street, where the elephant had finally been felled. Even so, he was not the first to arrive. Several of the Maharaja's bodyguards were already clustered around the shattered howdah, which itself lay several feet from the dead elephant.

The Inspector quickly surveyed the rest of the scene. Two constables stood a few yards to the left of him, mumbling uncertainly to each other, and beyond them a fresh crowd was already starting to build up.

'Get these people out of here!' Blackstone screamed at the constables. 'Do it now, while you've still got jobs!'

Ruddick and Calvert took their first steps like men who had just been snapped out of a trance, but within seconds their movements had become more fluid and they were starting to herd the crowd back.

The bodyguards were still in a tight, protective circle, but though they seemed to be concentrating on its centre, they were not entirely unaware of what was going on around them, and as Blackstone approached, two of them whirled round to face him, their daggers already in their hands.

'Police!' Blackstone said.

A small man with wire glasses appeared from the inner circle.

'I am Aggarwal, His Majesty's secretary,' he said. 'Do you have some identification?'

Blackstone produced his warrant card. The secretary peered at it, then spoke a few, rapid words in Hindi.

The circle parted, and Blackstone could see the Maharaja. He was lying on the ground, his head supported by the rolled-up jacket of one of his bodyguards. His eyes were closed, and he was not moving.

Blackstone took a couple of steps forward and knelt down beside the Maharaja. He noted two things immediately. The first was that there was a slight rise and fall of the other man's chest – the second, the strong smell of chloroform.

Blackstone straightened up and stepped back. 'Where is the Maharaja's son?' he said to the secretary.

The small man bent his head. 'Gone!' he said in what was almost a wail. 'His Royal Highness is gone!'

*   *   *

53

'My father took part in the Charge of the Light Brigade,' the Horse Guards' captain said mournfully. 'They rode up that valley under a barrage from hundreds of Russian guns. It was one of the greatest disasters in English military history – but it can't have looked any worse than this.'

Patterson glanced around him. All the cavalry were now back on their feet. But two of their horses were not, nor ever would be again, for the noble beasts had broken legs and had already been shot.

'You shouldn't blame yourself,' the detective told the captain. 'These horses of yours were never trained to deal with anything like this.'

The other man was not consoled. 'I'll be "Tiger" Lennox-Frith from now until the day I die,' he said. 'It'll probably even go on my tombstone.' He took a deep breath. 'Can my men and I be of any use here?'

'Shouldn't think so,' Patterson admitted.

'Then, with your permission, we'll withdraw to barracks and assess our losses.'

'Good plan,' Patterson agreed, for want of anything else to say.

Blackstone and the two constables were standing facing each other at the entrance to Jermyn Street. Both Calvert and Ruddick had their heads bowed – like errant schoolboys who had been summoned to the headmaster's study.

'Tell me, in your own words, exactly what happened,' Blackstone said.

Calvert quickly sketched out the arrival of the Indians and the discussion which had followed.

'And you had this pleasant little conversation while a bull elephant was actually charging you?' Blackstone asked incredulously.

'No, sir,' Ruddick replied. 'It was before that.'

The kidnappers had planned it well, Blackstone thought. Better than well! They had planned it brilliantly.

'So what happened next?' he asked.

'The man with the big rifle told us we should stand back

an' let him handle things. That made a lot of sense to us. You can't stop an elephant with a police-issue truncheon.'

The man in the flowing coat took up his position in the centre of the road as calmly as if he were just waiting for a delivery boy to arrive. He raised the gun and took careful aim. The explosion was as loud as a cannon. The elephant pitched forward, then almost froze for a second before toppling over.

'The howdah was thrown clear, was it?' Blackstone asked.

'The what, sir?'

'The seat.'

'Yes, it was thrown clear.'

'And you immediately went to see how the man and the boy were?'

'No, sir.'

'No? Why not?'

'We were told not to.'

'Keep back,' the man in the flowing coat said.

'But we're the policemen here!' Calvert protested.

'And we are His Majesty's true and loyal servants. It is not meet that your unbeliever's hands should touch his royal personage.'

'So these Indian blokes rushed over to the Maharaja and his son?'

'They rushed over to the man we'd *thought* was the Maharaja up to that point,' Constable Calvert said.

'And wasn't he?'

'No, sir.'

'And how would you know that?'

'Because the man with the gun told us he wasn't, sir.'

Flowing jacket ran back towards the constables, carrying the child in his arms. 'Treachery!' he shouted. 'Treachery and treason!'

'What are you talkin' about?' Ruddick demanded.

'The man lying beside the elephant is not our Maharaja. He is an impostor. A well-known enemy of the state.'

'And you believed him?'

'Oh yes, sir. He sounded very convincin',' Ruddick said.

He frowned. 'Why? Are you tellin' us he isn't an impostor after all?'

'I take it from what you've just said that it didn't occur to you to ask why, if the man dressed as the Maharaja *had* been an impostor, the few dozen people who were with him at the time hadn't noticed,' Blackstone said.

'No, it—'

'Or why, even if *they* were too far away to get a clear view of him, his son, *who was sitting next to him*, didn't spot it!'

'Perhaps . . . p-perhaps if we'd had time to think . . .' Calvert stuttered. 'But it all happened so fast, sir.'

Of course it did, Blackstone agreed silently. That was just how the kidnappers had planned it.

'So since you now believed this man was an impostor, you made an attempt to detain him, did you?' the Inspector asked.

'No, sir.'

'If he's not who he's supposed to be, we'd better arrest him,' Ruddick said to the man in the flowing coat.

'There would be little point in that,' the Indian replied. 'He is already dead.'

'And you just took his word for *that*, too?'

'Like we said, sir, he was very convincin',' Ruddick said.

'Don't tell me that was a lie as well.'

'What state was the young prince in?'

'He was unconscious, sir. Must have knocked his head when he fell off the elephant.'

'Are you sure he was unconscious?'

'Well, he certainly wasn't movin'.'

'You didn't happen to notice a strange smell, did you?'

Ruddick and Calvert exchanged uneasy glances.

'Indians *always* smell funny to me,' Calvert said unconvincingly. 'It's all them spices they eat.'

'So all you could smell was spices. Wasn't there, perhaps, the odour of some kind of chemical?'

'Might have been,' Ruddick said begrudgingly.

'Perhaps the odour of chloroform?'

'It's possible.'

'So, you were standing next to the Indian who had the young prince in his arms. Did you make any attempt to take the prince off him?'

'Yes, we . . . we did try.'

'Then why didn't you *succeed*?'

'The nigger talked us out of it.'

'*We must get the young prince away while we still can,*' Flowing Jacket said.

'*You can't go doin' that,*' Ruddick protested. '*He's a witness to a serious crime.*'

'*He is a small child who is in great danger of being assassinated. Will you take the responsibility for his death?*'

'*Well . . .*'

'*I thought not. In which case, please stand aside while I remove his Royal Highness to a safer place.*'

'An' that's when this cab pulled by two horses arrived,' Ruddick said.

'Who was driving it?'

'Another nigger.'

'Now wasn't that convenient?' Blackstone asked. 'The first five turn up with an elephant gun just as the elephant goes berserk, and at the very moment they need a cab to take the young prince away, one arrives. It's almost as if they'd known exactly what was going to happen, isn't it?'

Calvert muttered, 'I suppose so.'

And Ruddick said nothing at all.

Twelve

Patterson, shoulder-to-shoulder with the veterinary surgeon, watched as the four burly attendants from the London Zoological Gardens struggled to get the tiger into the back of the van.

'A fine specimen,' the vet said mournfully. 'Did they really have to shoot him?'

'He was running wild in the streets of London,' Patterson pointed out. 'And he *is* a man-eater.'

'Tigers aren't *particularly* attracted to human flesh,' the vet grumbled. 'Given the choice, he'd probably have eaten one of the horses. Or had a go at the elephant. And if he had decided on human *hors d'oeuvres*, so what? There's men and enough to spare in London – but there was only *one* tiger.'

Patterson wondered whether the other man was joking, then decided that he probably wasn't. 'Can you do some tests on him?' he asked.

'What kind of tests? Want to know how the poor creature died? I can tell you that now. He was shot by a bunch of irresponsible niggers. I've seen the bullet holes for myself.'

'I'm more concerned with the way he was acting earlier,' Patterson explained. 'A couple of the Horse Guards claimed that he didn't seem very steady on his feet. I was wondering if he'd been drugged in some way.'

'If he was drugged, then there was even less excuse to shoot him,' the vet said, with growing outrage.

'Could you find out about drugs?' Patterson asked patiently.

'Suppose so. I could do it while I was skinning him.'

'Skinning him? Why would you want to do that?'

'Look,' the vet said, 'I'm very angry that he was shot, but now that he *is* dead, his skin's no use to him – and it will make a very fine addition to my living room.'

'I imagine it will,' Patterson agreed.

The attendants had succeeded in cramming the tiger into the back of their van and had slammed the door on him.

'Well, that's another job done,' the vet said, starting to walk back towards the van.

'How long?' Patterson called after him.

The vet glanced over his shoulder. 'How long to skin him?'

'How long to carry out the tests for me.'

'Couple of hours. Maybe a little longer.'

The vet climbed on to the passenger seat of the van, issued a terse instruction to his driver, and was gone. Patterson looked around him. There was so much of the bloody mess still left to clear up that he had no real idea of where to start.

At least the Maharaja was no longer an immediate problem. His bodyguards had escorted him back to Claridge's the moment he'd been revived. His dancers, musicians and flower girls, on the other hand, had been left to their own devices, until they'd been rounded up like sheep by a couple of constables. Now they stood huddled together in a group. They looked lost, Patterson thought – exotic, dark little people who were completely out of place under an English sky which, even in August, must seem dull to them.

He walked over to the group. 'Does any of you speak any English?' he asked hopefully.

'Me. A little,' volunteered one of the drummers.

'Where are you staying in London?'

The drummer looked to his companions for guidance, and an animated discussion followed.

'Big palace,' the drummer said finally. 'Claridge Palace.'

'You're staying in Claridge's Hotel?' Patterson asked incredulously.

The drummer nodded. 'Some under roof, some down below floor.'

Some in the garrets and some in the cellars, Patterson translated. 'And can you find your way back there?' he asked.

The drummer nodded confidently.

'Then you're to return to the hotel and stay in your rooms until a policeman tells you that you can leave. Understand?'

'Unner'sand,' the drummer said.

Right, that was one more problem dealt with, Patterson told himself. Now he really must turn his mind to the elephant.

Messages had been sent out to intercept the coach which had whisked the Maharaja's son away, but though Blackstone had gone through the motions, he considered it a waste of effort. It was a slow, ponderous business, alerting all the coppers in London about *anything*, and by the time even half of them were informed, the kidnappers would probably have ditched the coach.

There had to be an easier way to keep in touch, the Inspector thought. Perhaps some day all policemen would be taught Morse code, and would carry little telegraphy keys around with them. Then he shrugged his shoulders dismissively. In an ideal world such devices would appear like magic, but the world he inhabited was far from ideal, and he couldn't imagine that anything so sophisticated would ever actually be developed.

He turned his attention to the two constables, who were still waiting in trepidation for him to pass judgement on them.

'I'm not blaming you lads for what happened,' he said.

'You're not?' Calvert said, with the gasp of a condemned man who's just been told that the hanging's off.

'No, I'm not,' Blackstone reiterated. 'You acted like a pair of bloody fools, right enough, but I'm not sure that anybody else put in the same position would have done any better.'

The constables still looked dubious. This was not the kind of good luck which ever happened to people like them, their expressions seemed to say. But Blackstone meant it. When all was said and done, if the gang could run rings round him, then what chance did the ordinary copper on the street have?

'So now I've put your minds at ease about that, let's turn to more important matters,' the Inspector continued. 'Tell me something that will set me off on the right track.'

The two constables tried to show their gratitude for their unexpected reprieve by making an ostentatious show of scouring their brains.

'I'm not sure that the man with the elephant gun was a real nigger at all,' Ruddick said.

'Why should you think that? Wasn't he dark enough?'

'Oh, he was dark. Very dark. But after he'd shot the elephant an' rescued the kid, I noticed that his face had gone a bit blotchy. It didn't really register at the time, but lookin' back on it, I think that his face may have been dyed, an' that in all the excitement the dye might have started to run.'

'What about the others? Did they all look as if they were in disguise as well?'

The two constables shrugged helplessly. 'It's hard to say,

sir,' Calvert admitted. 'You see, most of our attention was on the man with the gun.'

Which was just what he'd wanted, Blackstone thought. One man had to be very much exposed by the nature of the task, but the less the constables saw of the others, the better it would be for the whole gang.

'Describe the man with the gun to me,' he said.

'He was about six feet tall, an' had dark eyes,' Calvert told him.

'Did he have a big nose?'

'Not over-big, sir.'

'Did he have a lot of hair, or was he going bald?'

'Couldn't say, sir. He was wearin' one of them turban things.'

'What about the rest of his face? His chin? His mouth?'

'Couldn't see much of them, sir,' Calvert admitted. 'He had this big bushy beard, you see.'

'An' now I think about it, that might have been false as well,' Ruddick added helpfully.

Patterson walked slowly around the fallen elephant. It was the fifth or sixth time he had circumnavigated the body looking for a solution to his problems, and each time the huge beast just seemed to get even bigger.

It was a relief to see that Blackstone had finished talking to the constables, and was now headed in his direction.

'Learn anything useful, sir?' he asked hopefully.

'Yes,' Blackstone replied. 'I've learned that trained policemen are not much more use as witnesses than members of the general public. How are things going from your end?'

Patterson looked down at the mountain of grey flesh. 'I don't know what to do with this elephant,' he admitted. 'I'm sure there isn't a wagon in London big enough to put it on, so we'll just have to use a large team of horses. But that's only the start of our problems, isn't it? Even if we succeed in dragging it away, where do we drag it *to*?'

On a day which had started out badly – and could only

get worse – Blackstone felt the sudden need for a little light relief.

'The elephant's evidence of a crime,' he said, in a deeply official voice. 'Which means, according to regulations, that it should be stored in the evidence room back at the Yard until it's needed for further examination.'

'The evidence room,' Patterson repeated, recognizing Blackstone's game and falling in with it. 'That certainly might be one solution, sir. The only drawback to it I can see is that the elephant's probably bigger than the room it's supposed to be stored in.'

'Couldn't dump it in the Thames, could you?' Blackstone suggested.

'I think somebody would probably notice, sir.'

'Yes, there are far too many nosy buggers around in London these days.' Blackstone thought for a moment. 'I'll tell you what we could do – send one of the lads up to Smithfield.'

'To the meat market?'

'That's right. Tell him to find half a dozen butchers who fancy the idea of facing a real challenge.'

Patterson grinned, but only for a moment. 'You're completely serious!' he said.

'Can't think what else we can do with the beast,' Blackstone told his sergeant. He took out his pocket watch. 'All hell will be breaking loose at the Yard just about now, so I suppose I'd better get back there.'

'What do you want me to do here?' Patterson asked.

'Have a look at that van which your witnesses seem to think the tiger came out of. And see if you can find this Sergeant Simcox. Everybody's been talking about him, but I haven't seen hide nor hair of the bugger yet.'

Thirteen

The two men were waiting for Blackstone in his office. They were both total strangers to him. He hadn't invited them to be there. And he certainly hadn't given them permission to sit behind his desk.

One of the unexpected – and unwelcome – visitors was a tall man with a military bearing which was apparent even though he was sitting down. He had grey intelligent eyes and a greying clipped moustache. He must once have been a very dashing man, though the broken veins in his cheeks were evidence to the fact that hard drinking had ceased to be a diversion and was now a full-time occupation.

The other man was smaller and rounder. His frock coat had obviously come from Savile Row, the diamond in his tiepin would not have looked out of place on a princess's finger. He had brown eyes which were not so much hard as sulky. He looked, Blackstone decided, like a man who resented having been born with a mere silver spoon in his mouth, while most of the men he constantly rubbed shoulders with had come into the world with a whole *canteen* of cutlery in theirs.

Blackstone walked over to the coat rack and hung up his hat. So far, no one in the room had said a word. The visitors were obviously expecting him to speak first – if only to comment on the fact that his position had been usurped – but the rabbit does not make its move until it has divined the stoat's intentions.

The Inspector turned, walked over to his desk, pulled out a visitor's chair, and sat down. From the look on the round man's face, it was clear that he thought Blackstone would now have no option *but* to speak – so it must have come as some disappointment when, instead, the Inspector merely took out his cigarette case. The round man coughed, and even in that he managed to convey resentment of the world in general, and Blackstone in particular.

'My name is Sir Horace Fullerton-Smythe,' he said. 'My companion here is Major Cedric Walsh (retired).'

Blackstone lit up his cigarette. He inhaled, and let the smoke tickle his lungs before blowing it out through his mouth again.

'I'm Sam Blackstone,' he said, 'and, until very recently, I was under the impression that this was my office.'

Fullerton-Smythe frowned sulkily, but Walsh seemed to find the comment amusing.

'You are probably wondering why we're here,' Fullerton-Smythe said.

No I'm bloody not, Blackstone thought. You're here because you want to stick your noses into matters which you know bugger all about – and I've probably got no choice but to let you do just that.

'I am here as a representative of the India Office,' Fullerton-Smythe continued. 'Major Walsh is in attendance because he has some local knowledge of Chandrapore and its ruler.'

It must have been hard to make Walsh's Indian experience sound like little more than an insult, the Inspector thought, yet Fullerton-Smythe had somehow managed it.

Blackstone studied the Major's face. Either Walsh felt himself to be above such disparaging remarks, he decided, or else he no longer cared.

'You should be made aware of the fact that we, in the government, consider this situation with the Maharaja's son to be extremely grave,' Fullerton-Smythe continued. 'And as a consequence of that, we desire – nay, we insist on – a speedy resolution to the problem.'

'You can insist all you like, Sir Horace,' Walsh said, 'but if wishes were horses, beggars would ride.'

'And how am I to interpret that particular remark?' Fullerton-Smythe asked haughtily.

'Forget it,' Walsh said.

'No, I will *not* forget it. What did you mean?'

Walsh shrugged. 'I know Indian bandits better that any

man alive,' he said. 'When I was a political agent, I rode with them for several months and—'

'We are not here to listen to your reminiscences of your glory-days in India,' Fullerton-Smythe said cuttingly.

'I rode with them for months,' Walsh repeated, as though the other man had never spoken. 'I developed a grudging respect for both their nerve and their cunning, but even so I doubt if they could have carried out any operation as imaginative and disciplined as this kidnapping.'

'But that's neither here nor there, is it?' Fullerton-Smythe asked, both exasperated and puzzled. 'We are not in India. This is England.'

'True,' Walsh agreed.

'Well then?'

'I suspect there is not much difference between the average Indian criminal and the average British criminal.'

'You can't compare niggers with Britons,' Fullerton-Smythe said dismissively. 'The Indians are a very primitive people.'

'A very primitive people who nevertheless constructed the wonder that is the Taj Mahal.'

Fullerton-Smythe turned to Blackstone. 'Tell the Major he's talking nonsense,' he demanded.

Blackstone forced himself to hide his smile. 'Since I'm a patriot, I like to think that English criminals are the best robbers and cut-throats in the world,' he said. 'But on this occasion, I'm forced to agree with Major Walsh. There's not a gang in London who could have pulled off this particular job.'

'Then who *is* responsible?' Fullerton-Smythe asked.

'I have no idea,' Blackstone admitted, 'but whoever it is, they won't be easy to track down.'

'I'm not sure I like your defeatist attitude, Inspector,' Fullerton-Smythe said.

'And I'm not sure I can do anything about that, Sir Horace,' Blackstone countered.

The politician flushed and ran his index finger around the edge of his starched collar.

'Perhaps I should consider asking for this case to be reassigned to a more experienced and forceful officer,' he said.

'Perhaps you should,' Blackstone agreed.

'I am *serious* about that, you know, Inspector Blackstone!'

'So am I. I've never been one to pick up the poisoned chalice when I didn't have to – and this case is a poisoned chalice if ever I saw one.'

Fullerton-Smythe rose heavily and portentously to his feet. 'I intend to talk to your superiors immediately,' he said. 'You'll be hearing more – *much* more – of this in due course, Inspector Blackstone.' He turned to face the Major. 'Are you coming, Walsh?'

'I'm not sure I'd be of much use to you at this particular moment, Sir Horace,' the Major replied. 'You're the man with the political influence necessary to make any changes in how the investigation is run. All I have to offer is *some local knowledge* of Chandrapore and its ruler.'

'Perhaps you're right,' Fullerton-Smythe agreed, missing the point entirely. 'But there may be other matters for which I need to draw on your expertise. I will see you back at the India Office in two hours. And I *mean* two hours, Major. Do not be diverted by any drinking establishments on the way.'

'I'll be there,' Walsh promised.

Ignoring Blackstone, Fullerton-Smythe squeezed around the desk, opened the door and stepped out into the corridor. Once he had gone, Major Walsh stretched out his legs as if he could finally make himself at home.

'It's comforting to think that while our lads are out risking their lives in India, they have the backing of such a wise and strong man as Sir Horace Fullerton-Smythe,' he said. He pulled out his cigarette case, and with hands which trembled slightly, lit up a cheroot. 'Perhaps now that the idiot is gone, we can adjourn to the nearest convenient pub, and I can brief you on the situation as I see it.'

'I don't think there'd be much point in that, since the chances are I'll be off the case within the hour,' Blackstone said.

Walsh smiled broadly, as if he considered the comment hugely amusing. 'Do you *want* to be off the case?'

'Like I said, it's a poisoned chalice.'

'I asked a direct question,' Walsh pointed out. 'You didn't give me a direct answer.'

'No, I didn't, did I,' Blackstone agreed.

'I've known men – and I was one of them – who'd volunteer for duties that most other soldiers would refuse to undertake even if the only alternative was a court martial. Now why do you think that was?'

'You tell me,' Blackstone said.

'Because what one man sees as a suicide mission, another will view merely as a challenge. And you're one of the latter breed, Inspector. You like a good challenge.'

Blackstone could see no reason why he should feel unnerved by Walsh, but he most certainly did.

'You seem to know a lot about me, Major – considering we've only just met,' he said.

Walsh smiled again, sadly this time. 'Don't fall into the same trap as that stuffed-shirt Sir Horace Fullerton-Smythe did,' he warned.

'And what trap might that be?'

'Don't assume that because I've seen better days I'm now of no more use than a broken chair. There are still people of importance who are wise enough to both seek my advice and to confide in me.'

'I'm sure there are,' Blackstone said hurriedly.

'No, you're not,' Walsh corrected him. 'You're not sure at all. But at least your mind – unlike the one which passes for a mind in Sir Horace Fullerton-Smythe's balloon of a head – is open to the *possibility* that what I say may be true.'

'Go on,' Blackstone told him.

'A little while ago, you were involved in the case of a young man of good background who was found floating in the Thames with his throat cut. Isn't that correct?'

'It may be.'

'But it didn't take a smart chap like you long to realize that this was not a straightforward murder – that there were, in fact, serious political ramifications to the case. And not only domestic ramifications. Foreign powers were involved. Well?'

'You wouldn't expect me to confirm that, would you?'

'No, but I note you are not denying it, either.' Walsh smiled again. 'Let me tell you something you *don't* know. Your participation in that particular affair is too sensitive ever to become public knowledge, but given the great service you did for your country, there is some serious talk in the corridors of power about awarding you a medal in secret.'

'You're joking!' Blackstone said.

'Not at all. It is perfectly true. Of course, Sir Horace Windbag, for all his self-importance, knows nothing of this. But even he may begin to suspect he's not being given the whole picture when he's told that, despite his objections to you, you are to remain in charge of the investigation.'

'And you really think that's what will happen, do you?' Blackstone asked.

'I'm sure of it. What does the opinion of some jack-in-office matter, when weighed against the wishes of the two very important people who are convinced you are the right man for the job?'

'And who might these two very important people be?' Blackstone asked. 'Or is it a secret?'

'No secret at all – at least, from you,' Walsh replied. 'You have the strongest possible backing from both the Queen and the Prime Minister. Shall we go and have that drink now?'

Fourteen

The Horse Guards had returned to their barracks and the uniformed branch had cleared the area of sightseers. Patterson cut a solitary figure on the street, though he felt far from alone considering the dozen or so unanswered questions he had to keep him company.

At that particular moment he was wondering about the Black Marias. Were they genuine, or were they fake? If genuine, how had the kidnappers got hold of them? And why *two*? There had, after all, only been *one* tiger.

He stepped back, and the answer to this last question soon became obvious to him. The second Black Maria had a definite purpose, but that purpose had nothing to do with transporting anything. The van was there to complete the blocking off of Charles II Street – to ensure that when the tiger emerged, there was only one direction in which it could go.

A smile of quiet triumph came to Patterson's face, only to quickly melt away again as a new question popped into his head.

Why should the tiger have wanted to go *anywhere*? he wondered. The brute had been drugged – almost everyone he'd spoken to had agreed about that – so why hadn't it simply remained inside the van?

Patterson pictured his tall, thin mentor standing before him, and tried to imagine what Blackstone would have speculated in this situation.

'Imagine it was a drunken bloke instead of a doped tiger,' said a voice in his head, which sounded very much like the Inspector's. 'What would make him shift himself?'

'Something somebody else did to him,' a second voice – Patterson's own – replied.

'Then find out what that "something" is,' the Blackstone voice advised.

Fair enough, Patterson thought, stepping closer to the two Black Marias.

The doors of the right-hand van were wide open, whilst those of the one on the left were tightly shut. So it didn't take a trained detective to work out which van the tiger had emerged from, Patterson thought. It was so simple that even the Commissioner could have worked it out – given time. Besides, the back of the right van reeked of tiger. And if any more confirmation had been needed, the animal had left its calling card in the form of a large heap of tiger droppings.

Patterson climbed into the back of the van. Running around the walls was an elaborate system of rods and gears. There was no such mechanism in the back of a regular police Black Maria, and for a moment Patterson wondered what it was all in aid of. And then he had it!

He'd been wondering earlier what kind of man it would take to be brave enough – or stupid enough – to open the doors and let the tiger out. Now he saw nobody had undertaken the dangerous task – because nobody had needed to. It had all been done mechanically, by someone sitting on the driver's seat.

He advanced further into the van, stepping carefully to avoid any tiger shit lying in wait in the shadows. He noticed the small circles of light in the front wall almost immediately, but it was not until he got close to them that he identified them as a series of six small holes, drilled close to the floor, which were letting in daylight.

He wondered why anyone should have gone to so much trouble. Perhaps for ventilation. But if that had been the case, they would surely have been larger, and there would have been more of them.

Patterson squatted down. If the tiger had been standing up, the holes would have been at about the level of its knees, he thought. But the tiger probably hadn't been standing. In its doped condition, it would have been much more likely to have been lying down. And in that case, it would have been its trunk which was on a level with the holes.

'All the better to prick you through, my dear!' Patterson said aloud.

That was it! That had to be it! The man on the driver's side, having opened the doors, had then proceeded to taunt the tiger with a metal spike or sharpened wooden stick. And the tiger, tired of being poked, had decided to take itself elsewhere, which was exactly what the kidnappers had wanted.

Patterson backed out of the van and stepped down on to the street. After the stink inside, it was a relief to be in the open again, and he took in a lungful of good old smoky London air.

What next? he wondered.

There was a gap between the side of the right-hand van and the wall. It was not big enough for a full-grown tiger to squeeze through, but for a fit – if slightly portly – young police officer, it was quite another matter. And he supposed he *should* go to the other side, because it was always just possible that the kidnappers, who had not put a foot wrong during the rest of operation, had suffered from a sudden mental aberration and left what might turn out to be a vital clue on the driver's seat.

A body had been the last thing he had been expecting to find when he had eased his way through to the other side of the van, but the moment he saw the three stripes on the dead man's arm, he realized what had happened to Sergeant Simcox.

'Jesus!' he said.

Blackstone had been angry enough before. When he learned that one of their own had been killed, he'd hit the bloody roof.

Fifteen

M ajor Walsh walked over to the bar and ordered a double whisky for himself and a pint of bitter for Blackstone. The whisky came first, and while the pint was still being pulled, the Major knocked it back and ordered another one. Watching the whole incident from a table, Blackstone found himself wondering just how many state secrets *he'd* entrust the Major with.

Walsh brought the drinks over to the table, his hands now so steady that he did not spill a drop.

'Would you like to know why our friend Fullerton-Smythe is so concerned about Chandrapore?' he asked.

'Very much,' Blackstone said.

'Then perhaps, given that you must only have been a small

child when the Indian Mutiny occurred, we should begin with a brief history lesson,' Walsh said. 'You wouldn't object to that, would you?'

'Only a fool ignores history,' Blackstone replied.

'You're quite right about that,' Walsh agreed, 'though it would probably surprise you to learn just how many fools there *are* around. To begin then. The Mutiny started in 1857, when the sepoy regiments in several of the northern cities revolted. The British, both those in India and those back home, found it almost impossible to believe at first. Can you understand that?'

Blackstone nodded. 'If a dog habitually submits to your kicks, it comes as a great shock when it finally decides to bite back.'

'Quite so,' Walsh agreed, looking longingly at his already-empty whisky glass. 'But the fact was, the dog *had* bitten back. The Mutiny soon developed into a bloody business on all sides. The renegade troops massacred a great many wives and children of British officers and officials – though the actual figures were later considerably inflated by our government.'

'Why was that?'

'To justify the extent of the repression which followed. Some British commanders hung every Indian they could lay their hands on. Others were even more vindictive. Before he executed his prisoners, Colonel Neill forced the Hindus among them to eat beef and the Moslems to eat pork – the point being that they would not only know they were dying, but understand that they died damned. There are accounts of Sikh soldiers roasting mutineers over a slow fire, while British officers looked on.' Walsh looked down at his glass again. 'You wouldn't mind getting me another drink, would you?'

'Of course not,' Blackstone said.

He bought another whisky, making it a treble this time. Walsh cupped his hands around it as if it were a precious relic.

'The important question to ask is why the rebellion failed,' the Major continued. 'Consider this. There were only 21,000

72

British troops in the whole of India, whereas the combined sepoy regiments of Bengal, Madras and Bombay alone amounted to an excess of 277,000 native soldiers. In addition, there were many areas in which the civilians gave their wholehearted support to the revolt. So what went wrong, do you think, Inspector Blackstone?'

'The Sikhs remained loyal, as did some of the Hindu and Moslem regiments,' Blackstone guessed.

'Very good,' Walsh agreed. 'But in my opinion, that was not the decisive factor. Not by a long chalk!'

'Then what was?'

'Consider your own position, Mr Blackstone. Which are there more of in London – policemen or criminals?'

Blackstone grinned. 'Criminals. Without a doubt.'

'So why, with the numbers on their side, do the criminals not call the shots?'

'Because they're not united, and we are.'

'Precisely. And that was exactly the case in India. There was not *one* mutiny, you see, but a series of mutinies. Most of the rebels – including the rebel Indian princes – never looked further than their own state. If they had been united, they would have been harder – perhaps even impossible – to defeat.'

Walsh was making a great deal of sense at that moment, Blackstone thought, but that state of affairs wouldn't continue after he'd knocked back another whisky or two. It was time to get him to the point.

'What has all this to do with Chandrapore?' the Inspector asked.

'We'll come to that in a moment,' Walsh said. 'We must now shift our gaze from the Indian sub-continent to Europe, which is best seen as a very small cage inhabited by increasingly larger hounds.'

'Meaning what?'

'Meaning that Europe is too small to satisfy the ambitions of all the strong monarchs who now inhabit it. I do not know who we will have to fight when it comes to it. It may be Germany or Austro-Hungary, Russia or France. Possibly it

73

will be a combination of several of them. But we *will* have to fight – and within the next twenty years.'

'Is that a personal view?' Blackstone asked.

'Yes, but though it would never admit it openly, it is also a view that this government – and any government likely to succeed it – secretly shares. Consider the implications of that, Mr Blackstone. If we are to pursue a war in Europe, we will need not only peace in India, we will need that vast rich country's resources at our disposal. If India were to take the opportunity to revolt, however, we would not only be denied Indian troops for the European battlefield, but we would be forced to send precious British troops to India.'

'Not a pretty thought,' Blackstone said.

'Not a pretty thought at all,' Walsh agreed. He smiled again. 'You may relax, Inspector. I will come to the point I am trying to make long before I pass out from the drink.'

'I never thought—'

'Yes, you did, but that is only understandable. To get back to Chandrapore, then. During the Mutiny, the Maharaja stayed loyal. But he was a very different prince to the one who runs the state now.'

'You don't think we can rely on this one?'

'I served on secondment in Chandrapore for three years, and I got to know this Maharaja well. He's a very intelligent man and a very strong leader. This would not matter if he came from a small or poor state, but unfortunately Chandrapore is neither. Were he to lead a revolt against us, he would not make the mistakes his predecessors fell victim to. He would unite the whole of northern India – and perhaps the south as well – behind his leadership.'

'And is he likely to want to do that?'

'If you'd asked me yesterday, I would not have hesitated to say no. His aim then was simply to maintain his state, so that he could pass it on as an inheritance to his son. But what if he loses that son? Grief can do strange things to a man. If he is to be denied the glory of establishing a royal line, then perhaps he will seek personal immediate glory, and decide to become the emperor of India.'

'But surely, he has other sons who could carry on the line,' Blackstone said.

'You would think so, wouldn't you?' Walsh agreed. 'But his wife is dead. She died giving birth to Balachandra, her first and only child.'

'The Maharaja could marry again.'

'Yes, he could – but it would be a pointless exercise. Shortly after his wife died, he caught a particularly nasty strain of a social disease. He recovered his health, but lost his manhood. There will be no more children, however fertile the woman he takes as his wife.'

'So you're saying that returning his son to him is the key to maintaining stability in Northern India?' Blackstone asked.

'Yes,' Walsh replied gravely. 'That's exactly what I'm saying.'

Sixteen

Blackstone stood by his office window, watching dusk fall over the Thames. At least, that was what Patterson *assumed* he was doing, though since the Inspector hadn't spoken nor moved so much as a muscle for several minutes, it was difficult to say for certain. Perhaps the Inspector's eyes weren't taking in the view at all. Perhaps, though his body was still in the room, his mind was somewhere else entirely.

Patterson gave an involuntary shudder. This wasn't the hot anger – the hit-the-roof anger – that he'd been anticipating when he told his boss about Simcox's murder. This was a cold, chilling rage which was much, much worse.

Only once before had the sergeant ever seen his boss in such a state. They'd been investigating a series of razor attacks on prostitutes, and their investigation had led them to a room in a cheap boarding house in the East End. There'd been four people in the room when they arrived. One had been a girl – she couldn't have been more than thirteen –

who'd been lying in the corner, softly whimpering to herself and doing her best to staunch the blood which was flowing from the slashes in her cheeks. The other three had been men – big bruisers who claimed the right to most of the pittance which poor girls like this one earned on the streets.

Blackstone had told the men they were under arrest and that they should come quietly. But he hadn't wanted that, his sergeant had realized. He wanted them to resist – he wanted a chance to hurt them.

A carefully aimed kick had knocked Patterson out of the action right from the start, which had left one tall but thin police Inspector to deal with three heavy thugs whose occupation it was to hurt people.

Lying on the floor in agony, the sergeant had been a helpless witness to what followed. Later, he would describe it to his colleagues as a bloodbath, and there was no doubt that it had been. Blackstone was on sick leave for a week – and it had been a month before the police surgeon finally decided that the hooligans were fit enough to stand trial.

Blackstone turned around. The cold rage still showed on his face, but now he seemed to have it under control, and Patterson felt himself breathing a deep sigh of relief.

'Why do you think the kidnappers killed Sergeant Simcox?' the Inspector asked.

'Because the poor devil was unlucky enough to get in the way,' Patterson suggested.

'By which you mean that if he'd never gone round to the front of the Black Marias, he'd still be alive?'

'Yes, I suppose so.'

The Inspector nodded gravely. 'But if they hadn't murdered Simcox, they'd have found an excuse to kill another copper.'

'You think murdering a policeman was part of the plan?'

'Undoubtedly.'

'But why?'

'Why did they send that poor bloody kid's head back in a hat box?' Blackstone demanded. 'Why did they stage the kidnapping in the way they did, when they could just have stormed the Maharaja's suite in Claridge's?'

'An attack on the suite might have been expected,' Patterson pointed out. 'What they chose to do instead gave them the element of surprise on their side.'

'True,' Blackstone agreed. 'But wouldn't they have caused just as much confusion with a small bomb? Why use anything as elaborate and complex as a live tiger?'

'I don't know,' Patterson admitted.

'Because it *was* complex and elaborate! Because they wanted to show us just what they could do if they set their minds to it. Nothing has happened accidentally or as a spur of the moment decision. They cut off the kid's head and murdered Sergeant Simcox to demonstrate that they're serious. They'll hang for those murders, if we catch them. Not only that, but they know we know that they know it. It's their way of saying that they're not interested in half measures – they'll either get everything they want, or they'll die.'

'But what *do* they want?' Patterson asked. 'Shouldn't we have had a ransom demand by now?'

'Yes, and if it had been an ordinary kidnapping, we certainly would have. But we've already established that it *isn't* ordinary. They're not in a hurry, like most kidnappers. They're working to a timetable of their own – and they're banking on us not being able to find out anything about them while that timetable's still in operation.'

'They could be right about that,' Patterson said gloomily. 'We haven't got a thing to go on so far.'

'That's not true,' Blackstone contradicted him. 'They've left a mountain of clues. They couldn't have failed to, with an operation of this complexity.'

'Clues?' Patterson repeated. 'Like what?'

'The tiger, for a start. By the way, have you worked out *why* it was drugged yet?'

'Because that made it easier to get it into the Black Maria?'

'Possibly that's part of the reason. But why drug it so heavily? Wouldn't it have been better to have it fully alert when it came out of the van?'

'Yes, it would,' Patterson said. Then catching the look of

disdain on his boss's face, he quickly added, 'That is to say, no, it wouldn't have been better.'

'Why not?'

Why not indeed? Patterson wondered. And then he saw the way Blackstone's mind was working. 'Drugged or not, it would have frightened the horses, thus accomplishing half its function,' he said. 'And if it hadn't been drugged, it might have attacked the elephant.'

'So?'

'So the object of the exercise was never to harm the elephant at that point. Quite the reverse. All the kidnappers wanted was for the elephant to turn around and stampede back to where they were waiting for it.'

'Absolutely,' Blackstone agreed. 'Now we come to the second point. They had both the Maharaja and his son in their hands. Why did they only take the son?'

'That's easy. It'd be like killing the goose which laid the golden eggs.'

'Go on.'

'The kidnappers could be pretty sure that the Maharaja would pay the ransom to get his only son back. What they *couldn't* be sure of is that whoever took over in Chandrapore once the Maharaja had gone missing would be willing to raise the money to get *him* back.'

'We'll make a copper out of you yet,' Blackstone said approvingly. 'Now let's get back to the way in which the tiger might help us to get on to their trail. Suppose you wanted to get your hands on one of the beasts. How would you go about it?'

'There must be zoos and circuses that have tigers.'

'So you'd steal it from one of them?'

Patterson thought about it for a few seconds. 'No,' he said finally.

'Why not?'

'Because it's too chancy. I'd be running the risk of getting caught during the actual theft – which would mean that the real operation would be over even before it started. And even if I got away with it, the theft would create a sensation.

Everybody would be on the lookout for the beast. Moving it around the country would be almost impossible.'

'So you wouldn't steal it. What would you do instead? Buy one in India and have it shipped to England?'

'No, I wouldn't do that, either.'

'Why not?'

'Because I'd leave a trail connecting me with the tiger.'

'So you wouldn't steal it, and you wouldn't bring it in yourself. What's left?'

'I'd arrange it for someone else to bring it into the country, without them knowing that they were doing it for me.'

'And how would you go about that?'

Patterson scratched his head. 'There, I must admit, sir, you've got me completely stumped.'

'Think about it,' Blackstone ordered him. 'Where, in London, can you get whatever your heart desires?'

'I don't know.'

'Aren't there some organizations which make a positive virtue out of the fact that they can lay their hands on anything you want?'

'Not that I . . .' Patterson paused, and then grinned. 'The big department stores!' he said.

'The big department stores,' Blackstone agreed. 'Find out if any of them has fulfilled an order for a man-eating Bengal tiger, and if so, who placed that order.'

Seventeen

'It wasn't your tiger?' Patterson asked. 'You're sure of that?'

'It wasn't our tiger,' the general manager of Harrods' Pet Department replied firmly. 'I have told you that twice already, and if you put the question a hundred more times, the answer will still be the same.'

The manager, a man in late middle age with cotton-wool

hair and large belly, looked the epitome of Dickensian geniality. And possibly he would have been with a normal customer. But Patterson was not a customer at all. He was a policeman attempting to connect a very respectable business with a very reprehensible crime – which made him an enemy of the store.

'How can you be so *certain* it wasn't your tiger?' Patterson asked. 'Do you brand them with the Harrods trademark? Do you shave the name of the store into their fur?'

'Of course we don't. That would be absurd.'

'Then for all you know, it could well have been one of yours.'

The manager sniffed. 'Leaving aside for one moment your obviously mistaken impression that we sell tigers in much in the same way – and in the same volume – as we sell our famous fruit preserves, I still maintain that it is ludicrous of you to claim that the beast could be ours,' he said severely. 'Harrods has a reputation to consider. We would no more provide tigers for kidnappers than we would supply skeleton keys to house burglars.'

'So you *haven't* sold any tigers?'

'I did not say that.'

'Then you have?'

'I will need to check.'

As if it were something he would be likely to forget, Patterson thought, as he watched the manager lift a thick, leather-bound ledger on to the counter and slowly begin to thumb through the pages.

'Could you see whether you've sold any polar bears, while you're at it?' Patterson asked.

The manager looked up. 'Are you suggesting that a polar bear might also have been used for criminal purposes?' he demanded.

'No,' Patterson admitted.

'Then why . . . ?'

'Just curious.'

The manager shot the sergeant a look of intense dislike, then returned his attention to the ledger.

'Yes, it does appear as if we recently fulfilled an order for a tiger,' he admitted reluctantly.

'*How* recently?'

'How recently was it ordered? Or how recently did we deliver it?' the manager asked, using the delaying tactics which – it seemed to Patterson – every manager and minor official in the country was born with the innate ability to manipulate.

'Both,' Patterson replied. 'When it was ordered *and* when it was delivered.'

'You will appreciate that there is inevitably some considerable time lapse between those two pivotal points in the transaction?' the manager asked.

Patterson wondered how long it would take the store to get him a gorilla and – once it had arrived – how long it would take him to train it to beat up the supercilious manager.

'Give me both dates,' he said.

'It was ordered over a year ago.' The manager consulted the ledger yet again. 'And it was delivered two weeks yesterday.'

'And who was it delivered to?'

'It was delivered to a Colonel Howarth, who is, I believe, a retired military gentleman.'

Given that he was a colonel, such a supposition was a better than even bet, Patterson thought, but he contented himself with saying, '*Where* exactly was the animal delivered to?'

'To Colonel Howarth's estate in Berkshire.'

Which was just about as close to London as anyone could hope to keep a tiger-in-waiting, Patterson thought.

The British government had been sending emissaries to see the Maharaja almost from the moment he had returned to Claridge's. The first had been a fairly minor figure in the India Office. Then, as the afternoon wore on, and an appreciation of the implications grew, the visitors began to be more and more important. Their status did not matter to the Maharaja. He had refused to see any of them. In his current mood of despair, he would even have declined to see Lord Salisbury himself, should the Prime Minister have chosen to put in an appearance. Yet in contrast to all his refusals, he was willing to see the man waiting outside at that moment, even though the rank of the man in question was low – and his prospects even lower.

The secretary opened the door. The visitor stepped into the room and gave an unsteady bow.

'It is only late afternoon and already you are drunk, Major Walsh,' the Maharaja said sternly.

The other man nodded. 'You are quite right, Your Majesty,' he agreed.

'When I first knew you, you were a man I could put great faith in,' the Maharaja said. 'And did I not, as a symbol of that faith, entrust to you – rather than to any of my own people – the task of finding me a bride? Did I not send you to all the other Indian courts in search of an appropriate wife?'

'You did, Your Majesty. And it was both an honour and a privilege to serve you.'

'It is a decision I have never regretted taking,' the Maharaja said, 'for not only did you find me a wife who could strengthen my dynasty, but you brought me a woman I could love. I would have raised you to great heights for that act alone – even above the princes of the blood royal. But you made that impossible for me, did you not?'

Walsh looked down at the ground. 'Yes, Your Majesty.'

'A man can only follow one master, and you chose the bottle as yours. Within a year of my marriage, you were no use to your own queen and of no use to me.'

'That's quite true, Your Majesty,' Walsh agreed.

'So why am I wasting my time by talking to you now?'

'Only you can answer that, Your Majesty,' Walsh replied. 'Only you can say why you agreed to see me.'

'But you have your own thoughts on the matter?'

'Yes, Your Majesty.'

'And what are they?'

'A blunt knife is better than no knife at all, especially when all your other allies are carrying nothing but feathers.'

'Any idiot can quote wise sayings at me,' the Maharaja

told him, feeling his anger rising. 'Put your case into plain words.'

'Very well, Your Majesty. If you had been back in Chandrapore, you would already have known who was behind your son's kidnapping. You would have set your own people to work on it, and they would have found out – at whatever the cost to others. But this is not Chandrapore. You must rely on the British, and they do not understand the Indian mind at all.'

'Are you saying that my son was taken by *Indians*?'

'I do not know, Your Majesty. And neither do you. But we can both name people in your court who would not be displeased at what has happened today. And if Indians *are* involved, then you need a man close to the centre of the investigation who knows how they think.'

'And if Indians are *not* involved?'

'You will still need a man to represent your interests.'

'Are the *British* incapable of representing my interests?'

'No, but they also have interests of their own.'

'They do not want to see my son returned to me?'

'That would be the easiest solution for them, but their prime concern is to avoid trouble in Chandrapore. Thus, while some of their energy will be devoted to returning your son to you, some will also be devoted to developing a plan of action to follow if they cannot. That is why having your own representative at the heart of the matter is of vital importance.'

'And that representative would be you?'

'I cannot think of anyone else it *could* be, Your Majesty.'

The Maharaja nodded. 'What would I have to do to ensure that my "representative" is at the "heart of the matter"?'

'Very little. Simply insist that whatever my enemies in the India Office might say, I should be allowed to work closely with Inspector Blackstone.'

'And what is in this for you?'

'The honour of serving Your Majesty.'

'Only that?'

Walsh hesitated. 'I have fallen a long way,' he said, 'but

not yet so far that it is impossible to begin climbing again. If I succeed in having your son returned to you, I will have earned a great deal of credit with both Your Majesty and the British government. With new possibilities spread out before me, I might at last be able to triumph in my battle with my own weakness.'

'And what if you fail?'

'If I fail, I will be *persona non grata* everywhere in the British Empire. But that will not matter, since I will not live long under the weight of such indignity.'

'Why? Are you ill?'

Walsh laughed. 'No, Your Majesty. Apart from my liver, I am in excellent health. But you and I both know that if I fail you, I will be discovered in an alley one early morning – with an axe in my head.'

'You are suggesting that I would have you killed?'

'Of course not, Your Majesty. But perhaps one of your loyal subjects – motivated by a purely natural desire to please you – might think that was what you wanted and thus carry out the act.'

The Maharaja nodded. 'Even when you were at your drunkest and most useless, we still understood each other, didn't we, Walsh?'

'Indeed we did, Your Majesty.'

'Very well. I will use my influence to have you attached to Inspector Blackstone. But remember, as you have just pointed out yourself, I have *many* loyal subjects who would see it as no more than their duty to avenge me if you fail.'

'And so they should,' Walsh said. 'I accept Your Majesty's terms, both those stated and those implied.'

'Then you may go,' the Maharaja said, and watched unmoved as Walsh gave him another shaky bow and then backed uncertainly out of the room.

Eighteen

The lamp lighter made a slow but measured progress along the Embankment, stopping at every lamp standard and using his long pole to ignite the flame. His mind, not needed for the task in hand, was elsewhere. But even had he been more aware of his surroundings, he would still not have noticed the tall, thin figure who was watching him from the second-floor window in Scotland Yard.

'The illuminator,' Blackstone said softly to himself. 'The bringer of light. We could use a bit of that round here.'

'What was that, sir?' Patterson asked.

'Nothing,' Blackstone said gruffly. 'Just thinking aloud.'

In his orphanage days, when most of what he knew of the world had been observed through a barred window, he'd watched the lamp lighter whenever the opportunity had arisen. It had seemed to him, back then, that there could be no finer job in the world than to bring light out of the darkness. And he still believed that – though now he was old enough and wise enough to understand that there were many kinds of darkness a man might choose to grapple with.

He turned to face Patterson. 'So this Colonel Howarth ordered a tiger from Harrods, did he?'

'Yes, sir.'

'And he was the only one to do so?'

'You make buying tigers sound like buying jars of fruit preserve,' Patterson replied, unconsciously echoing the manager of the pet department.

'But you did check everywhere else, didn't you?' Blackstone asked. 'And I mean *everywhere*?'

'Yes, I did, sir. Zoos and circuses excepted, Howarth's is the only tiger which has been imported into England in the last ten years.'

'Then tomorrow morning, we'd better go and check if it's

still where it's supposed to be,' Blackstone said. He crossed over to his desk and sat down next to his sergeant. 'I've had a report on the two Black Marias,' he continued.

'Were they the real thing?'

'No. I never expected they would be. Stealing the cabs to stage that little fracas on Westminster Bridge was no real risk – they only needed them for an hour. Stealing Black Marias, on the other hand, *was* a risk – because they'd have had to do it several hours before the kidnapping, and that would have alerted us to the fact that something was wrong.'

'Must have been expensive to get fakes made,' Patterson said.

'Money doesn't seem to be a problem to this gang,' Blackstone said. 'Nor time. That's one of the things that makes it unique in my experience.'

'How do you mean?'

'I've never heard of a criminal who was prepared to wait for over a year to carry out his plan. But that's what these blokes have done – and we know that because of the tiger.' He paused, thoughtfully. 'How *did* they know they had so much time to get organized, do you think?'

'A great many of the Queen's engagements are fixed well over a year in advance,' said Patterson, who counted knowledge of courtly protocol among the many subjects he stored in his dustbin of a mind. 'Besides, they had a marker to pace themselves against.'

'And what marker was that?'

'The elephant.'

'Of course it was,' Blackstone agreed. 'Stupid of me not to have thought of it myself. Once they'd learned of the Maharaja's plan to have an elephant in his procession, they'd have known exactly how long they had to put their own arrangements in place.' He clicked his fingers, as if hit by a sudden thought. 'You know what this means, don't you?'

'I'm not sure that I do,' Patterson confessed.

'They could have learned about the Maharaja's visit from someone in London, but to know about the elephant they must have had a source in *India*.'

'Are you sure? Couldn't the Indian Office have been informed about it from the start?'

'Could have been – but wasn't. According to Major Walsh, the Indian Office wasn't told until last week.'

'Why the delay?'

'I expect the Maharaja's advisers thought that if our government found out about it earlier, they'd raise some objection. But so close to the date, they couldn't regard it as anything but a *fait accompli*. So the information had to come from India – possibly from inside the Maharaja's own court! And that's got to be as good a lead as we've had so far, hasn't it?'

Patterson seemed unwilling or unable to be caught up in his boss's enthusiasm. 'I'm sure the Maharaja has enemies enough in his own court,' he said. 'There's probably never been a king in the world who didn't. But even so, there's a hundred other ways the kidnappers could have found out.'

'For example?' Blackstone asked, reluctant to abandon what had seemed a promising line of investigation.

'Unless they walked the elephant to the nearest port in India – and Chandrapore's a bloody long way from the sea – they'd have to have made special arrangements with the railway company. They'd have informed the shipping company well in advance, too. And think how many hungry clerks there'll be working in the railway and shipping companies – clerks who'll only have been too glad to earn a few bob by passing on that kind of information.'

'True,' Blackstone agreed gloomily. 'So we'd better pray that when we take our trip out to Hertfordshire tomorrow morning we don't find the tiger happily frisking around his enclosure, just as he's supposed to be. Because if that happens, we'll have nothing. Bloody hell, lad, we'll have *less* than nothing.'

Aggarwal sat at his desk in the sitting room of the Maharaja's suite. He was pretending to study the papers which were spread out in front of him, but his mind was enveloped in the swirl of intrigues and plots which were the staple of life in the court of Chandrapore.

The prince had been kidnapped, but for what purpose? The obvious answer was that it was the work of ordinary criminals, intent on no more than collecting a ransom. But Aggarwal did not really believe that. His instinct, which had enabled him to rise from obscurity to a position of some power, told him that there was a plot afoot – a plot which, if he did not tread carefully, would bring about his downfall.

Yet though he was sure there *was* a conspiracy, it was not a conspiracy he had even begun to understand. If the object of the conspirators had been to seize power, then why kidnap the boy? Why not just kill him *and* his father by the side of the dead elephant?

A further series of questions presented themselves to him. Who were the conspirators? What did they want? And might it be to his advantage – once he had identified them – to go over to their side?

The knock on the door startled the secretary, but did not alarm him. There were six bodyguards on duty in the corridor, he reminded himself. In such confined spaces, even an army set against them would take some time to make headway. So he was safe – at least, for the moment.

There was a second knock on the door. 'Come in,' he said.

The door swung open. A liveried hotel porter stood there, his right hand tightly gripping the thin arm of a street urchin who could not have been more than eleven or twelve years old. Behind the man and the boy were the bodyguards, ready to take any action which should be called for.

'What is the meaning of this?' Aggarwal demanded.

'Begging your pardon, but this boy come up to me at the door,' the porter replied. 'Said he had an important message for the Maharaja.'

The urchin had been passive until that moment, but now he began to try to struggle free of the porter's grip.

'Are you 'im?' he demanded. 'Are you the boss nigger?'

'Why are you wasting my time by bringing this piece of vermin to me?' Aggarwal asked with distaste.

The porter opened his free hand. 'The boy had this with him,' he said.

It was a ruby – not a particularly valuable stone by the Maharaja's standards, but one which the secretary recognized as having formed part of the decoration on the young prince's turban.

'My men will take care of the boy – and the stone,' the secretary said to the porter. 'You yourself may leave.'

'Now just a minute,' the porter protested. 'I could have kept the jewel to myself, you know. Instead, I decided to do the honest thing and bring it to you. I'm surely entitled to some reward for that, ain't I?'

If the man had been an Indian servant, Aggarwal would have had him whipped within an inch of his life for such insolence. But that was not possible in this country, the secretary thought regretfully. Here, it was unfortunately necessary to employ gentler means.

'You will be well paid for the valuable service you have performed,' he assured the porter, 'but now we would like some privacy.'

The porter hesitated for a second, and then withdrew. The secretary gestured to one of the guards that he should take control of the boy and bring him closer to the table.

'*Are* you 'im?' the urchin demanded. 'Are you the boss nigger?'

'No.'

'Then where is 'e?'

'His Majesty is sedated at the moment,' the secretary explained.

The boy looked at him blankly.

'His Majesty is asleep,' Aggarwal amplified.

'Don't know nothin' about any majesties,' the urchin said. 'I was told to speak to the boss nigger.'

'Speak to me.'

'But you're not the boss.'

'True, but I am His Majesty's private secretary.'

'I s'pose it'll be all right to tell you then,' the urchin said cheerfully. "'Specially seein' as you're the one what'll be doin' all the dirty work.'

'What dirty work? I demand to know what you mean.'

'The bloke told me to say fings in the right order, so I wouldn't get confused,' the urchin said. 'The part about the dirty work only comes later.'

'Then start immediately, in order that we may reach that part as quickly as possible.'

'I was down on Mile End Road when this bloke come up to me,' the boy replied.

'What did this "bloke" look like?'

'Big bugger. Wearin' a top 'at an' a beard what looked as if it 'ad been made of rats' 'air.'

'Was he dark, like I am?'

'Could 'ave been anuver nigger. Then again, 'e might just 'ave spent a lot of time out in the sun – which ain't 'ealthy.'

'What did this man tell you?'

'Said he 'ad this message 'e wanted deliverin'. Said I was to tell the sekritury – that's you – to be standin' at Battle Bridge Steps at exac'ly eleven o'clock tomorrer mornin'. Said if you wasn't there at just the right time, the 'ole thing was off.'

'What whole thing?'

'Didn't say.'

'What happened next?'

'Then the bloke give me this jool. Said I'd need it to convince you I was on the up an' up.'

How deep did the conspiracy run? Aggarwal asked himself. Could even the boy be part of it – the skinny goat used to ensnare much mightier creatures? And if that were the case, might not the way he himself reacted now determine whether he was to live or die?

'There is one thing about your story which does not make sense,' he said cautiously.

'An' what fing is that?'

'Why did this man trust you with the jewel? How could he be sure that you wouldn't simply run away once he had given you the precious stone? Was it that he looked into your face and saw an honesty which was beyond question?'

The urchin gave the secretary a look which was halfway between contempt and pity.

'Course it bloody wasn't,' the boy said. 'I'd sell me own grandma for a tanner – if I knew 'oo she was – an' anybody can see that. So 'e didn't trust me. 'E didn't trust me at all. 'E brought me 'ere in a cab, an' stood across the road till he saw me show the jool to that bloke in the uniform.'

Aggarwal cursed himself for not asking the question earlier. If he had known that one of the kidnappers was in striking distance, the guards might have been able to lay their hands on the man. Then again, he thought, reconsidering the matter, perhaps it would have been a mistake to go on the offensive in such a manner. Perhaps the wiser course would be to bide his time until he had a clearer picture of what exactly the conspiracy involved. And it seemed he was to be afforded just that opportunity.

'I should be at Battle Bridge Steps at precisely eleven o'clock,' the secretary repeated. 'Is that correct?'

'Yes. An' there was one more fing. 'E said that you was to make sure that you come alone. Said that 'e'd 'ave 'is people watchin' you every step of the way, an' that if you 'ad a policeman or any of the uvver niggers with you, 'e'd 'ave to do somefink unpleasant to yer.'

A cold shudder ran through Aggarwal. 'Is that precisely what the man said?' he asked. 'That he'd do "something unpleasant"?'

'No,' the boy admitted, 'but it turns me stomach just to fink about what he *did* say.'

Nineteen

It was a foggy morning in London – it would not really have *been* London without the fog – but once outside the capital, the weather started to improve, and by the time the train pulled into Windsor Station the sun was shining benevolently and Blackstone felt it was almost possible to take an optimistic view of life.

While Patterson hailed a cab, Blackstone looked up at the majestic Windsor Castle and wondered if it were true that the Queen was thinking of awarding him a medal. If it was, he was not sure that he wanted it. Because though he had fought in the Army, it had not been for the greater glory of the Queen so much as to escape from the grinding poverty of his childhood. And though he was capable of intense loyalty, he reserved most of it for the people of the East End, where he had grown up. It was ironic then that he – who cared so little for her – had done the Queen greater service than most men in England and that, by working on this case to the best of his ability, he was continuing to further her interests.

Patterson had found a closed cab, and the two detectives climbed inside.

'Spill the beans on Colonel Howarth, then?' Blackstone asked.

'Spill the beans?' Patterson repeated, feigning a look of slightly injured innocence. 'We didn't even learn that he existed till last night, yet you expect me to know about him already?'

Blackstone grinned. 'Correct,' he said.

That was the thing about Patterson, he thought. Not only did he store vast amounts of information in his dustbin of a brain, but he knew who to ask for any he hadn't already absorbed. It was truly remarkable the number of people that the sergeant – a man still a couple of years off thirty – seemed to know. Blackstone was *almost* looking forward to the day when they conducted an investigation which *didn't* involve someone Patterson knew – a case in which the sergeant would be unable to greet a journalist or a lawyer, a chimney sweep or an itinerant chair-mender, on terms of familiarity. But whilst he might anticipate it, he wasn't holding his breath while he waited for it to happen.

'Well?' the Inspector asked.

Patterson returned his grin. 'I was talking to a pal of mine at the War Office last night,' he admitted.

'And?'

'Colonel Howarth's in his late seventies. He comes from a very good background, but not a particularly affluent one. He spent most of his Army career in India, where he served with some distinction and was decorated twice. He never married. When he retired, he bought a place in Warwickshire. He moved to Amritsar Lodge less than a year ago.'

'And that's all you've got, is it?' Blackstone teased.

'I did my best in the short time available,' Patterson protested.

They passed by a gatehouse, and got their first view of Amritsar Lodge. Sunlight shone on the rows of elegant Georgian windows. Peacocks strutted and preened themselves on the terrace. There was a stable block to the left of the house, and an artificial lake to the right. The lodge was not a palace, by any stretch of the imagination, but it was still a substantial enough dwelling for any country gentleman to be proud to call his home.

'Thought you told me that Colonel Howarth didn't have any money,' Blackstone said.

'I told you he wasn't *born* with money,' Patterson corrected him. 'But he certainly seems to have it now, doesn't he?'

'Yes, he does,' Blackstone agreed pensively.

They had announced their intention to visit in advance, and the footman who greeted them at the door took them straight through to the Colonel's sitting room.

The room told its own story. A crossed pair of hunting rifles were mounted over the fireplace, just above a regimental sword. An antelope's head on one wall stared across the room at an elephant's head mounted on another. Surrounding these trophies were dozens of fading, framed photographs, each depicting a group of men posing stiffly in military uniforms. There were several occasional tables with Benares brass tops and curly teak legs, and much of the floor was covered with silk carpets. It all reminded Blackstone of the officers' mess he had seen – though only through the window – while he had been serving in India.

The Colonel was sitting in an armchair by the fire. He made no move to get up when the detectives entered the room, nor seemed to feel the need to apologize for the fact. He was a completely bald man, but sported a white walrus moustache under his beak of a nose. He was wearing the red, blue and gold uniform of the 11th Hussars, which, over the years, must have undergone extensive alteration in order to still fit his corpulent frame.

'Policeman, are you?' he asked Blackstone.

'That's right, sir,' Blackstone confirmed.

'Not always been, though, have you?'

'No, sir.'

'Thought not. You stand like a soldier. Ever serve in India?'

'Yes, sir.'

'Don't suppose you were an officer?'

'I was offered a field commission,' Blackstone said.

'So why didn't you take it?'

'Couldn't afford to. I didn't have the private income necessary to meet the expenses it would have entailed.'

'Quite right to turn it down in that case,' the Colonel said. 'Admire you for it – in a way. Shouldn't wear the uniform if you can't afford to live the life. Still, you do realize that the fact you weren't an officer means I can't ask you to sit down?'

'Of course,' Blackstone said.

'That's all right then.' The Colonel glanced across at the window. 'Seen the view through there?'

Blackstone turned his head. 'Windsor Castle.'

'Windsor Castle! Used to live in Warwickshire when I first left the Army. Like it better here. Comfortin' to be so close to the monarch I served all my life. Convenient for London, too. Not that that makes much difference. Never go there now. Don't get out much at all these days.'

'Why is that?' Blackstone asked politely. 'Are you unwell?'

'Gout's got something to do with it,' the Colonel admitted. 'Cut a fine figure on a horse in my time. Going from that to being pushed around in an invalid chair like some frail old lady is a long way to fall. But that's only part of the reason I stay away from London.'

'And what's the other part?'

'Don't feel comfortable there these days. Probably never really did once I'd seen India. Can't understand these stay-at-home wallahs, and they can't understand me. Calcutta's my city.'

'Do you know the Maharaja of Chandrapore?' Blackstone asked.

'Knew his uncle. The current maharaja was no more than a boy at the time.' The Colonel paused. 'I've been ramblin' on, haven't I? Comes of gettin' so few visitors. Suppose I should really ask you what this is all about.'

'I thought you'd know already, sir.'

'Well, you're wrong. Haven't got a clue why you're here.'

'I take it from that that you don't read the newspapers, sir.'

'Damn right, I don't read them. See no reason why I should subsidize the anarchists and radicals who seem to be in charge of the press these days. Wouldn't have happened in India, you know. Over there, we knew how to use the so-called journalists as an instrument of government policy.' The Colonel paused again. 'Assumin' I did read the papers, would there have been anythin' of interest to me in this mornin's'?'

Blackstone smiled, and told the Colonel about the kidnapping.

'Damn clever,' Howarth said. 'A bit flash, but still damn clever. I had a tiger myself, you know.'

'*Had?*' Blackstone repeated.

'Brute died on me last week. Hadn't had him more than a few days.' A new thought seemed to strike the Colonel. 'Didn't think it was my tiger on Regent Street, did you?'

'We thought it might be a possibility. And we had to check.'

'Of course you did,' the Colonel agreed. 'Leave no stone unturned – that's always been my motto.'

'What did your tiger die of?'

'God alone knows. Some kind of tropical disease, I expect. Lot of them in the air in India. They say West Africa's the white man's graveyard, but let me tell you, India could run it a damn close second.'

'Do you mind if *I* ask you a question, sir?' Patterson said to the Colonel.

'Ask away, young feller. Never learn if you don't ask.'

'Why did you want a tiger?'

'Because I couldn't afford an elephant.'

'I beg your pardon?'

'Wanted something around me in my old age to remind me of India. Thought of an elephant at first, but I'm no maharaja, and it would have cost too much to ship it across. Settled on a tiger.'

'And where did you keep it?' Patterson asked.

'There's a walled-off area near the edge of the property which used to be an orchard. Kept the brute there. Why do you ask?'

'I wondered if we could see it.'

'Can't think why you should want to.'

'It's just curiosity on my part,' Patterson said, affecting a blush which made him look even more like a plump boy than he normally did. 'I've never got close to a tiger—'

'Told you, the damn thing's dead.'

'—but if I could just walk over the same ground as he once strode o'er, I'm sure I'd be able to feel something of his majestic presence.'

The Colonel gave the sergeant a long, penetrating stare. 'Sounds like a damn silly idea to me,' he pronounced finally. 'Fanciful! Not one of those nancy boys, are you?'

'No, sir,' Patterson said, the blush on his cheeks now more real than assumed.

Blackstone put his hand on Patterson's shoulder in an avuncular fashion.

'My sergeant's as normal as you or I, Colonel,' he assured Howarth. 'He's just not had our experience of the world.'

'That's obvious enough,' Howarth replied, sounding slightly uneasy.

'We've been to India. We've seen all the marvels the sub-continent has to offer. But my sergeant's hardly ever been out of London. So it wouldn't do him any harm to see the tiger's enclosure, would it? His ideas might seem a bit fanciful to you and me, but it's not really much different to letting your grandson have a sniff at the cork on the whisky bottle, now is it?'

'I suppose not,' Howarth said doubtfully.

'So you wouldn't mind if he had a quick look, would you? I promise I won't let him do any damage.'

The Colonel hesitated. 'I'm not sure—'

'After all,' Blackstone said cheerfully, 'it's not as if you've got anything to hide, is it?'

'No,' the Colonel admitted, reluctantly. 'It's not as if I've got anything to hide.'

'So how would we go about seeing this famous tiger's den?'

'On your way out ask the footman to take you to Tebbitt, my head groundsman,' the Colonel said, defeatedly. 'Served with me in India, did Tebbitt. A sound chap. He'll take you to where I used to keep the tiger.'

'Much obliged,' Blackstone said.

The Colonel relapsed into deep thought the moment his visitors had left.

'*You shouldn't necessarily expect a visit from the auth-orities,*' he'd been told, '*but you shouldn't be too surprised, either, if you do get one.*'

'*How should I behave if they turn up on my doorstep?*' the Colonel had asked. '*I'm no actor, you know.*'

The other man had laughed. *'No actor? After you've been playing the bluff, honest soldier – the warrior who knows no fear – for almost your entire life?'*

The young could be so cruel, the Colonel thought, but what had been said was not so far from the truth. Ever since he had first donned a uniform, he had had the guilty feeling that he was not so much *being* a soldier as *playing* at being one. Perhaps all British officers felt as he did, though he knew that they – like he himself – would die rather than admit it.

Now that the policemen had gone, he found himself wondering if, for once, he had failed to play the part up to the hilt. They should not have asked to see where the tiger had been kept, and when they did, he should have refused them. Yet how could he have done that without raising their suspicion?

'It's not as if you've got anything to hide, is it?' the Inspector had asked.

And what choice had there been but to agree with that?

The Colonel noticed that his breathing was becoming a little irregular. There was no need to panic, he told himself. It didn't really matter where the policemen had gone. They wouldn't find anything – because there was nothing to find.

Twenty

It had been a long time since Aggarwal had needed to look where he was going. In Chandrapore, whenever he travelled on foot – and that was rarely – he did so with an escort of his master's guards, and the common herd quickly divided so that he might pass unhindered.

But this was Tooley Street, not Chandrapore. He was unknown here, and was treated accordingly. Thus he was forced to dodge the long pole from which the beer-boy hung his cans. Thus the wharfingers – who, for all their air of self-importance, were no more than minor clerks –

pushed past him in their haste to reach ships which were waiting to sail. Thus even the lowly bill-stickers cursed him as he almost kicked over their buckets of paste. It was all a great humiliation for him to endure. But there had been many humiliations as he had climbed the ladders of life, and he knew from experience that, once he reached the top of any particular ladder, it was easy enough to push to the back of his mind what he had had to do during the ascent.

He had reached the end of Tooley Street and was at the entrance to Battle Bridge Stairs. Though he was only a dozen yards away from the bustling commercial thoroughfare, the atmosphere was now completely different. Back there, men had hurried from place to place. Here they lounged around, leaning against walls and chewing at toothpicks. On Tooley Street, there been a smattering of men dressed in top hats and frock coats, while here flat caps and mufflers were the norm.

He had reached the head of the Stairs. Below him, he could see half a dozen watermen. Two of them sat in their boats; the rest were squatting down on the quay, playing cards. He wondered if he should go down the steps or stay where he was. What, exactly, had the kidnappers meant when they said he should be *at* Battle Bridge Stairs?

He decided to go down to the quay, and gingerly placed one of his feet on slippery stone steps.

'Look 'oo's comin',' one of the watermen called out. 'A monkey wearin' a whistle.'

It had been a mistake to wear a suit, especially one of the Maharaja's good cast-offs, Aggarwal now realized. If he had bought some old clothes, the watermen might have taken him for a Lascar sailor, and not given him a second glance. And suddenly he found himself yearning for the same anonymity that he had so despised only moments earlier.

When he reached the jetty, one of the watermen – a giant of a man who seemed full of menace – stepped in front of him and said, 'Want a ride in my boat, Sambo?'

Aggarwal's throat was so dry that he could not speak, even though he wanted to.

'Well, do you want to go out on the river or not?' the man demanded.

'I . . . I . . .'

'He's my passenger, Jack!' said a voice from halfway up the steps.

'Like hell 'e is,' said the big waterman. 'It's first come, first served in this game, Lou Gammage. You wasn't 'ere when 'e arrived, so you doesn't get to row 'im out anywhere.'

'I don't want 'is money, 'cos I've already been paid,' the man called Lou said.

'You must fink I was born yesterday,' the other man replied, contemptuously.

Lou had now reached the bottom of the steps. 'Why don't you pay my mate Jack 'ere for the journey, but let me be the one that rows you out?' he suggested to the secretary. 'Fair enough, Jack?'

'Fair enough, if you're happy wiv that,' the other waterman agreed. 'But if you ask me, you want your bumps feelin'.'

'Give 'im a guinea,' Lou said the secretary.

'A guinea?' Aggarwal repeated, finally finding his voice. 'But a guinea is a great deal of money.'

'You can afford it,' Lou said. 'Besides, it ain't really you what's payin', is it?'

Perhaps he was one of the gang, Aggarwal thought, in which case it might be wisest to do as he said. The secretary reached into his pocket, extracted a guinea, and handed it over to Jack.

The giant waterman bit it to make sure it was genuine, then nodded that he was satisfied. With nothing more to impede them, Lou led the secretary down to his rowing boat.

'Where are you taking me?' Aggarwal asked nervously, as he climbed into the boat.

'Not far,' Lou said.

'To the other side of the river?'

'I told you, it's not far.'

The waterman pulled powerfully on his oars, and the rowing boat cut through the water, leaving Battle Bridge Stairs behind it. The river was, as always, busier than any

100

street in the very busy city. Cargo ships, moored midway between the two shores, were unloading their produce on to lighters. Steamers battled against the tide on their way upstream, and sailing ships floated downstream with it.

Aggarwal took little comfort from all the activity going on around him. His belief in Lou being a member of the gang had started to diminish. Now he was prepared to believe that the man was actually what he seemed – a genuine waterman – and he had read of cases in which watermen had drowned their passengers just to claim the police bounty for fishing them out of the river. Could that happen here? Would any of the people in these busy vessels even notice if an Indian in a good second-hand suit suddenly disappeared over the side of a rowing boat?

You must be calm, he told himself. If you are to turn this affair to your own advantage, you must remain calm at all times.

There was a long barge anchored in the middle of the river, and the waterman rowed straight to it.

'This is as far as I go,' he said.

The secretary was not sure he had heard correctly. 'I beg your pardon?' he said.

'I pull up beside the barge, an' you climb aboard,' the waterman explained, talking slowly, as if to a small child.

'But I don't—'

'See that flat bit at the back of the barge? Yer'll find some steps there that will lead you down to the cabin.'

'But who will I meet there, and how will I return to the shore?' Aggarwal asked in a panic.

'Beats me,' the waterman said. 'All I know is that when I was 'ired to bring you out 'ere, the bloke 'oo was payin' me made it quite plain that 'e'd be very cross – cross enough to break a few of my bones – if I didn't deliver you to the barge as promised.'

'Good place to keep a tiger, well away from the main house,' Blackstone said, looking at the walled orchard. 'Well away from *anything at all*, as a matter of fact.'

101

Tebbitt, Colonel Howarth's head groundsman, merely grunted. He was an old man with muscles as hard as knotted oak and skin the colour of worn leather. He had shown little enthusiasm when he had been introduced to the two detectives by the footman, and had not spoken a word as he had led them to the extreme corner of the estate, where the orchard was located.

The wall around the orchard was at least twelve feet high, Blackstone estimated. The only entrance was through a narrow door, which was secured by a large and heavy padlock.

As Tebbitt fiddled with the lock, the Inspector looked around him. There was no earthly reason why anybody should need to come near the old orchard, he thought, and even if they wanted to, all the notices which warned of danger would probably be enough to make them think again.

Having extracted the lock from the hasp, Tebbitt pushed open the heavy wooden door and the three men entered the old orchard. Half of the space was taken up by rotting fruit trees which had plainly been stricken by some kind of disease. The rest of the area was occupied by a large cage, at least forty feet square, which was made of thick wire.

'This be where we kept 'im,' Tebbitt said, pointing to the cage.

'Didn't last long in there, did he?' Blackstone asked.

'Never thought him would,' the old man said. 'Can't go bringing somethin' here from some foreign land an' expect it to flourish. Same with plants. Same with them darkies.'

'What darkies?' Blackstone asked.

'Them that have started visitin' the maister. Tha' could tell just by lookin' at 'em that them was more used to heathen weather than them was to ours. Not warm enough for 'em, tha' sees. If them catch one little cold, them'll be gone.'

'When did these darkies start to appear?' Blackstone asked casually.

'Few days before the tiger come here,' the groundsman replied. His eyes narrowed with suspicion. 'Why am tha' askin'?'

Blackstone chose not to answer the question. Instead, he said, 'I think I'll go for a walk around the tiger's enclosure.'

'Why should tha' want to do that?'

'Every man should experience what it's like to be locked up once in a while,' Blackstone said. He looked straight in Tebbitt's watery eyes. 'For some of us, it might be good practice for what's to come later.'

'Tha's lost me,' the old man said.

Blackstone studied him for a second. 'Yes,' he said thoughtfully. 'Yes, I probably have.'

Blackstone opened the door to the pen, and stepped inside. For a moment he just stood there, then he took a series of long strides from the gate to the far fence. Once he had completed this operation, he crossed the paddock again, this time diagonally.

'What am he doin'?' Tebbitt asked, sounding worried.

'Perhaps he's thinking of keeping a tiger himself,' Patterson said. 'Though after Colonel Howarth's experience, it strikes me as a foolish move.' He paused. 'Was the Colonel upset when his tiger died?'

The expression on Tebbitt's face told Patterson that the old man had no idea how to answer the question.

'Well, was he upset?' the detective prodded.

'Not particarlarly.'

'Of course, he must have been prepared for the worst,' Patterson pressed on. 'The vet would already have warned him what might happen.'

'Didn't have no vet.'

'Really? That *is* strange, don't you think?'

'Vets cost money.'

And so do tigers, Patterson thought.

Blackstone, who was crossing the tiger enclosure again, suddenly appeared to lose his footing and fell sprawling on the ground. Patterson would have gone to help him, but the Inspector was soon on his feet, dusting himself down and putting his handkerchief – which Patterson had not even seen him remove – back in his pocket.

'So what happened to the tiger when it died?' the sergeant asked the groundsman.

'I buried he,' Tebbitt said. He pointed towards one of the decaying apple trees. Most of the ground around it was covered with patchy grass, but there was one large rectangle which had recently been dug over. 'I buried he there.'

'And how long after the tiger's death did this burial actually take place? A few days?'

'No, it were done straight away. I went to the maister an' said, "The tiger's dead," an' him said, "Tha's better get he buried then."'

'How many men did it take to do that?'

'Hast tha' got cloth ears? I told thee, I buried he myself.'

'*All* by yourself?'

'Just me.'

'Wouldn't it have been easier to get some of the other servants to help you with the job?'

'Don't know nothin' 'bout that. Maister told me I mun bury he, an' I buried he.'

Blackstone seemed to have completed his examination of the cage, and returned to where the other two men were standing.

'Mr Tebbitt says he buried the tiger all by himself, sir,' Patterson told his boss.

'Then I'm sure he did,' Blackstone replied airily. 'We've just about done looking around here, Mr Tebbitt. Have you any idea how we might get back into Windsor?'

'Maister told the coachman he am to take thee back into town when tha's ready to go,' Tebbitt said.

'Then I suppose you'd better tell him we're ready now.'

There was a clip clopping of horses' hooves, and an open carriage appeared, travelling from the direction of the house.

'He'm comin' now,' Tebbitt said, unnecessarily.

The Colonel was being most helpful, Patterson thought. It was almost as if he couldn't wait to get them off his land.

Twenty-One

The waterman rowed rapidly away, leaving Aggarwal stranded on the barge in the middle of the Thames. For a moment the secretary considered hailing a passing boat and asking the oarsman to take him back to the shore.

But that would be both pointless and stupid, he told himself angrily. Because even if the kidnappers really were what they seemed to be, what would they gain by hurting him?

Three paths to the future lay open for him to tread. He could become the trusted servant of the Maharaja that he had always pretended to be. He could commit himself fully to the plot which had been hatched just before he left Chandrapore. Or he could throw in his lot with this new conspiracy. But before he could choose any of these options, he needed to know more about the third one – and he could see only one way to do that. Taking a deep breath, he tried the cabin door and found it unlocked. He pulled it open and began to descend the steps.

The portholes were covered with some kind of blackout material, and the few tiny diamonds of light which managed to permeate it only served to emphasize how dark the rest of the cabin was. The air was thick with the stink of oil, fish and sulphur, all overlaid with a smell of fear which – Aggarwal realized – was emanating from him.

He took each step carefully, first feeling it out with the toe of his shoe, and then gingerly testing it with his sole. It seemed to take an age until there were no more edges and he was standing firmly on the lower deck.

What should he do now?

He took a cautious step forward.

'That's far enough,' said a voice, from within the black bowels of the cabin.

What was the speaker's nationality? Aggarwal wondered.

Was he Indian? Or English? He had not said enough yet to know for sure.

The secretary cleared his throat. 'I am here on behalf of His Majesty—' he began, in a squeaky tone.

'We know who you are – and what you represent – Mr Aggarwal,' the voice interrupted him.

English! Aggarwal decided. Or perhaps an Indian who had been educated in Britain.

'His Majesty wishes—' the secretary said.

'I have no interest in what His Majesty wishes. And neither do you.'

'I can assure you that—'

'Why do you think we asked for you, rather than anyone else?' the voice demanded.

'I have no idea.'

'Because you're a nasty piece of work. Because you have the ambition of ten men and the ruthlessness of twenty. Because we can *use* you.'

'Use me? How? What are you planning?'

'That will become clear in the fullness of time,' the voice said. 'For the moment, it is enough that you fulfil the task we have assigned to you.'

'What is that task?'

'You are to convince the Maharaja that if he pays the ransom, his son will be safely returned to him.'

'And is that true?'

'Do you really care whether it is true or not – so long as you come out ahead of the game?'

'Yes, of course I do.'

In the darkness, the other man sighed theatrically. 'If you are to be a part of our venture, you must be honest with us,' he said. 'So I ask you again – do you care whether the boy is returned safely or not?'

'No,' Aggarwal admitted. 'I do not care.'

'Good,' said the voice. 'Then you will tell the Maharaja that the ransom will be one hundred thousand pounds.'

'That is a lot of money,' Aggarwal said.

'It is a fortune,' the voice corrected him. 'But it is a

fortune which the Maharaja can lay his hands on if he is forced to.'

'This is not a simple kidnapping, is it?' Aggarwal asked. 'It is part of a bigger game.'

'I am glad you asked that question,' the voice told him. 'If you had not, you wouldn't have been the man we took you for.'

'You still have not answered the question.'

'Yes, it is part of a bigger game. A *much* bigger game.'

'Then I must be told the details of that game.'

'No.'

'If I am not told, then I will not help you.'

The other man laughed. It was a dry, humourless laugh, like the sound of fire ripping its way through parched brush.

'You *will* help us, because you have no choice,' he said. 'Because refusal to do so would inevitably lead to your death.'

'You would kill me?'

'No, that would not be necessary. We would let the Maharaja know that you had tried to make a deal with us, and leave the rest up to him. He could devise a slower, more painful death for you than we could ever concoct ourselves.'

'Let me understand this,' Aggarwal said, doing all he could to keep his tone below that of a panicked scream. 'If I make a deal with you, I will be safe. If I do *not* make a deal with you, you will tell the Maharaja that I did, and he will have me murdered.'

'Very concisely put,' the voice agreed. 'I knew you were the right man for us.'

The businessmen having travelled down to the city earlier in the morning and the shopping wives planning their arrival to coincide with luncheon, the detectives had the carriage to themselves.

Patterson, who had rarely travelled in any coach other than 3rd Class, lounged back in his seat and savoured all the space. Then he sniffed. This might *be* a 1st Class carriage, he thought disappointedly, but in some ways it didn't smell any different to travelling 3rd.

'Have you learned anything of importance this morning, Sergeant?' Blackstone asked.

'I might have,' Patterson said cautiously. 'I believe the tiger's dead, but I don't think it died how, or where, the Colonel claims it did.'

'Go on,' Blackstone encouraged.

'The tiger must have cost a small fortune, but according to Tebbitt, the Colonel never called the vet in to have a look at it.'

'Some men do make foolish economies. You'd be surprised how many are prepared to spoil the ship for a ha'porth of tar.'

'All right, then consider this. When the tiger supposedly died, the Colonel told Tebbitt to bury it. And Tebbitt says he did. He even showed us the grave. But how did he manage it, all by himself? You saw the size of that dead tiger on Regent Street. It took four big men to shift, and even then they were struggling.'

'Tebbitt probably hitched horses to the corpse, and had it dragged to where he buried it.'

'Horses don't like tigers. That's another thing we learned from what happened on Regent Street.'

'The Regent Street tiger was alive,' Blackstone pointed out. 'If we're to believe Howarth, his tiger was dead.'

'Alive or dead, it would still smell like a tiger,' Patterson said, wondering again about the unpleasant stink which seemed to be permeating the carriage. 'Alive or dead, it would still be difficult to get a team of horses to go near to it.'

'But not impossible.'

'But not impossible,' the sergeant conceded. 'But if I had no other argument to make my case, there's still the fur.'

'What about the fur?'

'I spoke to the vet from London Zoo when he came to collect the tiger. He liked tigers. In fact, I'd say that he much preferred tigers to people. But as fond of them as he was, he was going to skin that one. And why? Because tiger skins are very valuable. Do you see where I'm leading with this, sir?'

'Maybe,' Blackstone said. 'But you're the one who's mounted the horse. Let's see you ride it all the way to the finishing post.'

'Colonel Howarth's sitting room is full of souvenirs of India – stuffed heads, tables, rugs. A tiger skin would only have enhanced the look the place. Yet the moment the tiger dies, Colonel Howarth tells Tebbitt to bury it. I can't see that.'

'So Tebbitt knows what actually happened?'

'Yes, Colonel Howarth had no choice but to take him into his confidence. Someone had to look after the tiger while it was there, and tell the other servants – after it was gone – that it had died.'

'After it was gone?'

'We both know what really happened to the tiger, don't we?' Patterson asked.

'Do we?'

'The kidnappers took it away – probably in one of the Black Marias they used on Regent Street.'

'And when did this happen?'

'Two or three nights ago. The kidnappers wouldn't have wanted to run the risk of having the tiger in their possession for longer than that.'

'But the Colonel said the tiger died last week.'

'He did that to protect himself. If he'd said it had died the day before the attack on Regent Street, it would have looked more suspicious.'

'Yet how could he have got away with saying the tiger was dead when it was still very much alive?'

'Easy. The orchard's a long way from the main house, and the servants were probably instructed never to go near it. Even if they did get close, they'd never see over the walls.'

'What if the tiger roared? Wouldn't they have heard it?'

'What would it have had to roar *at*? Besides, we know it was drugged when it was let out of the Black Maria – perhaps they'd been *keeping* it drugged for a week or more.'

'You do realize, of course, that this is all pure conjecture!' Blackstone told his sergeant.

'Are you saying I'm wrong, sir?'

'No, I'm not saying that at all. I'm just saying that you can't prove it. But fortunately, I can. Do you remember me falling over in the tiger's cage?'

'Of course I do.'

'Rather clumsy of me, wasn't it?'

'It certainly seemed to be.'

'I could just have bent down, I suppose. But Tebbitt would have seen me doing it, and wondered why. And I didn't want him wondering at that particular moment.'

'So you're saying you deliberately fell over?'

'That's right. Did you happen to notice anything in my hand at the time?'

'Your handkerchief.'

Blackstone beamed with pleasure. 'Good lad!' he said.

He reached into his pocket and pulled out the handkerchief. Patterson could not help but notice that the smell which had been bothering him earlier was even stronger now.

'What have you got in there, sir?' the sergeant asked.

Blackstone opened the handkerchief, and held out its contents for Patterson to inspect. 'What does it look like to you?'

'It looks like a lump of shit,' Patterson said, holding his nose.

'That's exactly what it is,' Blackstone agreed. 'My guess is it's *tiger* shit. And since it still pongs, I'd be willing to wager that it's not more than thirty-six hours old.'

Twenty-Two

There were people enough in the Admiral Nelson when Lou Gammage entered it, but very few who had the price of another drink on them. Gammage jingled the coins in his pocket, and looked around contemptuously at them all – at the dockers who had not been taken on for work that morning; at the costermongers who had pawned their barrows to pay the fines the magistrates had imposed on them for fighting; at the crippled ex-soldiers who made their living by begging; at the flower girls and prostitutes.

"Oo fancies a drink, then?' he asked in a loud voice.

The air of quiet desperation which had hung over the bar disappeared as if by magic.

Hands went up, people shouted out their requests. Gammage grinned, and slapped a guinea down on the counter. 'Give them whatever they want,' he told the man behind the bar.

As the landlord struggled to meet the sudden wave of orders, a new man entered the pub. He was dressed in the same kind of second-hand clothes as the rest of the customers. But he did not seem to be at all at ease in them. The rough shirt he was wearing looked as if it were making him itch. His expression showed disdain over the fact that his trousers lacked a sharp crease. Had anyone deigned to notice him, he would have stuck out like a sore thumb immediately – but with the offer of free drinks on hand, nobody did.

The man walked over to the bar. When the landlord told him that there was no need to pay because the 'gentl'man there' was buying all the drinks, he merely nodded and asked for a glass of the house's best whisky. He sniffed at his glass when the landlord slid it across the counter to him. It plainly did not come up to his expectations of what a good whisky should be, but he made no comment. Instead, he walked over to a corner table, and quietly took a seat.

111

Lou Gammage had already knocked back enough gin on an empty stomach to make himself quite drunk. 'You see before you a man of some means,' he announced to the bar in general. 'An' not just means today, but means tomorrer as well, because I 'ave found the money river, an' whenever I'm broke I'll just drop a bucket into it an' pull some more out.'

'Where is this money river?' one of the other customers asked, doing his best to mask his greed with a veneer of indifference.

Gammage wagged his finger drunkenly at the man. 'You'll not find it,' he slurred. 'The money river's only for the Quality an' for them as knows them. An' I know them.'

''Oo are they?' the other man asked.

'You'd like me to tell you, wouldn't you?' Gammage asked. 'An' maybe I will – when I've 'ad another drink.'

It would never have occurred to Blackstone to choose the dust-heap in the County Council depot as a rendezvous point, but that was where his contact had told him to go, and so that was where the Inspector went.

It was the first time Blackstone had been to such a place, and he was not enjoying the experience. The rubbish was piled high, though – with due deference paid to the laws of gravity – it was not stacked vertically but rose to its peak by means of a steady slope.

It was like a small mountain chain, Blackstone thought, remembering his days in the Hindu Kush – a particularly hellish, *unnatural* mountain chain.

Even more depressing than the rubbish itself were the people around it – the trash mountaineers. Most were women – though there were a few men – and all of them carried cheap wicker baskets.

Some stuck close to the foothills of the pile. Others, more adventurous souls, were closer to the summit, up to their ankles in refuse.

Standing watching them was a man in a greasy bowler hat and a canary yellow waistcoat. It was only two days since

112

Blackstone had gone down to the Wellington Arms to talk to Tommy Keogh about the kidnapping, but already it felt like a lifetime ago.

Blackstone walked up to the other man. 'This doesn't look like the kind of work you'd be thinking of going into,' he said.

Tommy Keogh chuckled. 'Just checkin' on me investments, Mr Blackstone,' he said.

'All these people work for you?'

'No, Mr Blackstone. This country of ours is driven by the spirit of enterprise. They work for themselves. But when they've finished their task, they take what they've 'arvested to some of my lads.'

'And what do they "harvest"? Bottles?'

Tommy Keogh chuckled again. 'Bottles?' he repeated. 'You really are a card, Mr Blackstone. Bottles is too valuable to 'ave got this far along in the chain. Any *bottles* will 'ave been 'ad away a long time ago.'

'So what *do* they hope to find?'

'Bits of metal. Old hats. Rags. Odd boots that somebody might be glad to wear as part of an odd pair.'

'It doesn't seem like much of a living.'

'It's 'ardly any livin' at all,' Keogh said. 'But a crust of stale bread beats starvin' to death, any day of the week.'

'And how much of their pittance do you steal from them?' Blackstone asked, feeling an anger – which he already knew he was unwise to allow – starting to rise up inside him.

'I don't steal nuffink,' Tommy Keogh said, taking no offence. 'I provide a service, I do.'

'A service?'

'Certainly. You don't fink these are the only people who want to pick through the rubbish, do you? If they wasn't under my protection, they'd soon be kicked off by some bunch 'oo had anuvver gentleman givin' them 'is support. An' he'd probably take a damn sight more off 'is lot than I want from mine.'

'You're a saint, Tommy,' Blackstone said.

'No, I ain't,' Keogh replied. 'I'm just a bloke what takes the world as 'e finds it an' tries to make the best out of it. But my little businesses ain't what we're 'ere to talk about, are they?'

'No,' Blackstone agreed. 'They're not.'

'So let's get down to the subject in 'and. It shook me rigid what 'appened on Regent Street. Honest, it did. There's never been nuffink like it that I can remember.'

'Who did it, Tommy?' Blackstone asked bluntly.

'It beats me,' Keogh confessed.

'Remember what I said last time we met?' Blackstone asked. 'If you don't want an army of coppers swarming over your territory, you'd better tell me what you know.'

'That ain't a bad threat, as threats go,' Keogh admitted. 'But it still don't make no difference. I won't help yer 'cos I *can't* help yer. An' I *can't* help yer 'cos, as far as I know, there isn't a gang in London 'oo could 'ave pulled that snatch off.'

'You must have something for me, or you'd never have taken the time to meet me,' Blackstone pointed out.

Keogh hesitated. 'I might be able to give yer a hint that'll set yer off on the right lines. But before I do that, yer've got to promise that yer'll never tell anybody that yer heard it from me.'

Blackstone took a closer look at the other man, and saw Keogh's right eye seemed to have developed a twitch.

'You're scared, aren't you?' he said, incredulous.

'I'm bloody terrified,' Keogh replied.

'You don't *look* like a man who's frightened of death.'

'Nor am I,' Keogh said. 'I'd never 'ave got where I am if I 'ad been. But there's fings worse than death. There's losin' yer position in society. There's findin' out that yer not the man yer took yerself to be.'

'You're serious, aren't you?' Blackstone said wonderingly.

'There's people around the docks that 'old me in more fear an' respect than they 'old the Queen 'erself, you know,' Keogh said. 'I'm a big man on the river, an' I tell meself that I could take on these new blokes easy,

114

if I 'ad to. But I don't want to put it to the test. That's why I'm not goin' to do nuffink to draw undue attention to meself.'

'Understood,' Blackstone said. 'So what have you got for me?'

What Keogh had was the tale of an Indian in an expensive suit who had been ferried out to a barge in the middle of the Thames.

'Do you know who owns the barge?' Blackstone asked.

'Course I know. It's on my river, ain't it? The bloke 'oo owns it is a Dutchman, but I've already checked an' he don't know anyfink about anybody else usin' it for a meetin'.'

'Are the Indian and whoever he was meeting still on the barge?' Blackstone asked hopefully.

'Nah. Both of 'em's long gone – the Indian in a rowin' boat, the other bloke – 'ooever 'e was – in a launch. But yer've still got Lou Gammage, ain't you?'

'Assuming he knows something,' Blackstone said.

' 'E knows somefink, all right. 'E's got a pocket full of money, an' 'e didn't earn that from just rowin' people across the river.'

'And where will I find him?'

'My lads tracked 'im down to the Admiral Nelson in Rother'ithe. 'E should be there till 'e falls over.'

'Then I'd better have him picked up while he still makes sense,' Blackstone said.

'But remember – don't mention my name,' Tommy Keogh said. He paused. 'Whenever I walk into a pub,' he continued, his voice thick with sadness, 'I see all the little toe-rags already there start to develop the shakes. I've often wondered what it'd feel like to be one of them. Now I know.'

There were any number of Indian seamen in London. They were easily identifiable by the light cotton jackets and trousers – which they wore whatever the weather – and by their turbans and their oiled hair. Yet they were rarely seen, except around one of the special hostels which had been established for them, so their arrival in the bar of the Admiral Nelson caused quite a stir among the drinkers.

'We don't serve niggers in here,' the landlord said, though not unkindly.

The Lascars paid him no attention. Instead, they looked across at the man in the corner, who nodded towards Lou Gammage.

'Did you 'ear me?' the landlord asked, his tone not quite as friendly now.

The Lascars walked over to the bar, where Lou Gammage – now so drunk that he was using the counter for support – was standing.

'You come wiv we,' one of the Lascars said, in broken English.

'Sod off, you heathen bugger,' Gammage said.

The Indians took an arm each, and began to hustle the waterman towards the door.

''Ere, you can't do that!' shouted one of the dockers, who had no wish to see the source of his free drinks dragged away.

''Elp!' Lou Gammage cried, as drunk as ever but now aware of his predicament. 'Save me from these niggers.'

The docker and two of his drinking companions stood up and blocked the doorway. The Lascars seemed unconcerned. While keeping a firm grip on Gammage, each reached into the waistband of his trousers with his free hand, and produced a wicked-looking knife.

The docker and his pals weighed up their options. It didn't feel right that a couple of heathens should treat a white man like this – especially a white man who still had money in his pocket. On the other hand, the Lascars were bloody big blokes and looked as if they really knew how to use those knives. After scarcely a moment's contemplation, the three men returned to their seats, abandoning Gammage to his fate.

The Lascars bundled their captive through the door and into a cab which was waiting outside. Once the cab had pulled away, the man in the corner stood up and left as quietly as he had entered.

Twenty-Three

The assistant manager of Claridge's escorted Blackstone from the foyer of the hotel, to the head of the stairs which opened on to the second floor, then came to an abrupt halt.

'This is as far as I'm allowed to go,' he said apologetically. 'The Maharaja's bodyguards have prohibited any of the hotel staff from passing beyond this point.'

'But you're the *assistant manager*!' Blackstone pointed out.

The other man shrugged. 'That doesn't make any difference. Even the manager himself isn't allowed up here.'

'So how do the other guests on this floor feel about the fact that they can't call for a porter, or have a meal delivered to their rooms?'

'There *are* no other guests. The Maharaja has engaged the whole floor.'

Blackstone whistled softly. 'Jesus! What's that costing him?'

'More than you would ever wish to imagine,' the assistant manager said. 'Good luck.'

Then he turned, and began to descend the stairs.

Blackstone looked in both directions down the long, empty corridor, and found himself wondering just how easy it would be for an assassin to get at the Maharaja.

One step – so that his left foot actually made contact with the corridor itself – and he had his answer. From out of nowhere, the Maharaja's bodyguard appeared. The last time Blackstone had seen them, they'd been carrying elaborate ceremonial muskets, but now they were all toting the latest Winchester repeating rifle – and all these rifles were pointing at him.

'Police!' he said. 'Inspector Blackstone!'

One of the bodyguards advanced towards him, while the rest continued to keep him in their sights.

'You will please to stand facing the wall with the palms of your hands flattened against it,' the bodyguard said.

'But you know me. I'm from the police.'

'You will please to stand facing the wall with the palms of your hands flattened against it,' the bodyguard repeated.

The guard ran his hands expertly up and down the Inspector's body.

'Come,' he said, when his search was completed.

Still under close scrutiny from the other bodyguards, Blackstone followed the man down the corridor and into the parlour of one of the suites.

The Maharaja was there, sitting imposingly on an exquisitely carved throne. Various servants hovered in the background, ready to satisfy his slightest wish. Aggarwal sat at his feet, in front of a low table, like a faithful dog.

Blackstone made a quick study of the Maharaja's expression. There was haughtiness there, as might be expected on the face of a man who had the power of life and death over his subjects. But there was grief, too – the grief of a father who did not know how he would survive if anything should happen to his son.

'You have found the men who took my golden child from me, Inspector?' the Maharaja asked, without preamble.

'Not yet, Your Majesty,' Blackstone admitted.

But we *did* have a lead, at least for a while, he thought.

Lou Gammage might have told them much! But by the time Blackstone's men reached the Admiral Nelson, Gammage had gone. Not for ever, of course. He would almost certainly turn up again – but probably as a corpse, floating in the river.

The Maharaja shook his head sadly. 'Of course you haven't found the kidnappers. You will *never* find them. They are far too clever to be caught.'

'May I ask if there has been a ransom demand?' Blackstone said.

'Yes, there has.'

'How much do the kidnappers want?'

'One hundred and twenty thousand pounds,' the Maharaja replied, and Blackstone noticed that Aggarwal, still at his master's feet, blinked.

'Can you raise that kind of money?' the Inspector asked.

The Maharaja's lip twisted in contempt that the question should even have been asked.

'The money will be raised,' he said, 'but it will take a little time, for even *I* do not carry so much currency with me on my journeys.'

'I would like one of my men – perhaps my sergeant – to be the person to deliver the ransom,' Blackstone said. 'Are you willing to agree to that?'

'No!' the Maharaja replied emphatically.

'He will not interfere with the transaction in any way, but when he sees the kidnappers at first hand, he may perhaps be able to notice something which will give us a clue as to where—'

'No!' the Maharaja said again.

'We know that these men are capable of killing their victims, because they have already done so.'

'And that is precisely why I am prepared to do exactly what they ask of me.'

This was an impossible situation for any policeman to find himself in, Blackstone thought. Under normal circumstances, the victim would have to co-operate with him whether he wanted to or not, because he represented the law. But the Maharaja *was* the law in Chandrapore – and even outside it he was powerful enough to exert his will, should he wish to. This hotel stood on English soil, for example, but as long as the Maharaja was there, its second floor had become a part of his kingdom.

'I must be brutally frank, Your Highness,' Blackstone said, hoping that fear might work where logic had failed. 'The kidnappers may kill your son however willing you are to co-operate with them. They may have *already* killed him.'

'They have not,' the Maharaja said.

119

'How can you be so sure of that?'

The Maharaja gestured towards his secretary. 'Show him the photograph.'

Aggarwal reached on to the low table, picked up a photograph, and handed it wordlessly to Blackstone.

It was a hasty piece of work which reminded the Inspector of the snaps which seaside photographers took of visitors wandering along the promenade. Though the boy in it was obviously Indian, he was dressed in the clothes of a London street urchin. He was standing against a brick wall. He seemed unhappy and looked as if he might have been drugged – but he was clearly standing unaided.

'Are you sure this was taken recently?' Blackstone asked.

'Do you think I would have allowed my son to be dressed in rags while he was still under my protection?' the Maharaja retorted.

Blackstone examined the photograph again. The brick wall did not look new, and neither was it crumbling. It was about as anonymous as any wall could be, and might have been located in hundreds of streets in London – or thousands of streets anywhere else, for that matter. He turned the picture on its side, looking for some detail which might help him pinpoint the place more accurately.

Nothing!

There was not even a shadow which would have allowed him to guess at what time of day the photograph was taken.

'As you can see, His Royal Highness is quite safe,' the secretary said.

'I can see that he was quite safe when the picture was *taken*,' Blackstone countered. 'But there's no guarantee that he still is. And even if the kidnappers haven't harmed him yet, they may well do once they have got their hands on the money. They know that if they're caught, they'll hang for what they've done already, so what's to stop them deciding it will be safer to kill the prince?'

'Because letting him live will put them in no extra danger,' Aggarwal said. 'They have assured me that they have been masked at all times, and the prince would be unable to identify them.'

'And you believe their assurances, do you?'

'Within limits. Only a complete fool would call a gang of kidnappers honourable men. Yet from the way they spoke to me I believe that they are not quite devoid of normal human decency. Perhaps they have children of their own, and can understand the suffering His Majesty is enduring. Whatever the case, they have promised to return the prince safely once the ransom is paid, and I am prepared to accept their word for it.'

'And I am prepared to accept the judgement of my secretary,' the Maharaja said.

'They have already killed twice, and may kill again,' Blackstone reminded him.

'This I know,' the Maharaja said dismissively. 'But there is a great difference between butchering a few commoners and spilling the blood of a prince. Will they risk such a thing – especially if I have done exactly what they asked? I do not think they would dare.'

He didn't understand, Blackstone thought desperately. He simply could not come to terms with the idea that even to an *ordinary* kidnapper, the prince was not royal at all. To them he was no more than the son of an unfairly rich nigger, and his life counted for virtually nothing. And these men were *not* ordinary kidnappers. He had realized that after his visit to Amritsar Lodge. He yearned to save the poor, frightened child, but the father was not helping at all!

'Return the photograph to my secretary,' the Maharaja said.

'I'd prefer to keep it for a while,' Blackstone said. 'It might just provide me with a—'

'Return it to my secretary,' the Maharaja repeated firmly.

With a sigh, Blackstone gave the picture to Aggarwal. 'I wonder if I might be permitted to question your secretary, Your Majesty,' he said.

The Maharaja nodded. 'By all means, ask him whatever you wish.'

'I . . . er . . . think it might prove more useful if we were allowed to talk in private.'

'And why might that be? Do you think he is keeping secrets from me? Do you think that he would even dare to *dream* of doing such a thing?'

'Of course not, Your Majesty. But he may find himself overwhelmed in the presence of his ruler, as I am sure I would be in the presence of mine. Perhaps he would be able to think more clearly if we were alone. Will you grant us that opportunity?'

'I will consider it,' the Maharaja told him.

Twenty-Four

B lackstone looked across his desk at the man lounging in his visitor's chair. Walsh seemed relatively sober, taking into consideration the fact that it was already late afternoon.

'So you talked to the Maharaja, did you?' Walsh asked.

'Yes, I did.'

'And there has been a ransom demand?'

'Yes.'

'How much do the kidnappers want?'

'A hundred and twenty thousand pounds.'

'And what did the Maharaja say about the ransom? That he was willing to pay it, and you were not to interfere in any way?'

'Who told you that?'

Walsh smiled. 'I did not need to be told. No one in the world knows the Maharaja better than I do.'

'No one?' Blackstone asked sceptically.

'There may have been those in the past who knew him better, but since having such knowledge is dangerous, they are all now dead,' the Major said, matter-of-factly.

'The secretary met at least one of the kidnappers, and he

believes they will return the child unharmed,' Blackstone said.

'Did he tell you this in private, or when the Maharaja was listening?'

'When the Maharaja was listening.'

'Then he may only have been saying what he thought the Maharaja wanted to hear.'

'I know. That's why I asked the Maharaja's permission to talk to him privately.'

'And did the Maharaja give his permission?'

'You claim to know him. What do you think he said?'

Walsh stroked his chin pensively. 'He said he would think about it.'

Blackstone shook his head in admiration. 'And *why* did he do that?'

'It's not his practice to grant a request the first time it's made. Normally it is necessary to ask – to beg! – four or five times, even when what you want to do is what he already wishes done. Perhaps in your case – since you are not one of his subjects and are concerned to capture the men who kidnapped his son – he may well grant your request at only the second time of asking.'

Blackstone had always suspected that he needed Walsh. Now – seeing the Major as a lantern which could lead him through the dark subtleties of the Maharaja's mind – he was certain of it.

'During your time in India, did you ever come across Colonel Howarth of the 11th Hussars?' he asked.

'If you're in India long enough – and I was – there are not many colonels you *don't* come across,' the Major said, lighting up one of his cheroots. 'What surprises me is that *you* seem to have heard of him. How did that happen?'

'What can you tell me about him?' Blackstone asked.

'Not going to answer *my* question first, old boy?'

'No.'

The Major shrugged. 'Fair enough,' he said philosophically. 'In my opinion, some soldiers are born, and some soldiers are made. If you're born to it, you know almost

123

instinctively what to do. If you're not, and you have any sense, you wrap yourself so tightly in all the paraphernalia of soldiering that any part of you which might *not* act like a soldier is never allowed to spill out. You live strictly by the regulations. You worship the ritual. You believe that whatever we do is always right – because it is we who do it. And conversely, of course, whatever the other chap does is always *wrong*.'

'Is Howarth, in your opinion, one of the soldiers who was made?' Blackstone said.

'Yes, he is,' Walsh agreed. 'But please don't take that as a slight on the man. For every Julius Caesar, Henry the Fifth or Robert Clive, there are a thousand Colonel Howarths. It's only if they're really unlucky that they turn out to be disasters. Most of the time they muddle through well enough. Some of them may actually achieve something.'

'Who could induce Colonel Howarth to commit a criminal act?' Blackstone asked.

Walsh's mouth fell open wide enough for his cheroot to fall out of it. 'I beg your pardon?' he said, as he bent down to pick it up.

'Oh, I think you heard me well enough,' Blackstone told him.

Walsh placed the cheroot back in his mouth and frowned. 'Criminal act?' he mused. 'Who could induce him to commit a criminal act? Let me see. The Queen, of course – but whatever he did for her couldn't, by its very definition, be considered criminal. Nor would he cross the line for his family because, as far as I know, he doesn't have any.'

'How about money as a motive?'

'Money?'

'He suddenly seems to have plenty of it. He's just moved into a very fine estate near Windsor.'

'I couldn't see him committing a crime *for* money,' Walsh said.

'But?'

'But I suppose it's *just* possible that having already committed it, he might be prepared to accept a reward for his services. Yet I must come back to the point that I don't think he'd ever contemplate anything anti-social, unless it was under orders from someone higher in the—'

Walsh came to a sudden halt.

'Yes?' Blackstone said.

'There are certain codes of conduct which apply even to drunken ex-officers who jumped shortly before they would have been pushed. I don't think I'm prepared to discuss Colonel Howarth any further – unless, of course, you can provide me with a really compelling reason why I should.'

'Perhaps you'll consider this compelling. We believe that Colonel Howarth played a part – admittedly small, but nevertheless significant – in the kidnapping of the Maharaja's son.'

'That's absurd!'

Blackstone quickly outlined what he had learned at Amritsar Lodge.

'The Colonel had a tiger, now he doesn't,' he concluded. 'So where is it? My guess would be that it's lying on a stone slab in the London Zoo infirmary, full of bullet holes.'

'But if he is involved, that must mean that—'

'That he's not the only Army officer who's part of the plot? That someone else, possibly someone who outranks him, is also involved?'

'I suppose so,' Walsh admitted.

'Thinking it over, I'm surprised this kind of thing hasn't happened before,' Blackstone said. 'How many soldiers would you say leave the Army with the conviction that they've had a raw deal? Or, at the very least, that they haven't been sufficiently compensated for all their efforts?'

'If you'd asked me that question a few years ago, I'd have said none at all,' Walsh replied. 'Back then, it was enough to know that you had done your duty. But times have changed. When one sees some common northern industrialist – a man without breeding or education – spending money like water, it's hard not to feel that something has gone wrong with the world. So there may well be a few bitter old soldiers around. Still, I refuse to believe that any officer who's had the privilege of serving under Her Majesty's colours—'

'They have the expertise, and they have the discipline,' Blackstone interrupted. 'I should have thought of the Army from the very start. Who else would be capable of pulling off such an operation?'

Walsh's brow furrowed in deep thought. 'I wish I could provide you with a ready answer, but I can't actually think of anyone else,' he said mournfully, after perhaps two minutes had passed.

'Well, then?'

'You're not the kind of man who would be cruel enough to deliberately undermine everything I've based my life on without some purpose,' Walsh said. 'So what *is* that purpose? What are you seeking?'

'I need your help. I want to know who Howarth was close to during his time in India. Not his superiors, they'll mostly be dead, but men who served under him and now probably outrank him – and, of course, are in England at the moment.'

'I'll feel like a Judas, but I'll do it,' Walsh said.

'And Major Howarth's house has to be watched. It's not really a job for the police. You'll need to use your influence to call in the secret service.'

Walsh's mournful expression disappeared, and he burst out laughing. 'The what?' he asked, between chortles.

'The secret service,' Blackstone repeated.

'And what, exactly, do you know about the secret service?'

'About the *British* secret service, I know nothing. It wouldn't really be very secret if I did. But I had some dealings with the Okhrana – the Russian secret service – a few months ago. *It* seemed to have an extensive web of agents, so I can only assume that—'

'Then you'd assume wrong,' Walsh said. 'In India, our political officers garner their information from paid native informers, which means that what they learn is, at best, unreliable. For God's sake, man, the Indian Mutiny took us completely by surprise! Do you think that would ever have happened if we'd had a decent intelligence-gathering network?'

'Perhaps there have been failures in India, but surely—'

'Do you know how we've learned about Russian advances in Asia in the last forty years? Through the efforts of individual Army officers who used the time they should have been spending on leave to travel through hostile territory!'

'Are you serious?' Blackstone asked.

'Quite serious. And you haven't even heard the worst yet. Sometimes, while carrying out these missions, they pose as explorers. And that's not just to deceive the people they're spying on – it's to deceive the Foreign Office as well.'

'The Foreign Office!' Blackstone repeated, dumbfounded.

'The Foreign Office doesn't like us spying. It has no power to avenge our deaths, should we be killed, and it feels that such activities could upset the cosy diplomatic relationships it periodically establishes with the Russians. So the Army's not only given the almost impossible task of having to defend a huge frontier against possible enemy incursions, it has to do it while it's blindfolded.'

'What you're saying is that we can't use the secret service to watch Colonel Howarth, because the most powerful nation in the whole world doesn't *have* a secret service!'

'Correct,' Walsh agreed. 'Insane, isn't it?'

Twenty-Five

The servants who had to be up before first light had long since retired to their beds all over England, while those of a higher status had turned in shortly after seeing their employers to theirs. It was, in other words, that rare hour of the night when there is perfect silence and complete darkness in even the largest country house.

Colonel Howarth, hovering uneasily on the border between consciousness and sleep, tossed and turned in his bed.

Thoughts of the inspector from London were still troubling him. In the old days, people like Blackstone would not have been a problem. The only policeman likely to have visited Amritsar Lodge back then would have been the local bobby, and it would never have occurred to him that he might be granted any audience with the squire. No, he would have considered himself well done by if he had been offered a cup of tea by the housekeeper, and then sent on his way.

But things were much changed. The old respect for authority was disappearing. The very qualities which had made Britain into *Great* Britain were being discarded as if they were no more than trash. Only in India was there any sign of the natural order being maintained – and India, much to the Colonel's perpetual regret, was a young man's country.

There was a sudden click from across the room. The Colonel, still wrapped in his semi-dreams of the days when even the hint of insolence could be answered with the horse whip, did not register it at first, but when the click was followed by stealthy footsteps, he recognized the danger for what it was and reached for the loaded revolver which he always kept on his bedside cabinet.

'There is no need to be alarmed, Charles,' said a reassuring voice from the darkness. 'We are both a long way from the Northwest Frontier now.'

The visitor struck a match, located the oil lamp, and lit the wick. A small circle of light filled the area around the Colonel's bed.

'Better put the gun away before there's an accident, don't you think?' the visitor suggested.

'Of course,' Howarth agreed, placing the revolver back on his cabinet. 'But what's all this about – midnight visits, and so forth? Bit dramatic, ain't it?'

'We live in dramatic times,' his visitor replied. 'A policeman – an Inspector Blackstone – came to see you this morning, did he not?'

'That's right,' Howarth agreed.

'It was always pushing our luck to use the tiger, but we knew we would reap great benefits from such an action,'

128

the visitor said. 'Do you remember the durbars which the Viceroy used to hold for the Indian princes?'

'Indeed I do,' the Colonel said fondly.

'The Viceroy would sit on his throne and wait for the prince to approach him. There would be thousands of troops on display. No expense was spared in the effort to put on an impressive show.'

'Happy days,' the Colonel murmured.

'Those durbars were more of a pageant than a political negotiation. But the fact that they *were* pageants was political in itself. Before we ever got down to talking business, we had demonstrated to the prince how powerful and impressive the British Empire truly is. The tiger served a similar function. There may have been more efficient ways to carry out a kidnapping, but none which could have had so much impact – none which could have served as such an inspiration for the future.'

'I know that. That is why I agreed I would go along with it.'

'Yet when you run a risk, you must be prepared to pay the price for dealing with its consequences. We had hoped that the police would be too stupid to trace the tiger back to its source, but sadly, as Blackstone's visit demonstrates, that has not proved to be the case.'

'I think I managed to pull the wool over the Inspector's eyes quite well,' the Colonel said, with more confidence than he felt.

The visitor shook his head sadly. 'You did not. Blackstone knows that the tiger came from here. Though he has gone away, he will return. And before he can do that, action must be taken.'

'What kind of action?' the Colonel asked, with a growing unease.

'Your groundsman, Tebbitt, knows enough of what has gone on to make him a danger.'

'He served me in India for over twenty years,' the Colonel said. 'You can depend on him to keep our secrets.'

'We can depend on no one,' the other man told him. 'At

any rate, he need concern us no longer. But he is not our only problem, is he? This particular end of the chain has two weak links.'

'And I'm the other one?' the Colonel asked tremulously.

'Unfortunately so.'

'Are you here to murder me in my own bed?'

The visitor laughed. 'Of course not. You are a brother officer. A comrade in arms. Whatever the damage you could do to the project, we would never condemn you to such an ignominious fate. But something *does* have to be done.' The visitor paused. 'Where is your best dress uniform?'

'It's . . . it's in the wardrobe.'

'Shall I fetch it for you?'

'No, I . . . yes, if you would be so kind.'

The visitor crossed the room and returned with the uniform. 'You cut a fine figure in your younger days,' he said. 'I see this uniform, and I can see you on the *maidan*, wearing it. What fear you inspired! What respect! What service you did for the Crown during your time in India!'

'I did do the Crown some service,' the Colonel admitted.

'But the greatest is yet to come. When the history of these times is finally written, you will emerge as a towering figure – an inspiration to generations yet unborn.'

'Do you really think so?'

'I *know* so!' The visitor held out the uniform. 'Would you care to get dressed now.'

'Of course,' the Colonel said, climbing stiffly out of bed.

'You should have a valet to dress you, but you do understand that it would have been too great a security risk to bring one with me.'

'Yes. Naturally.'

'So instead I will serve as your valet.'

'You couldn't do that! It would be—'

'I can, and I will.'

'You do me great honour,' the Colonel said, feeling a lump forming in his throat.

'No, it is *you* who do *me* the honour,' the visitor assured him. 'Can you not imagine what a privilege it is for me to be with you at this truly heroic time?'

Since the Colonel was not used to being dressed by inexperienced hands – and since the visitor, having never dressed another man in his life, was about as inexperienced as it was possible to be – the whole process took some time. But finally it was done.

'You *still* cut a fine figure,' the visitor said in admiration. 'A little portly, perhaps, but every inch a soldier.'

'What happens next?' the Colonel asked.

'I am needed in London, and so, regrettably, I will have to leave you.'

'How will you travel?' the Colonel asked, wishing to prolong the departure as long as possible.

'I have a horse tethered at the edge of your estate. Do not worry, I will be back in the capital before I am missed.'

'So what—?'

'You should give me at least an hour to get clear of the area. That will present no difficulties, will it?'

'None.'

The visitor smiled. 'Forgive me for even asking, Charles. I deal with so many of the new kind of soldier that it is sometimes hard to remember that men of your stamp still exist. But perhaps, through our noble enterprise, we will see men like you rise to the fore again. And that will make all our sacrifices worthwhile.'

The Colonel looked from his visitor to his night table, and then back to his visitor again. 'Shall I leave a note?'

The visitor shook his head. 'A note would only create unnecessary complications. But never fear, Charles, your heroism will not go unremarked. A hundred years from now, bookshelves will groan under the weight of volumes celebrating your life and achievements.

When the visitor had left, the Colonel walked over to his night table and picked up the service revolver. It had served him well over the years, and had taken at least three enemy lives. And in all that time he had never thought – even in his

131

wildest imaginings – that the last time he fired it, the barrel would be aimed at his own head.

Twenty-Six

A great deal had happened in the previous twenty-four hours, Blackstone thought, as the open carriage made its way up the drive towards Amritsar Lodge. A ransom demand had been made for the safe return of the prince; a waterman called Lou Gammage had been abducted by a couple of Indians dressed as Lascar sailors – and a retired Army colonel had been found dead in his own bed with a bullet from his own gun through his skull.

'It's not as rare as you might imagine for retired colonial officers to end up shooting themselves,' said the man sitting next to him in the carriage.

'Isn't it?' Blackstone replied. 'And why is that? Because you have to have a few screws loose to become an Army officer in the first place?'

'I think that was a little uncalled for,' Major Walsh said mildly.

Yes, it was, wasn't it, Blackstone agreed silently.

He wondered why he kept giving in to the urge to snipe at Walsh. It wasn't as if he didn't like the man. He *did* like him. Perhaps, despite the Major's weakness for the bottle, he even *admired* him.

He was sure that if they'd been sergeants in India together – or both inspectors in Scotland Yard – they'd have got on famously. But the problem was, they hadn't been either of those things. They weren't equals, nor were ever likely to be – and somehow the upper classes always brought out the worst in Blackstone.

'You're quite right,' he said aloud. 'The remark was uncalled for, and I apologize for it.'

'Don't give it another thought,' Walsh said – and sounded

as if he meant it. 'As a matter of fact, you may be right. Possibly we *do* all have a few screws loose. But I was talking about the fact that it's sometimes very hard to give up India. It's like a drug.' He paused. 'You were there yourself, weren't you? Surely you know what I'm talking about.'

'We were in two different countries,' Blackstone told him. 'When you talk about the effect your India could have on a man, what you mean is the effect it could have on an *officer*. I was in the ranks myself.'

'And was that so very different?'

'There was a world of difference.'

'So what *did* it mean to the common soldier?'

'It meant heat and dust. It meant the possibility of dying of a particularly nasty disease he'd never have caught if he'd stayed at home. It meant—'

'Damn!' Walsh said, patting his pocket. 'Damn and blast!'

'Something the matter?' Blackstone asked. 'Is the truth a little too close for comfort?'

'What?' Walsh said distractedly.

'The truth?' Blackstone repeated, suspecting that he was being unfair to Walsh again, yet unable to restrain himself. 'Was it too close for comfort?'

'Oh, I see what you mean,' the Major said. 'No, it's nothing like that. Fact is, I seem to have lost my cheroots. Must have left the damn things on the train. Dashed annoying. But let's get back to the lot of the common soldier in India. Surely there must have been something that the other ranks liked about the country?'

'There was. They liked kicking the Indians around. But if they ever stopped to think about it – and a few of them did eventually – they realized being a "nigger" is nothing to do with the colour of your skin.'

'Come again?' Walsh said.

'They'd been the "niggers" once themselves – back in England. And when they finally returned to the mother country – if they lived that long – they'd be the "niggers" again.'

'How cynical you can sound. You're not some kind of radical, are you?'

'No. I'm a policeman. And if a policeman is to do his job properly, he has to look at things as they are, rather than as he'd like them to be. Tell me about the India you and your fellow officers knew.'

'If you were very rich, then I don't suppose it was much different to being at home,' Walsh said. 'But if your family was only moderately prosperous – as mine was – you suddenly found yourself living like a king. You could employ all the servants you wanted to. You could play polo to your heart's desire. Birth still mattered – a lord's a lord wherever he is – but it didn't matter as much as rank.'

'Very nice,' Blackstone said dryly.

'But it wasn't just that. You didn't get to love India for purely selfish reasons. You felt useful there. Sometimes you even felt heroic. You were defending what Disraeli called "the brightest jewel in the English crown". It was a privilege to be of service. That's why leaving it could be such a shock. That's why there are so many suicides.'

'And are all the suicides as quick as Colonel Howarth's? Or do some of the old India hands just decide to drink themselves to death?'

'Are you trying to insult me?' Walsh demanded, showing anger for the first time since Blackstone had met him.

'No,' the Inspector said, only slightly disingenuously. 'I'm just doing what I'm supposed to do – what you told me to do. I'm drawing on your expertise.'

Walsh's anger disappeared as quickly as it had arisen, and he laughed.

'It's true that some officers do decide to drink themselves to death once they come home,' he said, 'though if suicide is *my* aim, it's a process which began long before I ever left India.'

The carriage pulled up in front of the house, and was met by a middle-aged, uniformed inspector with thinning hair and a slightly bemused expression.

'The name's Downes,' he said, shaking Blackstone's hand with a vigour which showed his relief that someone else had finally arrived to take over the whole unpleasant business. 'I'll take you straight to the body, shall I?'

134

'You sound like you think there's a rush,' Blackstone replied. 'Colonel Howarth's not got any other plans for today, has he?'

'Well, no.'

'In that case, I think we'll stroll round the grounds while I pick your brains.'

The two detectives walked around the side of the house, with Major Walsh following discreetly a few paces behind. They climbed the steps to the terrace, and Blackstone turned to inspect the peacocks.

There were two of the birds in the garden. If either of them had any sense of the drama which had been played out in the house, they showed no sign of it. Instead, they concentrated all their efforts on creating a fine display for the benefit of their drab concubines.

They were so full of pride and self-importance, whatever the circumstances, Blackstone marvelled. In that way, he supposed, they were a bit like the British in India!

'Any chance the Colonel's death *wasn't* a suicide, Mr Downes?' he asked the local policeman.

Downes frowned. 'According to his servants, the Colonel always kept the pistol on his night table, so I suppose there's always a chance that the shooting *was* an accident.'

'An accident!' said Blackstone, who had never for a moment considered such a possibility.

'I know what you mean,' Downes said – though he obviously didn't. 'If he'd been cleaning his gun, there'd have been an oily rag around somewhere. And there wasn't. Besides, you don't put on your best dress uniform to do a messy job like that.'

He hadn't even considered the possibility that the Colonel had been murdered. And why should he have? Murders didn't happen in nice places like Windsor, especially when – as the royal standard flying from the flagpole at the castle proclaimed – the Queen herself was in residence.

And though the local inspector's reasoning was seriously flawed, the conclusion it led him to was more than likely correct, Blackstone thought.

The Colonel probably *had* died by his own hand – the dress uniform seemed to confirm that – but it was quite likely that it had not been at his own *suggestion*.

'Will you be wanting to speak to the servants?' Downes asked.

'Probably. Where will I find them?'

'I had all the staff – outside as well as inside – sent down to the servants' hall.'

'Any of them missing?'

'As a matter of fact, there is. One of the groundsmen. We've been to his cottage to look for him, but he isn't there. He's a chap by the name of . . .'

'Tebbitt,' Blackstone supplied.

'Yes, that is his name.'

'You say you've been to his cottage. Is he married?'

'No, he lives alone. He normally eats with the rest of the servants, and the housekeeper sends a parlour maid over to his cottage sometime during the day to pick up his washing, dust around, and so forth. So far as we know, he spends the evening by himself.'

'So none of the servants will have touched his cottage since yesterday?'

'Correct.'

'In that case, I'd be grateful if you'd send a couple of your lads over to the cottage to do a thorough search.'

'Glad to. Err . . . what will they be looking for, exactly?'

'Anything out of the ordinary,' Blackstone said airily. 'If they can find his cash box, they should check to see if there's any money in it. They should try to establish whether or not any of his clothes are missing. And, of course, they should keep their eyes peeled for bloodstains.'

'Bloodstains?' Downes repeated.

'Bloodstains,' Blackstone confirmed.

Twenty-Seven

The butler was a distinguished-looking man in his late fifties, who – like most of the staff and all of the furniture – had come with the house. He had not even raised an eyebrow when he had been instructed to go to the Colonel's sitting room for questioning, and now, though both Blackstone and Walsh were seated while he stood, he still managed to look very much in charge of the situation.

'We'd like to ask you a few questions about the Colonel's visitors,' Blackstone told him.

'Certainly, sir. Providing I can give such information without being indiscreet.'

'The Colonel *is* dead,' Blackstone reminded him.

'That is true, but I have always believed that we have an obligation to those who employ us which goes well beyond the grave.'

Major Walsh chuckled. 'Oh, now I get the picture. Like that, was it?'

'Like what, sir?'

'The odd painted lady arriving on the London train? Or did the Colonel prefer fresh young things with big country bosoms.'

'I'm afraid I couldn't possibly comment on anything of that nature, sir,' the butler said stonily.

'Of course not,' Blackstone hastily assured him. 'Major Walsh was only joking. Our sole interest is in the Colonel's more conventional visitors. The owners of neighbouring estates, for example.'

'The Colonel had very little to do with his neighbours.'

'And why was that?'

The butler hesitated for a second. 'In part, it was of their doing,' he admitted. 'Living as close to the castle as they do, birth has become something of a preoccupation with them.'

'The Colonel wasn't good enough for them?'

'Let us just say that it did not take long for them to establish for themselves that the Colonel was not someone they would be comfortable with socially. But I would not wish you to believe that this hurt the Colonel – he showed no interest in cultivating such relationships either.'

I'll just bet he didn't, Blackstone thought. Socializing with the locals would have interfered with the job for which he had been plucked from obscurity and sent to Windsor.

'Did the Colonel often have visitors from outside the area?' the Inspector asked.

'Not often, no. And none of them stayed . . .' the butler faltered for a second, '. . . and none of them stayed overnight.'

'Do you remember the names of any of his visitors?'

'I remember the names of all of them,' the butler said frostily. 'Their ranks, too, since, given the Colonel's background, they were all military men.'

He quickly reeled off a list which included two generals, one colonel, three lieutenant colonels and one major.

'And all of the visits were short?'

'Usually no more than two hours.'

Blackstone paused for a moment before posing his next question. 'You hesitated when you were about to say that none of them was here overnight. Why was that?'

'There was one occasion when the Colonel had a visitor without informing me of the fact,' the butler said, his tone suggesting that the failure was his and not his employers.

'If he didn't inform you that he'd had a visitor, then how can you know that he did?'

'The incident to which I refer happened at the start of last month,' the butler said reluctantly. 'At eleven o'clock in the evening, I escorted the Colonel to his bed chamber, as was my normal practice, and then took my leave. When I arrived at his chamber with the breakfast tray, at seven o'clock the following morning, I knew immediately that he had had a visitor during the course of the night.'

'*How* did you know?'

'There was a small patch of dried mud on the floor, which I would suspect, from its shape, had come from the edge of the sole of a riding boot. I had left the cushions on the armchair plumped up, but now they were flattened, even though the Colonel never sits in that particular chair himself. I am used to the smell of the Colonel's cigars in the air, but there was also the hint of a much inferior brand. And though I always leave the Colonel two drinking glasses, one for whisky and the other one for water, both of them had been used for whisky.'

'You'd make a good detective,' Blackstone said.

The other man smiled almost imperceptibly at the comment. 'A good butler must be the master of many skills.'

'And you have no idea who this mysterious midnight visitor might have been?' Walsh asked, looking him straight in the eyes.

'None,' the butler replied, returning the gaze.

'Tell me about the tiger,' Blackstone said.

'There is very little to tell. It arrived one afternoon in a Harrods van, and was taken directly to the pen which had been prepared for it.'

'Didn't you think it strange that your master should have bought a tiger?'

'It was not my place to think about it one way or the other.'

'So you say the tiger was taken straight to its compound. How often did you see it after that?'

'Never.'

'Never?'

'The Colonel summoned all the staff together. He told us that the tiger was a very dangerous creature, and that, for our own protection, we should keep well away from it. To reinforce his warning, he said that anyone who was caught near the tiger's enclosure would be instantly dismissed.'

'So none of the staff saw hide nor hair of it. When were you told it had died?'

'Last week.'

'And you believed it?'

'Why would anyone wish to lie about the death of a tiger?'

139

There was an urgent knocking on the sitting-room door, and Inspector Downes entered the room.

'Don't know how you ever worked it out, Mr Blackstone, but you were quite right,' he said.

'Quite right about what?'

'You told my men to look for bloodstains, and bloodstains were what they found.'

The cottage was a modest one, but with all the services of the big house available to him, Tebbitt would have needed no more. It consisted of a scullery, a workshop, a parlour and a bedroom. It was in the bedroom that the bloodstain had been discovered. It was not clearly visible, and had not the conscientious constable gone down on his hands and knees at the side of the bed, the search might have missed the telltale stain altogether.

Walsh lowered himself on to the flag floor to take a closer look. Blackstone, on the other hand, seemed more interested in other aspects of the room, and instead of joining Walsh, he first examined the contents of Tebbitt's wardrobe and chest of drawers.

'Very interesting,' the Inspector said.

'What have you found?' Walsh asked, looking up at him.

'It's not so much what I found, as what I *didn't*,' Blackstone said enigmatically. 'That really is blood, is it?'

'No doubt about it,' Walsh confirmed.

'Then here's what I think happened,' Blackstone said. 'Tebbitt was in bed when his attackers entered the room. They woke him up, ordered him to get out of bed, and then clubbed him to death.'

'Wouldn't it have been easier just to attack him while he was asleep?'

'Easier, but messier. There'd have been blood all over the sheets, and it would have been more difficult for the attackers to make it look as if Tebbitt had left of his own accord.'

'Is that what they tried to do?'

'Yes. That's why they removed most of his clothes. They didn't want us to think there'd been any murders at Amritsar

140

Lodge, because that would have led to further questions and speculations. A suicide and a flight were another matter entirely, and that is what they tried to simulate.'

'Have you considered the other possibility?'

'And what is that?'

'That there was no attack at all. That the single drop of blood might have come from some injury Tebbitt had sustained during the course of his day. That he really did run away.'

Blackstone examined the floor, then repositioned himself so that he was clear of all the furniture.

'What do you notice about the flagstones immediately around me?' he asked.

'They're a little darker than the others,' Walsh said.

'And why is that?'

'Possibly because they're damp.'

'And why should they be damper than the flagstones in the rest of the room?'

'Because they've been washed more recently.' Walsh paused, and a look of comprehension came to his face. 'And the reason for that is to wash away the blood!' he continued.

'Which is what the murderers did – apart from one tiny spatter which ended up close to the bed.'

Twenty-Eight

'I've been a fool,' Major Walsh said suddenly, as the cab which was returning them to the railway station entered Windsor.

'A fool?' Blackstone repeated.

'More than that! I've been a complete bloody idiot.' Walsh patted his pocket for his cheroots, then remembered that he had lost them. 'I have something important to say, but before I begin, can I tell you a story about my soldiering days?'

'Why not?' Blackstone asked, intrigued.

'When I was a raw young 2nd lieutenant, I was posted to Calcutta. One of my first assignments was to work under a captain who had been given the task of investigating serious losses from the quartermaster's store.'

'What kind of losses?'

'Riding tackle, guns, ammunition, medicine – anything, in other words, for which there would have been a ready market outside the cantonment.'

'Go on,' Blackstone encouraged.

'The captain began working on the assumption that the guilty parties must be among the native workers attached to the stores. He questioned them all, and had several of them flogged to within an inch of their lives. When it became apparent – even to him – that the Indians were not responsible, he turned his attention to the enlisted men. But in the meantime, I had been doing some thinking of my own, and had decided that even if these common soldiers were guilty of assisting in the crimes, they were not the chief culprits.'

'And what had led you to that conclusion?'

'I can probably best explain if I take one robbery as an example. A hundred saddles had gone missing. A hundred! Now how would the common soldiers ever meet the kind of Indian who had sufficient cash to purchase a hundred saddles, even at knock-down prices?'

'*He* might have approached *them*,' Blackstone suggested, playing devil's advocate.

'All right,' Walsh conceded. 'Let us assume that, without them even seeking him out, they had already had a buyer. How would they manage to smuggle a hundred saddles out of the cantonment all at once?'

'Perhaps they didn't smuggle them all at once. Perhaps they only took a few at a time.'

'Where would they store the rest while all this was going on? You know what a barracks is like, Inspector. There's barely the space for the men to store their own equipment. And what other areas would they have access to – areas where they could be assured their hoard would not be discovered by one of their superiors? None! The whole thing would have been impossible without the active co-operation of at least one officer.'

'You told the captain this, did you?'

'I did. I put forward to him the same arguments as I have put forward to you. He wouldn't hear of it. He refused to contemplate the notion that an officer could ever be involved in such a sordid business. And I thought him a fool to be swayed by his prejudice to such an extent that he would refuse to see the logic of my argument. Yet am I any better? After the way I have been acting since you told me of your suspicions, am I any less of a fool?'

'So you're prepared to accept that Army officers are behind the kidnapping of the Maharaja's son?'

'Yes. I do not say *active* officers – perhaps they are all retired, like Colonel Howarth – but certainly officers of some sort. I don't want to accept it, but I'm forced to – especially now we have been given the names of the men who visited Colonel Howarth.'

'You recognized one of them?'

'I recognized *all* of them. But there was one in particular which stood out. May I return to my story about Calcutta for a moment?'

'Of course.'

'The captain, as I have said, refused to accept any of my conclusions. Eventually, he arrested a sergeant and a corporal. They were tried and found guilty. As they stood before the firing squad, they were still protesting their innocence. I believed them, and I determined, then and there, to carry on my own investigation in secret. I was ruthless in my approach – I owed it to those two dead men to be so. I deliberately put aside my personal prejudices and preferences. That a man was my friend – that I would trust him with my life – did not exclude him from my scrutiny. It took me months to reach my conclusions, but in the end, by a process of elimination, I found that the finger pointed very clearly at one man. I could not prove he was guilty, but I was convinced in myself that he had to be. He was a major at the time, and his name was Roderick Pugh.'

'According to the butler, a *General* Pugh visited Colonel Howarth recently. Could it be the same man?'

'It *is* the same man. I have been following his career ever since my time in Calcutta. I kept hoping that, though I was unable to bring about his downfall myself – though I was unable to make him pay for standing by while two innocent men were executed – someone else would eventually unmask him for what he truly was. But it was not to be. Whatever his other faults, he was a good soldier in the field. He was promoted to colonel, then to general. It is possible that as he grew older, he grew more honest. But I, for one, do not believe it. A leopard does not change his spots – especially a vile, avaricious, ruthless leopard, which was what I had discovered Roderick Pugh to be.'

'Do you know where he is now?'

'He retired about three years ago. He lives somewhere in the Home Counties in quiet respectability. And if you are looking for a man capable of organizing the kidnapping of the prince and the murders attendant on it, then you need look no further.'

Twenty-Nine

Night had fallen in Agra, bringing with it a little relief – but *only* a little – from the glue-like stickiness of the day.

It was simply not a white man's climate at this time of year, Captain Donald Threlford thought as he abandoned his rickshaw and covered the last few yards to the General's bungalow on foot. Not a white man's climate at all!

In this part of India the sun was not the benevolent, smiling face it was at home. Rather it was an angry ball of fire, hurling its cursed heat down on those below. Even before it had reached its height, the sweat which gathered under the armpits would become as thick as a swamp, as sticky as treacle. And it would get worse as the day progressed, so that by evening a man would feel as if not just his uniform, but also his skin, had begun to rot away.

General Greer was sitting on his veranda, somewhat cooled – though not enough, *never* enough – by the punkah-wallah's fan. He was gazing into the night towards distant Chandrapore, and seemed so absorbed in his own thoughts that he did not even notice his aide was approaching.

Threlford took a handkerchief out of his pocket, paused to wipe his perspiring brow, and wondered if he was about due to endure another tirade against the Princely States.

'They're nothing but a damned nuisance!' the General would tell his own officers, the occasional official visitor, the British merchants of the city – and anyone else he could back into a corner at a social function. 'A damned nuisance and a damned inconsistency. We already have direct rule over a good part of the country, do we not? Then why not over all of it?'

Agreeing with him – saying you shared his views entirely and without question – would do nothing to staunch the flow once he had got started.

'Does the government really think that the native princes do as good a job of running their states as we could?' he would continue. 'Has the Prime Minister – God rot him! – ever considered what a provocation it is to our niggers to see other niggers ruled by one of their own kind? And wouldn't the niggers in the princely states be much happier under British rule?'

A slight contradiction there, the listener would think. Either the natives would prefer to be ruled by the Raj or they wouldn't. He couldn't have it both ways. But they were wrong. Despite the logical inconsistencies, Greer was still the commanding general, and thus could have it as many ways as he liked.

'And why should the princes grow fatter and fatter on money which would be much more useful in the British treasury?' he would conclude.

Why indeed? his listeners would sincerely agree, whatever their personal opinion of the General. The princely states were there for the picking. All that was needed was someone with the will to harvest them.

Greer noticed the arrival of his aide-de-camp, and gave him a warm beam of welcome. 'Wonderful evening, is it not, Donald?'

Threlford agreed – just as he would have agreed if his commanding officer had said it was raining frogs – and found himself wondering just what had caused Greer to abandon his usual sour demeanour.

'We're going to see a bit of action at last,' Greer said. He handed Threlford a piece of paper. 'First thing in the morning, I want you to instruct the company commanders on this list that their men should be ready to move out at two hours' notice.'

Threlford ran his eyes down the list, and quickly calculated that the soldiers involved in the General's plans – whatever those plans *were* – accounted for two-thirds of the entire garrison.

'Are we going on manoeuvres, sir?' he asked cautiously.

'No, we most certainly are not. What we will be doing, my dear Donald, is marching into Chandrapore.'

Despite the heat, Threlford paled slightly. 'I wasn't aware that we'd received any orders from the Viceroy on such a course of action, sir.'

'Nor have we,' the General agreed jovially. 'Wait for orders from that old fool, and you'll wait for ever.'

'So the order came from London?'

'Not from there, either. Those stuffed shirts in the India Office are more concerned about their next visit to their favourite brothel than they are about the Empire.'

'Then if the order didn't come from the Viceroy and it didn't come from London, I don't quite see how we can—'

'The commander on the ground – which in this case, I should remind you, happens to be me – is allowed to use discretionary powers if the situation is deemed to warrant it. And that's just what I'm doing – assuming discretionary powers because the situation warrants it.'

What situation? Threlford wondered. Had the Old Man been sitting out in the sun for too long? Had he finally gone off his chump?

'We're marching into Chandrapore to restore order,' the General said, reading the obvious doubts on his subordinate's face. 'No one should be able to argue with that. And should I decide to continue to occupy the state once order *has* been restored,' the General gave his aide a broad wink, 'then who's to blame me? Can't be too careful with these excitable niggers, now can we?'

Threlford swallowed hard. There were procedures laid down for dealing with a superior who had gone completely doolally, but it would be a brave man who attempted to enforce them.

'You look troubled, Donald,' the General said, obviously enjoying himself hugely.

'Well, yes, sir. I . . . it's just that . . .'

'Spit it out, man!'

'I take your point about your discretionary powers, and so on and so forth. And you're quite right when you say that it's the duty of the Army to restore order, should the need arise. But . . .'

'But what?'

'But there hasn't *been* any trouble in Chandrapore. If there had been then I, as your aide, would have been the first to hear about it.'

The General laughed. 'You're quite right, of course,' he conceded, 'there hasn't been any trouble *yet*. But I received one telegram this morning, and I'm expecting another tomorrow. And let me assure you, my dear Donald, that soon after that second telegram arrives, there'll be trouble enough in the so-called "princely state" to more than justify whatever course of action I deem necessary.'

147

Thirty

When the Maharaja had informed Blackstone that he would need time to raise the ransom the kidnappers demanded, he had been lying. The safe in the corner of the suite was proof of that, for even as he had delivered his lie, it had contained one hundred and fifty thousand pounds. It did not contain that much money now. The bundles of banknotes were as thick as they had ever been, but their value had been considerably reduced.

The only man who was aware of the true state of affairs was sitting at the Maharaja's feet at that moment, fighting the temptation to keep his eyes on the safe door. Not that there was much danger the Maharaja would notice even if he did, Sapan Aggarwal thought. The man had not spoken for more than an hour, and but for the occasional sigh, it would have been possible to believe that he was unconscious.

Aggarwal had closed two of the three paths which had been open to him. The first – actually becoming the loyal retainer he had pretended be for so long – had been blocked the moment he removed the money from the safe. There was no going back on that now. The second – allying himself with the kidnappers – he had rejected on the grounds that at least *some* of the leaders of the plot appeared to be white, so the chances of a poor Indian getting a fair deal out of them was practically negligible. Thus, he was left with the one course he had already been committed to when he arrived in England. He would play a significant role in the planned palace coup, and be rewarded accordingly.

The telephone rang, its piercing shriek making both the Maharaja and the secretary jump. Though Aggarwal wanted to leap to his feet and grab the phone, he restrained himself. It would not do to seem too eager. Besides, there was protocol to be observed. It was the function of one of the servants – his *only* function – to answer the telephone, and there was nothing to be done until the proper procedure had been followed.

The servant picked up the phone, answered it in his broken English, and then bowed in the Maharaja's direction.

'There is a man who wishes to speak to your secretary, Your Majesty,' he said.

'Who is it?' the Maharaja asked.

Who do you think it is, you bloody fool! Aggarwal thought viciously. It is the kidnappers, of course! Who else would ring *me* – a man with no existence of his own outside the whim of his master?

'They do not say who it is, Your Majesty,' the servant replied. 'They say only that it is urgent they speak to Mr Aggarwal.'

The Maharaja nodded to his secretary, who then climbed to his feet and walked over to the telephone.

'Aggarwal?' the voice asked at the other end of the line.

'Yes.'

'Do you have the money?'

'Yes, I have the money.'

'Then listen carefully. You are to place the notes into a leather attaché case and take the case to Bank underground railway station. You are to be alone. No other servants, and none of the Maharaja's bodyguards, are to accompany you.'

'I will arrange for a cab to collect me, and—'

'No cabs. Policemen can hide in cabs. You will walk.'

'But it is very dangerous to be alone on the street with so much money. I may be robbed.'

'You will not be. From the moment you leave the hotel, you will be guarded every step of the way.'

'But—'

'Shut up and listen! You are to buy a ticket at Bank Underground Station – it will cost you tuppence, so make sure that you have the coins with you – and then you are to board the first train available.'

'And then?'

'Did I say there *was* an "and then"?'

'No, but there surely must—'

149

'You have been told all you need to know. Follow the instructions or face the consequences.'

There was a click and then the line went dead.

Aggarwal felt sweat starting to form on his brow. He had based all his calculations on having five minutes unobserved in order to do what needed to be done. He had not even considered the possibility he might be watched as he made his way to the rendezvous point.

He pictured the kidnappers checking through the piles of banknotes. They were *clever* men. It would be *obvious* to them what he had done. And even though he would not have cheated them – since he would have brought them all they asked for – they might not see it that way.

What was he going to do? What was he going to *do*?

They would not begin to have him under observation until he actually left the hotel, he realized with a huge rush of relief. And that was all the opportunity he needed! For surely, somewhere between the suite and the hotel's main door, he could find a quiet room – or even a cupboard – where he could take the necessary steps.

'What did they say?' the Maharaja asked anxiously.

'They want the money delivered now, Your Majesty.'

'And then they will return my son to me?'

'Yes, Your Majesty. But only if we do exactly as they say. They will have people watching me on the street. No servants or bodyguards must follow me, or they will regard it as a breach of faith.'

The Maharaja nodded his acceptance. 'Take the money from the safe,' he said.

Aggarwal walked over to the safe and began to extract bundles of money – the *right* bundles of money.

'You will not be followed, but one of the guards will escort you as far as the street,' the Maharaja said.

Aggarwal's hands froze. 'That . . . that will not be necessary, Your Majesty,' he gasped.

'Do you dare to defy me?' the Maharaja asked, astonished.

'No, Your Majesty, but—'

'Once you are outside, the kidnappers will make it their

business to see that you are not robbed, but as long as you are within the hotel the money is still mine and I *will* have it guarded. Is that understood?'

'Yes, Your Majesty,' Aggarwal said miserably.

He should have thought of this possibility, he told himself. Whatever the risk, he should have tried to bribe the guards earlier. But now it was too late! So what was he to do? How the hell could he get rid of the rubbish?

Thirty-One

The club servant walked along the corridor of the United Services' Club with the long, perfectly measured strides of a man who had served in one of the elite guards' regiments. Behind him, Blackstone matched his pace precisely, though Patterson – who had had no military training himself – was finding it hard to keep up without giving the impression of being hurried.

At the door of the smoking room, the porter came to an abrupt halt.

'Wait here,' he told the two detectives, before opening the door and disappearing into the room.

He returned a minute later. 'General Pugh is willing to see you now.'

He seemed surprised that a distinguished military man like the General would condescend to spend time with a couple of ordinary policemen.

And so am I, Blackstone thought, for he had never imagined it would be *this* easy to see Pugh.

The porter led them into the smoking room. It was a large room, full of big leather armchairs and thick with the aroma of cigars. There were perhaps a dozen members in the room. Some were talking, some reading the early editions of the evening papers. All gave the impression of being very much on home territory.

General Pugh sat in splendid isolation, a large balloon glass of very pale brandy in his hand. So this was the man whose career Major Walsh had been following for nearly twenty years – the man who had stood by while two common soldiers were executed for crimes he had committed himself.

There should be more evidence of his life history etched into his face, Blackstone thought. A man like Pugh had no right easing so comfortably into stocky old age. He had no right to look so at peace with himself.

Pugh looked up at the two policemen. 'Well, don't just stand there like mutes at a funeral,' he said.

'I beg your pardon, sir?' Blackstone said.

'The reason that the club puts chairs in this room is it expects people to want to sit down on them, so now you're here you might as well take the weight off your feet.'

Blackstone eased himself into a chair which had probably cost more than he earned in a year. The General had a very different approach to that of Colonel Howarth, he thought. Howarth had made him stand, Pugh had invited him to sit. But the Inspector had long ago stopped confusing courtesy and politeness with honesty and decency.

'Read in the paper that Charlie Howarth topped himself,' the General said. 'I assume that's why you wanted to talk to me.'

'It is, sir,' Blackstone agreed. 'You visited the Colonel a couple of months ago, didn't you?'

'That's right, I did.'

'Might we know why?'

He fully expected Pugh to tell him to mind his own damned business, but instead the General said, 'I visited him because he asked me to.'

'Was there a purpose behind the visit?'

'Yes,' Pugh agreed hesitantly. 'A definite purpose, at least from his standpoint – but I'm still not entirely sure what it was.'

The conversation had already started to take turns that Blackstone had not anticipated. 'Could you explain that last remark to me, sir?' he asked.

'Certainly willing to do my best. When we old buffers get together, it's inevitable we talk about our days in the Army. Not that it's usually much of a *talk* – in fact, it sounds more like an artillery barrage.'

'Artillery barrage? I'm not sure I understand.'

'Did you know that I was the best soldier ever to serve in the British Army?' Pugh asked. 'Are you aware that, compared to me, Wellington was nothing but a bungler and Wolfe little more than a choir boy?'

Blackstone coughed, awkwardly. 'No, I didn't realize that, sir.'

Pugh laughed heartily. 'Of course you didn't. And there's good reason for that. It isn't true! But every old war horse likes to think of himself as the greatest soldier who ever trod the earth – and when we get together it's not usually to listen to what the other chap has to say about himself, but to brag about our own exploits. *That's* what I mean about an artillery barrage – we all want to have our say, and it's the one with the loudest voice who usually wins.'

Blackstone nodded. 'I get the point now, sir.'

'No you don't,' Pugh said, 'but you look a sharp enough chap, and you will in a minute. When I went to see Charlie Howarth I expected him to want to tell me how he saved the Empire single-handed, but all he seemed interested in were *my* exploits.'

'Any exploits in particular?'

Pugh gave him a hard stare. 'Know the answer already, do you? Can't bear the kind of chap who asks questions he already knows the answer to. Damned annoying'

'I don't know the answer,' Blackstone promised. 'It just seems to me that since Colonel Howarth invited you, rather than anyone else, it must be because of something which was unique to you.'

Pugh nodded. 'Smart thinkin',' he said. 'As a matter of fact, Charlie Howarth *was* interested in somethin' in particular. Wanted to know about the leave I took in '80.'

Blackstone recalled Walsh talking about the way in which some soldiers had chosen to use their leaves.

'I assume you took this particular leave in Central Asia,' he said.

'Are you certain you don't know this story?' Pugh demanded.

'Positive,' Blackstone assured him. 'I'm just making an informed guess.'

'Then your information must be very good,' Pugh said, 'because that's exactly where I did go. Went to the eastern end of the Caspian Sea, to be exact. Took me months to get there, and involved crossing some of the most desolate places on God's earth. Probably no idea what it's like yourself, but I can tell you that a man can travel for hundreds of miles without seeing another living soul.'

'Was the purpose of your expedition to gather military intelligence?'

'Yes, it was. Suppose there's no harm in admitting that now. Heard rumours that the Russkies were planning to invade a place called Merv, which would have given them a vital staging post on the route to India. Rumours said they were already assembling a large army on the shores of the Caspian. Wanted to see if it was true.'

'But you didn't do this openly, did you?' Blackstone asked. 'To disguise your true intentions, you probably said that you were conducting a geographical survey?'

'Not quite such an informed guess this time, Inspector,' Pugh said gleefully. 'Didn't so much disguise my intentions as disguise *myself*. Pretended to be an Armenian horse-trader. Had to, otherwise the British Diplomatic Mission in Tehran might have heard what I was up to. And if they'd reported it back to the Foreign Office, there'd have been hell to pay. Of course, once I'd actually *collected* the information, the government was glad enough to hear it. Did some good, too, I think. By the end of the year, the Tsar was giving the Queen his personal assurances that he had no interest in conquering Merv.'

'And that's the story Colonel Howarth wanted to hear?'

'Yes, in a way. Except that he didn't seem very interested in the *details* of the expedition. Didn't seem interested in the *expedition* at all, as matter of fact. Was more concerned with what might have happened if I *hadn't* decided to go to Transcaspia.'

'Why was that?'

'Kept asking me if I thought the Empire had survived more by luck than judgement. Wondered whether the day of the amateur spy was over. Said the Army had become professional in every other way, and wasn't it about time we became more professional in the way we gathered our intelligence?'

'Did you agree with him?'

'Suppose I did – on a practical level. But in my heart I'm against it. Wellington said the Battle of Waterloo was won on the playing fields of Eton. Not at some kind of Germanic *staff college*, you understand, but back at school – where a man's character is formed. Think he was right about that. We English have always been a nation of amateurs, and it hasn't served us badly so far, now has it?'

That depended, Blackstone thought. If you'd served in the 2nd Afghan War under General Roberts – as he had – then you'd probably agree with Pugh and Wellington. If, on the other hand, you'd served in the *1st* Afghan War and survived the retreat from Kabul under Elphinstone – and only one man had – you'd probably be forgiven for wishing that your commanding officer *had* attended some kind of Germanic staff college.

'What were you guided by when you gave your answer to Colonel Howarth's question?' the Inspector asked. 'Your heart or your head?'

General Pugh smiled, perhaps a little sadly. 'I answered with my head,' he admitted. 'It's all very well for us old dogs to dwell on our past glories, but we have to think of all the puppies coming up. If you send a man into battle, you owe it to him to arm him as well as you can – and that includes arming him with the best possible intelligence.' He paused. 'Funny thing, Howarth wasn't a particularly emotional sort of chap, yet he seemed quite overcome when I told him that. Thanked me for visiting and told me I'd put his mind at rest. Had absolutely no idea what he meant by that. Do you?'

'No,' Blackstone admitted.

Nor did he, though he was sure that the answer Pugh had given had been very important to Howarth – and that whatever had impelled Howarth to feel the need to ask the question was very important to the case.

Thirty-Two

For the first fifteen minutes of his journey to Bank Underground Railway Station, Sapan Aggarwal did all in his power to spot the men who were tailing him.

It proved to be a hopeless task. The streets were crowded, and he soon lost the ability to decide whether the man in the top hat, who was behind him at that moment, was the same man who had been on his heels at the corner of Oxford Street and Wardour Street.

Besides, who was to say that his hidden escorts would be so obvious as to wear top hats at all? Why couldn't the beggar heading in the same direction as he be one of the kidnappers? Was that hansom cab travelling so slowly because the cabby was a cautious soul – or because one of his unknown watchers was sitting inside it? Didn't the man pushing the barrow weighed down with vegetables look altogether too healthy to be a real costermonger?

It was impossible to know if he was being observed continually or only at intervals, but he was certain that if he fell into the hands of the kidnappers before he had had time to adjust the contents of the attaché case, he would find himself having to answer some very unpleasant questions.

Coming down Cheapside, he saw a dome rising above a flat roof. It reminded him of his own country – of the mosques in which the Maharaja generously allowed his Moslem subjects to worship, once they had paid an additional tax. But this was no mosque. The dome concealed the workings of the hydraulic lifts which took passengers down to the platforms of the Bank tube station, and it told him that he was nearly there – and still had not solved the problem of what to do with the extraneous contents of his case!

Lombard Street! he thought with a sudden burst of inspiration.

There were banks on Lombard Street. There was *his* bank on Lombard Street. A man could go into a bank and do what he had to do without drawing undue attention to himself. In truth, the curiosity which would have seemed only natural on the street would be construed as extreme rudeness within the confines of that august institution.

So relieved that he paid little attention to the traffic – and was almost knocked down by a grocer's delivery cart in consequence – Aggarwal crossed the road in front of the Mansion House and stepped into Lombard Street. That his own bank – the Anglo-India Bank – was so close to the tube station, could only be taken as a sign that fortune was on his side in this enterprise, he thought.

He entered the bank full of almost light-headed optimism. But he must not relax, he warned himself – he must not lower his guard even for a second. The chances that one of the kidnappers was already in the bank were so minimal as to be non-existent, but he must still make sure that the desk he chose gave him a clear view of anyone entering or leaving by the main door.

Aggarwal unbuckled the straps on the attaché case, opened it slightly, and looked down at the bundles of bank notes. It was a fortune, he thought – but not quite as big a fortune as some people might believe.

Blackstone and Patterson sat in the public bar of the Crown and Anchor – a pub which boasted neither the royal nor the nautical connections that its name seemed to promise and owed most of its business to its proximity to Scotland Yard.

Blackstone had ordered a pint of stout with – unusually – a whisky chaser, and for the previous five minutes had sipped the two alternately with so little sign of pleasure that he could have been drinking ditch water.

157

'Do you want to tell me what's troubling you, sir?' asked Patterson, whose sociable nature took no great pleasure in being alone with *its* own thoughts.

'What was that?' Blackstone said, distractedly.

'Is there something on your mind?'

'Yes, there is,' Blackstone admitted. 'General Pugh isn't at all how I'd pictured he'd be – especially after what Major Walsh told us about him.' Patterson grinned. 'Oh, I get it, sir. Pugh's supposed to be one of the villains of the piece, so he should have a black eye patch and big scar running down one cheek!'

Blackstone returned the grin, somewhat sheepishly. 'No, I suppose not,' he said, 'but . . .'

'But what?'

'Put yourself in his shoes for a minute – or rather, put yourself in the shoes that, up to now, we've been *assuming* he occupies. You're a ruthless kidnapper – part of a conspiracy.'

'All right,' Patterson agreed, attempting to harden his plump features into an appropriate criminal mould.

'Perhaps you read about Colonel Howarth's death in the newspapers,' Blackstone continued. 'Or perhaps you've been told in advance that he's *going* to die. Whatever the case, you know that it's highly likely the police will get your name from Howarth's butler, and will want to know why you visited him. So what story are you going to tell me when I ask?'

'General Pugh said—'

'I know what *he* said. What I asked was what *you* would have said in his place. Bear in mind that you have secrets to guard, and that you don't have to stick to the truth.'

Patterson slipped into the role. His spine stiffened, and from the way he began to hold his nose it was almost possible to see a heavy military moustache underneath it.

'Charlie Howarth told me that he'd overreached himself in buying Amritsar Lodge, and asked me for a loan for old times' sake,' he said in a fair imitation of Pugh's voice.

'Not bad. Now give me another explanation.'

Patterson thought for a second. 'Howarth has no close

158

living relatives and wanted my advice on who to leave his estate to.'

'Even better. Give me another.'

'He asked me down to his estate because he needed cheering up. Said there'd been times recently when he'd felt quite suicidal. That's why I wasn't surprised when he shot himself.'

'One more, and we'll call it a day.'

'He wanted advice on the best way to look after the tiger he'd ordered from India.'

'That's four possible explanations, and all of them pretty convincing,' Blackstone said. 'What was it that made you – thinking as General Pugh – choose any, or all, of those stories?'

'I couldn't tell the police the truth about my visit – that it was to do with the kidnapping – so I needed to come up with a story which was both simple and plausible.'

'Exactly!' Blackstone agreed. 'The whole object of the exercise, from your point of view, was to send me away satisfied – to put me in a frame of mind in which I'd rule you out of the investigation. So that is indeed the kind of story you'd have told me. What you certainly *wouldn't* have done is spin me a tale which threw up any number of *new* questions. But that's just what Pugh did do, didn't he?'

'I suppose he did,' Patterson agreed.

'For the last fifteen minutes, I've been asking myself why Howarth should have wanted to know about Pugh's expedition to the Caspian Sea,' Blackstone continued. 'And you see what the fact that I've even been considering that means, don't you?'

'It means that you're taking it seriously. That you don't think it's a story at all. That what Pugh *claims* was said actually *was* said.'

'And that in turn means what?'

'That you don't believe Pugh is a member of the gang?'

Blackstone nodded. 'Exactly so! Are you still on drinking terms with any of the clerks at the India Office?'

'I keep in touch with a few,' Patterson said warily. 'Purely in case I need to talk to them in the line of duty, of course.'

'Look them up this evening. See what you can find out about General Pugh's time in India. I'd be particularly interested in the period he spent in Calcutta, while he was still a major.'

'Couldn't Major Walsh tell you about that?'

'Walsh already has,' Blackstone reminded his sergeant. 'And I'm not sure he's given me the whole picture. I like Walsh. He's intelligent, perceptive – and as reliable as anyone who drinks as much as he does could be. But we've never put all our faith in a single source of information before, and I don't see why we should start now.'

Thirty-Three

Sapan Aggarwal had only ever been underground once before – to talk to a prisoner in the deep dungeons below the Maharaja's palace. It had not been a pleasant experience for him, but it had at least been made bearable by the knowledge that the visit was only temporary – that while the prisoner was still festering and suffering, he would be back at ground level, smelling the clean air and sipping warm, fresh tea.

The underground at Bank Station was quite a different matter. There were no bodyguards there to make him feel secure, no reassurance that a pleasanter time lay just ahead. And though he prided himself on being as sophisticated as any Briton, he did not share the obvious assurance of his fellow passengers that the tons of rock overhead would *stay* overhead.

He paid his two coppers and took the crowded lift down to the platform. What should he do next, he wondered? Get on the waiting train? Or wait to be contacted?

*   *   *

The cricket ground was not as full as it would have been if the match had been held on a bank holiday. Nonetheless, the very fact that Surrey were playing their old rivals, Sussex, was enough to ensure that a large number of clerks had rung in sick, that a small legion of boys had decided their education would not unduly suffer from missing one day's schooling, and that at least a quarter of the House of Lords had weighed up the pros and cons and reached the conclusion that the legislation on the floor of the house that day was not particularly important.

It had been a hard-fought match thus far, and it was becoming uncomfortably hot. Many of the spectators had tucked handkerchiefs or newspapers under their hats, to protect their necks from the sun. Some of the players were visibly wilting. Yet no one would have wished to leave the scene at such a nail-biting point in the match.

It was midway through an over when the phone call came. The steward who answered it, furious at being dragged away from the action, was more than willing to give the caller short shrift. Then he heard what the caller had to say and his expression changed from annoyance to disbelief – and then genuine concern.

'This isn't a joke, is it?' he demanded.

'No joke,' said the man with the Irish accent at the other end of the line. 'We think you've got fifteen minutes – but the mechanism's not always reliable.'

As the steward hung up the mouthpiece, he saw that his hands were shaking. Instinctively, his gaze was drawn to the edge of the ground – to the huge, dull-red cylinders of the gasworks.

'Something wrong?' one of the stewards asked him.

'Something's very wrong,' the first steward replied. 'That was the Fenians.'

'Get on the next train to come into the station!' said the voice behind Aggarwal, as if the man it belonged to had been reading his mind and gauging his indecision.

Aggarwal began to turn around.

'If I'd wanted you to see me, I'd have stood in front of you!' the voice growled.

Aggarwal froze. 'Can I not just give you the money now?' he asked tremulously.

'I'm the dispatcher, not the collector,' the other man said. 'And you are nothing but the messenger boy. You don't ask questions – you just do as you're told. Understand?'

'Yes,' Aggarwal mumbled.

'Good. Then listen carefully. Stay on the train until the fifth stop, then get off. You'll be met outside the station.'

'*Who* will meet me?' Aggarwal asked.

But there was no answer, and when he finally plucked up the nerve to glance over his shoulder, he found that the man had gone and the space had been filled by a woman and two small children.

The train entered the station. The carriages it was pulling were of the old-fashioned type – the ones that Londoners called 'padded cells', because they had no windows and the upholstery of the seatbacks reached almost to the ceiling. Aggarwal, a novice in the underground, did not know this, yet as he stepped into the carriage he still felt as if he had entered some kind of lunatic asylum.

The man with the megaphone held to his mouth walked slowly around the boundary of the pitch, shouting his remarks at the crowd.

'Gentlemen, due to circumstances beyond our control, we regret that the day's play is now being brought to an end. The management request that you evacuate the ground as soon as possible, though please do so in an orderly manner.'

The spectators were as puzzled as the players obviously were. There was not a cloud in the sky, and the match still had some time to play. Why should they leave, when there appeared to be no reason for it?

'Please evacuate the ground now!'

Nobody moved. They had all paid their entrance fee and were determined to get their money's worth.

162

Faced with such recalcitrance, the man with the megaphone saw no alternative but to tell the truth.

'We have just received a telephone call from the Fenian Movement,' he said. 'They claim that there is a bomb planted somewhere in the ground.'

At each stop of the rattling journey, the guard called out the name of the station – London Bridge, Borough, Elephant and Castle, Kennington.

Aggarwal had been feeling more and more of his confidence seep away with each passing second, and by the time the train reached the next stop – his destination – his nerves were quite shattered. On legs which felt as if they were made of rubber, he walked towards the exit, sustained only by the knowledge that he would soon be clear of this dim underground hell.

What he saw as he approached the steps both stopped him in his tracks and dashed his hopes. A great wave of men was approaching from the opposite direction. They seemed in a great hurry – perhaps even in a panic. As they pushed and shoved each other in their angling for position, Aggarwal tried to move, and found that he could not.

The wave converged on him. He found himself being pushed backwards, and would no doubt have been dragged back into the booking hall, had not a hand grabbed his arm and pulled him clear.

The two detective constables – at least a dozen yards behind Aggarwal, and in a narrower section of the passageway – saw what was happening but could do nothing about it. Push and shove as they might, the fleeing crowd had now become jammed into an ever-tighter space, and all their efforts were to no avail.

'Shit!' one of the constables said.

'Double shit!' the other replied.

They had done a brilliant job in keeping Aggarwal in their sights for so long, but now that it really mattered, they had undoubtedly lost him.

Thirty-Four

It was not a large room, but the absence of any furniture save for a plain deal table and two upright chairs made it seem perhaps bigger than it was. There was only one small window and even that was masked by heavy sacking so that very little light was allowed to penetrate from the outside. What illumination *did* exist came from two wall-mounted gas-mantles, which – though they would have seemed perfectly normal in most circumstances – had taken on a sinister air in Aggarwal's mind, and seemed to flicker and hiss with true menace.

Once the blindfold had been removed, the Maharaja's secretary had been instructed to sit at one of the chairs. Facing him, at the opposite side of the table, was a man in his late fifties with iron-grey hair, a clipped grey moustache and pale, cold eyes. He had introduced himself as 'Mr Jones'.

'We have met before,' the secretary said, hoping that this fact would make the exchange which followed somewhat easier.

'You are mistaken,' the man said frostily. 'We are strangers to each other and strangers we will remain.'

Yet though the man's tone allowed no scope for further discussion, Aggarwal was now sure that they *had* met. It had been in Chandrapore, he remembered, and then Jones had had quite some other name – with the title 'Colonel' before it – and had been wearing a military uniform.

There were two other men in the room with them. They were younger than Jones – not more than in their middle thirties. Their speech was not as refined as his, and their attitude to him was clearly subservient. Jones introduced them as Brown and Green, and once Aggarwal had sat down, they positioned themselves behind his chair – Brown just to the left, Green just to the right.

Jones lifted the attaché case Aggarwal had brought with him, turned it upside down, and shook it vigorously. Bundles of bank notes spilled out on to the table. Jones spread his arms, pulling all the bundles of notes towards him.

'These are all issued by the same bank, are they not?' he asked.

'Yes,' Aggarwal said.

'And that bank is the Bank of England, not some obscure little institution in Yorkshire or Cornwall?'

Forgetting for a moment the perils of his situation – and the fear that they engendered – Aggarwal felt a sudden burst of resentment that his competence should be questioned in such a manner.

'You asked for Bank of England notes, and it is Bank of England notes I have delivered,' he said snottily. 'I am not some minor clerk sweating it out in a counting house in Bombay – I am the private secretary to the Maharaja of Chandrapore.'

Jones laughed. 'Our friend here seems to think that because he is working for the biggest monkey in his own particular jungle that means they have both come down from the trees,' he said to the two men behind Aggarwal's chair.

'What do you mean by that?' the secretary demanded.

'Shut up!' Jones ordered him. 'It will take me some time to count this cash, and while I am doing so you will keep your mouth closed and desist from picking your fleas.'

No soldier nor official in Chandrapore – however high his rank – would have dared to speak to him – a man with the Maharaja's ear – in that manner, Aggarwal thought. Yet it was the fear, not the anger, which was dominant in him once more, and thus he held his peace.

Jones slowly and carefully went through each bundle of notes.

'Why are the bundles of different thickness?' he asked, about halfway through the process. 'Why do some contain a thousand pounds, and some less than fifty?'

'It is all there,' the secretary said. 'Why should you care how thick or thin each bundle is?'

165

'Very true,' Jones agreed. 'Why should *I* care?'

Jones licked his finger for the second or third time, and continued to count off the notes in hundred pound batches.

'I have told you it is all there,' Aggarwal said. 'Why will you not take my word for it?'

Jones ignored him and continued to count. 'Ninety-nine thousand five hundred, ninety-nine thousand six hundred, ninety-nine thousand seven hundred, ninety-nine thousand eight hundred, ninety-nine thousand nine hundred, one hundred thousand.'

'You see! Did I not tell you not to waste your time by counting?' Aggarwal asked.

Jones frowned. 'Where is the rest?'

'The rest? What rest? When we met on the barge, you asked me to bring you one hundred thousand pounds. And that is what I have done.'

'True,' Jones agreed. 'But you did not ask the Maharaja for a hundred thousand pounds, did you? You asked him for a hundred and *twenty* thousand. And why was what? So that you could keep the twenty thousand for yourself?'

'It is an insult even to suggest such a thing,' Aggarwal protested.

'We were not surprised when you asked the Maharaja for more than we had demanded,' Jones said easily. 'In fact, it was what we fully expected you to do.'

'You did?'

'Indeed. The assumption that you would be greedy, if given the opportunity, was built into our plan.'

'I do not understand. You are talking complete nonsense and utter rubbish,' Aggarwal said, realizing that he was starting to jabber.

'Of course you don't understand,' Jones said agreeably. 'Nor is your understanding necessary – at least for the moment. Let us move on to another matter on which I would like to hear your opinion. Tell me, Mr Aggarwal, if the Maharaja gave up his throne, and assuming his son was not there to take his place, who would be most likely to succeed him?'

'I am a simple man,' Aggarwal blabbered. 'I know nothing of the ways of the high ones.'

Jones gave a slight nod, and Aggarwal felt a searing pain just above his left ear.

'If you wish to avoid further punishment, I suggest you answer my questions truthfully,' Jones suggested, as Aggarwal gingerly rubbed his aching face with his left hand. 'Let me put it to you again – who would replace the Maharaja on the throne if his son were not able to?'

Aggarwal wanted to turn to look at the man who had hit him – and might yet hit him again – but he lacked the courage.

'Well?' Jones asked.

'It cannot be known with any certainty,' Aggarwal said, raising both arms in what he already knew would be a vain attempt to protect his head. 'Please, do not have them hit me again. I speak nothing but the truth. There are many claimants, yet only one can succeed.'

'Then who is the likeliest candidate?'

'Prince Nagesh, His Majesty's cousin.'

'And he is a close friend of yours, is he not?'

'No. I would not dare to be the friend of one of His Majesty's closest rivals for the throne.'

'Yet in the months prior to your departure from Chandrapore, you were seen to spend a great deal of time in Prince Nagesh's company.'

'That was on His Majesty's instructions.'

'Indeed?'

'It is true. I swear to you it is true. His Majesty *ordered* me to befriend Prince Nagesh. It was my duty to discover if the prince was harbouring any disloyal thoughts.'

'And you threw yourself into your duties with commend-able zeal, didn't you? Tell me, when Prince Nagesh comes to the throne, will you still be a humble secretary or will you be raised to a much more exalted position?'

'I serve the Maharaja as his loyal servant. If Prince Nagesh ever came to the throne, he would probably banish me – along with all the others who were known to support his predecessor.'

'You really must learn to give an honest answer to a straightforward question,' Jones said, shaking his head almost sorrowfully.

The blow this time was so forceful that it knocked Aggarwal clear off his chair. The secretary hit the floor with some force, but was scarcely given time to assess the nature of his injuries before a pair of strong hands plucked him up and slammed him back down in his seat.

'Ask me what the Afghans say about Sergeant Brown,' Jones said.

So now Brown had a rank, Aggarwal noted, between waves of pain.

'Ask me – unless you'd like more of the same treatment again!' Jones threatened.

'What do the Afghans say about Sergeant Brown?' Aggarwal muttered, gasping with pain.

'They say that though they pride themselves on their ability to inflict hurt, they take their hats off to him. Do you understand what that means, you snivelling little nigger?'

'Yes, I—'

'They say that never have they known so skilful and patient a torturer as Sergeant Brown – nor any man who seemed to enjoy that kind of work as much as he. And so far, the sergeant has inflicted no more than a gentle tap on you. That is why it would be wise of you to tell me what position you would hold if Nagesh were Maharaja.'

'I would be his chamberlain,' Aggarwal said resignedly.

'How grand,' Jones said in mock admiration. 'But isn't there a slight obstacle to you achieving your ambition? Even if the Maharaja loses his son, he is still a comparatively young man, isn't he? It could be another thirty years before you achieve your ambition. Another thirty years of being what we English would call "the Maharaja's dogsbody". Could you tolerate that?'

'I am a patient man,' Aggarwal said.

He realized his mistake the moment the words were out of his mouth – which was perhaps a tenth of a second before Sergeant Brown knocked him to the floor again. This time, however, it was worse than the previous occasion – far worse – because the beating did not stop even when he screamed, even when he pleaded . . . even when he soiled himself.

But eventually the beating *did* stop, and the aching secretary was lifted back into the chair.

'So you claim you are a patient man,' Jones said meditatively, 'a man who is prepared to wait thirty years to become chamberlain, if that is what it takes. Is that the truth?'

'No.'

'No?' Jones repeated, expressing a deep surprise which he obviously did not feel.

'Prince Nagesh is planning to seize power,' Aggarwal admitted.

'Seize power? Or *assume* it?'

'What is the difference?'

'Don't play games with me! While the Maharaja lives, he must *seize* it. If the Maharaja dies of a sudden, mysterious illness, Nagesh has only to *assume* it. Which of the two will it be?'

'Prince Nagesh will assume it,' Aggarwal confessed.

'In other words, he plans to kill the Maharaja?'

'Yes.'

'How?'

'With poison.'

'And you will assist him in this poisoning?'

'Yes.'

'Because the Maharaja trusts you?'

'Yes.'

'Shall we get back to the question of the money, now?' Jones asked.

'What money?'

'Why, the twenty thousand pounds the Maharaja handed to you as part of the ransom, but which now seems to have somehow disappeared. Where is it? And before you answer, think of the consequences of lying to me.'

'I have placed it in a safe deposit box in the Lombard Street branch of the Anglo-Indian Bank,' Aggarwal said.

'And what did you intend to do with the money?'

169

'I intended to give it to Prince Nagesh.'

'In order to help finance his grab for power?'

'Yes. Many will support him because they love him, but others will need to be bribed.'

'Then if that's your plan, we will certainly not stand in the way of it,' Jones said. 'In fact, after all the inconvenience we've put you through, I think that the least we can do is to assist you in your scheme.'

'Assist me? How?'

'We will help you to send the money to Chandrapore.'

'You do not want the twenty thousand pounds yourselves?' the secretary asked, totally confused.

'No.'

'Even though you know how you may easily lay your hands on it?'

'You stole it, not us. You have the right to do with it as you please.'

'I do not understand.'

'No, you probably don't,' Jones agreed. 'But you soon will.'

Thirty-Five

'There was really nothing we could do, sir,' Detective Constable Dyson said, looking across the desk at Blackstone and speaking in a tone which was half-explanatory, half-self-justifying. 'The crowd came from out of nowhere. We could see Aggarwal being dragged away, but we just couldn't get at him.'

'It was like everybody had suddenly gone completely mad,' his partner, Detective Constable Tasker added.

Blackstone nodded. 'They'd been told there was a bomb planted in the Oval. If there really *had* been one – and it had gone off – it would have taken the Kennington gasometer and most of the surrounding area with it. Under those circumstances, *most* people would try to get themselves underground as quickly as they could.'

'So, you see, sir—' Tasker said.

Blackstone raised a hand to silence him. 'I'm not blaming you,' he said. 'The kidnappers were three steps ahead from the very start, and there's nothing you could have done about it. What I *am* interested in, is what went on in the bank.'

'Well, sir, Aggarwal opened this attaché case he had with him and started fiddling inside,' Dyson said.

'And where was he looking while he was doing that? At the door?'

'No. Into the bag. Whatever he was doing, he couldn't manage it just by touch. He needed to *see* what was going on.'

'What happened next?'

'He walked over to the nearest waste-paper basket, and dumped a load of stuff into it.'

'You saw what it was that he dumped, I hope.'

'Yes, sir,' Dyson said. 'When Aggarwal left the bank, Tasker followed him, but I went straight over to the bin and took out the contents.'

'And were the contents at all illuminating?' Blackstone asked, without much hope of a positive response.

'No, sir. The whole bin was full of rectangular pieces of paper. I thought they might have had writing on them, so I handed the basket over to one of the cashiers and told him to take care of it until we returned.'

'Which is what we did after we'd . . . after we'd . . . lost Aggarwal,' Tasker said.

His partner shot him a black look. 'After circumstances dictated that we could no longer *follow* Aggarwal,' he amended. 'Anyway, we took the pieces of paper into one of the offices, and we examined them. They were blank. All of them. We thought maybe someone had written on them with invisible ink, but we held a few under a flame, and nothing showed up.'

'Was this paper thick or thin?' Blackstone asked.

'Thick, sir,' Dyson said. 'Top quality. I've got a sample on me, if you'd like to see it.'

'Perhaps that might be a good idea,' Blackstone agreed.

The constable reached into his pocket and produced the rectangular piece of stiff plain paper. 'This is it, sir.'

'It's roughly the size of a banknote, wouldn't you say?' Blackstone asked.

'Might be, sir,' Dyson agreed. 'But I wouldn't know for sure. I've never actually seen a banknote that close up.'

Aggarwal had experienced a certain nervousness when he'd been placing the twenty thousand pounds in the safe deposit box the day before, but it had been a nervousness which had sprung from excitement.

A lesser man would have taken the money and disappeared, he had told himself. He, on the other hand, being a *superior* creature, had seen beyond short-term greed to a longer, more golden future. For why should a man choose to live like a lord when, with but a little patience, he could live like a king? And that was how he would live! As Nagesh's most trusted adviser, he would enjoy all that the new maharaja enjoyed. Perhaps even more – since he himself was a highly intelligent man, while Nagesh's intellect only just fell on the right side of stupid.

Yes, that was how he had felt closing the box.

Opening it again, less than twenty-four hours later, was a different matter. This time the nervousness stemmed from fear.

'We will not be able to see you while you are in the strong-room,' Jones had told him, *'but once you emerge we will have you in our sights again, and if you do not do exactly what we have told you, you will be a dead man.'*

And Aggarwal believed him – believed that not only would Brown kill him but that the evil sergeant would make sure it was a slow painful death.

The box was open. With clumsy fingers, Aggarwal transferred the notes from it to the leather attaché case which had quickly become so much a part of his existence.

'Do you wish to replace the box now, sir?' the clerk said, laying perhaps not quite as much emphasis on the last word as he would have done if his client had been a white man.

'Do what you will with the box,' Aggarwal said dismissively. 'I have no further use for it.'

The clerk consulted his ledger. 'But you paid a year's rental for it only yesterday,' he said, clearly scandalized at even the *possibility* of such profligacy.

'I do not care if I have paid rental for a thousand years,' Aggarwal said. 'I have done with the box.'

'Then perhaps you would return the key to me,' the clerk said, holding out his hand.

Aggarwal dropped the key into his palm. The clerk put it, together with the bank's key, into his waistcoat pocket.

'And now, if that is your wish, I will escort you off the premises?' the clerk said.

If only he could leave! Aggarwal thought. If only that were possible!

'I have other business in the bank,' he said miserably. 'I wish to open an account.'

The clerk took Aggarwal to the appropriate counter, then beat a retreat in search of other customers who might, perhaps, have a little more of the gentleman about them.

'So you wish to open an account,' the counter clerk said. 'And how much do you intend to deposit in it?'

His sneering tone suggested that he expected Aggarwal to say a guinea, though he would not have been surprised if it were as little as a shilling.

'I wish to deposit twenty thousand pounds,' the secretary said.

The counter clerk's jaw fell. 'How much?'

'Twenty thousand pounds,' Aggarwal repeated. 'I am a busy man. I have no time for jokes of such a nature.'

'See for yourself,' Aggarwal said, opening the attaché case. 'Count it, if you wish.'

The counter clerk gaped at the contents of the case for a moment, then rang his bell to summon a messenger.

'Fetch the manager,' he told the messenger.

'But it's his day off!'

'What does that matter? He'll be in his apartment above the bank. He always is.'

'He won't like bein' disturbed.'

'Tell him it is vitally important that he comes at once. Tell him I will take full responsibility.'

The messenger shrugged. 'It's your neck,' he said.

'And my neck!' Aggarwal thought, glancing across at the corner of the bank, where Sergeant Brown was pretending to fill in a form. 'And my neck, as well.'

'What do you make of it all, Patterson?' Blackstone asked his sergeant, when he had dismissed the two detective constables.

'I don't know,' Patterson admitted. 'I'm like Constable Dyson in that respect. I've not seen many banknotes, either.'

'I'd be worried if a man on your wages had,' Blackstone replied.

'I imagine you'd have to be quite a big spender to ever feel the need to carry one,' Patterson continued. 'For blokes like me, coins are usually enough to meet my wants.'

'For blokes like me, as well,' Blackstone agreed. 'But what I really meant was, why did Aggarwal cut up the paper in the way he did?'

'I haven't a clue.'

'We've no doubt that he was delivering the ransom when he set out this afternoon, have we?'

'No doubt at all.'

'Which means that when the Maharaja told me yesterday that he didn't have that amount of money in cash, he wasn't exactly being truthful with me?'

'Definitely.'

'Then consider this. When the Maharaja told me how much the ransom was, I noticed his secretary suddenly looked shifty. And at the same time it struck me that one hundred and twenty thousand pounds was a rather odd figure for the kidnappers to ask for.'

'Odd?'

'*Very* odd. Think about it, Patterson. If you fancied throwing away your money on the horses, would you place a bet of one and fourpence ha'penny?'

'Of course I wouldn't.'

'Why not?'

Patterson grinned. 'Because it's an awkward amount. I'd bet either one and threepence or one and six.' The implications of his own remark sunk in. 'So what you're saying, sir, is that the kidnappers would have asked for either a hundred thousand pounds or a hundred and twenty-five thousand pounds?'

'Yes, but the secretary decided to lie about it. And since I can see no reason why Aggarwal would round the figure *down*, my guess is that the kidnappers asked for a hundred thousand.'

'And Aggarwal planned to keep the rest for himself?'

'Exactly. But having once decided that, he gets to the tricky part. The money was probably in some kind of safe in the Maharaja's suite. Agreed?'

'Agreed. With all those armed men around him, it'd be a waste of time putting it in a bank.'

'So the Maharaja gave Aggarwal permission to remove a hundred and twenty thou. But *when* should he remove it? What would happen if he only took a hundred thousand with him when he went to meet the kidnappers?'

'He'd be running the risk that the Maharaja would have the safe checked while he was out, and realize he hadn't taken the full amount.'

'So when he returned, he'd the problem of explaining away why he hadn't taken the whole ransom with him. And even if he got away with that, he'd have no excuse to remove the other twenty thou' later.'

'On the other hand, if he took a hundred and twenty thou with him, there's a good chance the kidnappers would relieve him of the lot!' Patterson said.

'So what did he do?'

'He removed the twenty thou beforehand.'

'But to avoid it being noticed, he took all the money from the centre of the bundles and replaced it with pieces of paper. The only problem that left him with was that he couldn't let the kidnappers see the paper, or they'd start to ask questions.'

'So he ditched the paper in the bank on Lombard Street. But if that's true, where's the extra money now?'

'A very good question,' Blackstone agreed. 'Where *is* the bloody money now?'

Given the huge amount of money involved, it was no surprise at all that the manager of the Anglo-Indian Bank had agreed to abandon his day off in favour of conducting business. Now, sitting behind his desk with his tie carelessly knotted and his boots clumsily laced, he was finding it hard to mask his excitement.

'Twenty thousand pounds!' he said with awe, as he helped Aggarwal to fill in the form. 'And may I ask, sir, if I may be so bold, where such a fortune came from?'

'I act on behalf of the Maharaja of Chandrapore,' Aggarwal replied.

'Of course! The Maharaja of Chandrapore! A most respected and valued client of the bank.'

The application was made, the money hastily deposited in the vault.

'And now,' Aggarwal said, 'I would like to transfer the money by telegraph to an account in your Chandrapore branch.'

'All of it?' the manager asked, clearly disappointed.

'Perhaps I will retain a pound, for appearance's sake,' Aggarwal told him.

'The Maharaja should be made aware of the fact that this bank is as safe as any of our branches in India, and that should he wish guidance on investments, we are very well placed here to—'

'I am instructed to transfer the money,' Aggarwal said firmly.

And it was no more than the truth. He had been instructed

to do so by a homicidal British army sergeant whom even the Afghans treated with kid gloves – a sergeant who might, at that very moment, have his hand resting on a knife or a pistol.

'Very well, we will transfer the money as you requested,' the manager said, attempting to put on a show of good grace. 'If you would just give me the Maharaja's account number—'

'The money is not to go to the Maharaja's account,' Aggarwal interrupted.

'Then to whose?'

Even at this late point, Aggarwal found himself wondering about his chances of making a break for freedom – but he quickly decided that they were not at all that good.

'I wish to transfer the money to the account of Prince Nagesh,' he said, swallowing hard.

Thirty-Six

The sole purpose behind Blackstone's visit to the Anglo-Indian Bank on Lombard Street was to learn more about Aggarwal's activities while he had been under Dyson and Tasker's observation. Thus, it came as a surprise to be told that the secretary had made a second visit later in the day.

'You're sure it was the same Indian both times?' he asked the manager.

'I couldn't swear to it, because I wasn't here the first time, but my clerks are of the opinion that it was – and they're trained to notice faces.'

'But on the second occasion – if indeed, it was the second – he opened an account and placed a substantial amount of money in it?'

'That's correct. Twenty thousand pounds. All in Bank of England notes.'

'And then he immediately had most of the money transferred by telegraphic exchange?'

'Again, that is correct. The money was transferred to the account of a Prince Nagesh in our Chandrapore City branch.'

'What happened after that?'

'Once his business was completed, the Indian gentleman left.'

'Alone?'

'Er . . . yes.'

'Why the hesitation?'

'Two other customers left at almost the same time. Or rather, two other *men* – because as far as I can ascertain, they'd didn't actually do any business.'

'Could you describe them to me?' Blackstone asked hopefully.

The manager thought for a moment. 'Both big men. I'd estimate they were in their mid-thirties. Both quite well dressed – they'd never have been allowed through the door if they hadn't been – but somehow they didn't seem quite comfortable in good suits.'

'You're saying they'd have been happier in uniform?'

'Possibly,' the bank manager said.

'Could you be a little more explicit about exactly *how* they made their exits?'

The manager frowned. 'One was standing to the left of the main door, the other to the right. When Mr Aggarwal reached the door, they fell in beside him.'

'Like an escort.'

'I suppose it was rather like that.'

What a fool I've been! Blackstone thought angrily.

His working assumption had been that if soldiers *were* involved in the plot, they were driven purely by mercenary motives. But that assumption had been totally wrong! If personal gain *were* their only aim, why would they have overseen the transferral of funds to Prince Nagesh? There was a deeper, darker plot at work, and because he had allowed himself to be side-tracked by thinking of the soldiers

178

as ordinary criminals, he was only now starting to get the first glimmerings of what that plot might be.

'I should have kept my mind focused on the tiger,' he said aloud.

'What was that you said?' the bank manager asked.

'The tiger!' Blackstone repeated. 'I shouldn't have given up wondering about why they used the tiger!'

Though he was not accustomed to queuing, General Sir Harold Templeton Harcourt recognized that, as long as he was going under the name of Jones, it might be prudent to act as if he were no more than a member of the common herd. Thus, as he stood in line at the telegraph desk, he showed none of the impatience that those under his command had soon learned to know and fear.

The telegraph, Harcourt had long ago decided, was the greatest invention man had ever known – or was ever likely to know. Without steam power, factories could easily be run by sheer brute force. Without rifles, the ordinary soldier could fight with sword and spear, as his ancestors had done. But without the telegraph – without the rapid communications it facilitated – there would have been a limit to the growth of the British Empire, just as there had been limits to the growth of all the mighty empires which had preceded it.

Harcourt pictured the world as it had been when he'd joined the Army and contrasted it with the world as it stood at that moment. With every drop of British blood spilled, the map had grown redder and redder, until now the Queen reigned over a third of the globe.

And there was no reason why it should stop there!

Britain could never conquer the rest of Europe, and only a fool would believe that she would ever recapture her American colonies – but most of the rest of the world was still up for grabs. And Harcourt saw it as his duty to do all he could to ensure that the grabbing was done by the country he had sworn to defend with his life.

He had reached the head of the queue at last, and reached into his pocket for the two telegrams he had written earlier.

'Hurry up!' the clerk said imperiously. 'There's other people waiting.'

Indeed there were, Harcourt thought. But not one of them had a telegram to send which was of a millionth the importance of the ones which he now held in his hand.

He slid the forms under the grille. 'They are both for India,' he said.

'Issuin' the Viceroy with his weekly instructions, are you?' the clerk asked jovially.

As Harcourt, the General damned the man's impudence. But as Jones, he smiled as though he was genuinely amused and said, 'No, I thought I'd give the Viceroy a miss this week.'

The operator ran his eyes quickly over the messages. 'One's to this Prince Nagesh and the other's to a General Greer,' he said. 'Have I got that right?'

'Yes, you've got it right,' Harcourt agreed.

One for the pampered prince with the heart of a snake, the other for the general with the instincts of a mad bull. There was one more message to be sent – that one delivered by hand – and the job would be over.

'If you want to, you can pay for the replies in advance,' the operator advised him.

'I'm not expecting any replies,' Harcourt said.

Nor was he. The moment the prince and the General had read their telegrams, they would be far too occupied with other matters to think about responding to his warnings.

Aggarwal sat in the back of the cab, with the soldiers – Brown and Green – on either side of him. He had no idea where he was, for the blinds on the windows were pulled firmly down. What he *did* know was that they had been travelling for at least half an hour, and that while there had been other noises outside to distract him at the start of the journey, there was now only the clip-clop of hooves from the horses pulling the cab.

'Where are you taking me?' he asked, for perhaps the tenth

180

time. 'Mr Jones promised me that I would be released once I had completed my task in the bank.'

'An' you are bein' released,' said the sergeant who called himself Brown.

'Then I will get out of the cab now,' Aggarwal said, trying – in vain – to squeeze himself from the wedge in which he was held.

'We're not to let you go until we reach your hotel.'

'Is that where we are going? To my hotel?'

'Yes.'

'But if that is my destination, we should have been there by now.'

Brown sighed. 'That's the trouble with you niggers. We try to make things easier for you, but you won't have it.'

'What do you mean?' Aggarwal asked, noticing how his voice trembled.

'Ignorance is bliss,' the sergeant said. 'If somethin' nasty is goin' to happen to you, it's best not to know about it in advance.'

'And . . . and *is* something nasty going to happen to me?'

'What do you think?'

'I promise you that if you release me now—'

'You've seen too much. You *know* too much.'

'I will scream!' Aggarwal threatened. 'I will call for help until someone comes.'

'Scream as much as you like,' Brown told him. 'We should be at the East India Docks by now. When people hear a scream down here, they turn around and head in the other direction.'

'Please . . .' Aggarwal begged.

'I'm gettin' sick of this nigger's whinin', Sarge,' Green said. 'Can't we finish him off now?'

'What! An' have him bleed over all this nice leather upholstery?' Brown asked. 'Have a bit of decency, lad.'

181

Thirty-Seven

Sitting in the saloon bar of the Crown and Anchor, Blackstone checked his pocket watch. It was an hour to closing time. If things had gone according to plan, Patterson should already have been sitting opposite him and providing him with the missing pieces of information which would almost magically shine a bright light into all the dark corners of the investigation. But Patterson *wasn't* there, and in his absence Blackstone found himself involved in a solitary mental wrestling match.

Part of the puzzle already had been explained. He knew what the kidnappers had done with the twenty thousand pounds, and, more importantly, *why* they had done it. But he still couldn't *quite* see why the tiger had been used – could not *quite* understand what it had to do with the events which had already begun unfolding in Chandrapore.

The door opened, and Patterson made his entrance. The sergeant weaved his way erratically to the bar and fumbled in his pocket for some loose change. It was a good thing that the drinkers in this pub knew he was a policeman, Blackstone thought – because if they hadn't, at least one of the men he'd bumped into would have taken a swing at him.

Pint in hand, the sergeant walked over to his boss's table, the concentration on his face at least equivalent to that of a tightrope walker caught in a sudden high wind. Even when he had reached his destination without major incident, Patterson's problems were not over. For at least half a minute he stood there gently swaying, as he pondered on which manoeuvre to attempt next. Finally – and sensibly – he decided that he would first place his drink on the table, and then risk trying to sit down.

'You look a bit the worse for wear,' Blackstone said, as his sergeant established a precarious balance on his seat.

Patterson giggled. 'If I don't, I'm suing that bloody brewery,' he said. 'Thing is, sir . . . thing is . . . it was all in the line of duty.'

Blackstone nodded sympathetically. 'Let me guess what happened. You met the blokes from the India Office as you'd agreed.'

'Perfec'ly correct.'

'They were more than willing to talk about their work, but only to their pals – and by that they meant their *drinking* pals.'

'Their *heavy* drinking pals,' Patterson said resentfully. 'Their *very* heavy drinking pals.'

'So you've had a skinful?'

'Yes, if the skin in question belonged to an elephant. I'll tell you something, sir – I wouldn't like to be me at about three o'clock tomorrow morning.'

Blackstone patted his sergeant on the shoulder, only to regret it when Patterson winced.

'I hope that you learned something useful to compensate you for your suffering,' he said.

Patterson tried a nod, then thought better of it. 'Kept nipping out during the session and making notes, just in case the alcohol drowned my brain quicker than I expected it to. Got it all written down. Want to read it?'

'Maybe later,' Blackstone said. 'At the moment, I'll settle for what you remember.'

'Remember?' Patterson said, as if he'd completely forgotten what it was that he was supposed to be recalling.

'General Pugh,' Blackstone prompted him.

'Highly thought of both by the Army and by the government. Was a sple . . . a splendid commander, never reluctant to put himself on the front line.' The sergeant swayed on his chair a little. 'Greatly missed by all now that he's retired.'

'Was there any suggestion that he might once have been involved in something corrupt?'

'None at all.'

'You're sure?'

'Absol . . . absol . . . definitely.'

183

Blackstone stroked his chin thoughtfully. 'Yet if he was as dirty as Major Walsh claims he was, you'd have thought there'd have been at least a *whiff* of a suspicion,' he mused.

Patterson burped. 'Found out about Walsh, as well. Didn't mean to. Didn't ask. Just came up in the conversation.'

'Go on.'

'Everybody agrees that right from the start he was a brilliant man. Excellent soldier, very good leader. Picks up all the local languages at the drop of a hat, if not sooner. Had a golden future ahead of him. Natural choice to send to a ticklish place like Chandrapore. Just the kind of chap you'd want handling a difficult character like the Maharaja. So that's where he's sent. To Chandrapore. Does very well, at first.'

'At first?'

'Maharaja isn't married then. Gets Walsh involved in the process of finding him a bride.'

'Walsh mentioned that. And she had to be the right kind of bride, didn't she?'

'Exac' . . . exac'ly. Chaps like the Maharaja don't marry for love – marry for political considerations. Walsh travels all over India on the Maharaja's account – and on *our* account as well, of course.'

'Of course.'

'Visits every Indian ruler with a child of marriageable age. Eventually narrows the choices down to one. Beautiful creature. Well educated, too, for a woman. Most important of all, from our point of view, her father's known to be pro-British. Marriage takes place. Maharaja very pleased. Viceroy very pleased. India Office very pleased. Walsh riding on the crest of a wave.'

'Then what happened?'

'Maharani gives birth to a child. Dies in the process, but succession is assured. Maharaja very pleased. Viceroy very pleased. India Office—'

'I get the picture. Walsh was fulfilling all expectations. So what went wrong?'

'Shortly after the young prince is born, Walsh starts

drinking. Powers-that-be try to ignore it at first – brilliant young officer, great promise, etc. – but the drinking gets worse and worse. Soon Walsh is no good to man nor beast. People start to worry he might do something disastrous. Throw up on the Maharaja's throne, f'rinstance. Get in a fight with the palace guard f'rexample. That kind of thing. Anyway, he's called back to London, and since he's supposed to be an expert on that part of India, he's attached to the India Office. Doesn't do much there – more a case of being rewarded for his past achievements than being paid for what he's doing now. Still, nobody seems to mind that. Glad to hear what he has to say when he's there, get along fine without him when he isn't. Then the young prince is kidnapped.'

'And Walsh isn't just *an* expert any more, he's *the* expert.'

'Quite so. Told to work with us. Comes to see you. And there we are – bang up to date.' Patterson clapped his hand over his mouth. 'Mind if I go to the lavatory, sir?' he mumbled.

'No,' Blackstone said quickly. 'In fact, I think it's a very good idea.'

The Inspector watched his sergeant stagger to the door, then took a thoughtful sip of his pint. He'd been quite prepared to accept Walsh's assessment of General Pugh at face value initially. Then he'd met the General, who'd seemed both open and honest. And now that impression had been confirmed by Patterson's friends at the India Office.

So what was the truth? Was Pugh the smartest dissembler Blackstone had ever encountered? Or had drink destroyed more of Walsh's brain cells than even he'd realized?

The familiar smell of a cheroot drifted under Blackstone's nose. He looked up, half-expecting to see Major Walsh standing there, but instead the smoker was a local pawnbroker.

It was odd that Walsh should smoke cheroots rather than cigars. Perhaps it was a habit he'd picked up in India. Or perhaps, now that he was no longer a high-flyer, it was all that he could afford.

The sound of breaking glass announced the fact that

Patterson was back, and had barrelled into a waiter carrying a full tray. He really must do something about sobering the lad up in a minute, Blackstone told himself.

He let his mind drift – as lazily as smoke itself – back to Walsh. The man was obviously almost as addicted to cheroots as he was to alcohol, he thought, remembering how irritable and nervous Walsh had been when he'd misplaced his cheroots on the way to Amritsar Lodge.

Patterson – after having apologized to the waiter for crashing into him and being assured that he would be more hindrance than help in picking up the mess – had finally returned to the table.

'Not too steady on my pegs,' he slurred. 'Not too steady at all.'

'But did he?' Blackstone said, almost under his breath.

'Beg pardon, sir?'

'Did Walsh really *lose* his cheroots? Or was he just looking for an excuse not to have to smoke one?'

Thirty-Eight

Anyone with little on them worth stealing might walk down this particular street with only minor foreboding in the daytime. Once night fell, however, it was a different matter entirely. The darkness brought with it a sense of desperation. Prostitutes, trying to scrape together enough to pay for their night's lodging, would lower both their already pitiful fees and their already pitiful standards. Robbers would kill a man for a penny, for his life was not worth even that much to them. Drunken dockers might attack a passer-by for no other reason than the frustration which came from living a life on the edge – a life dependent on tides and weather, and on rich merchants who did not care what misery they might bring to a struggling dockland family.

Such dangers did not worry the man who was calling

himself – at least for the moment – Mr White. He had fought bandits on India's Northwest Frontier. He had battled Afghan warriors in an unofficial war which was forever being waged in the Hindu Kush. And though what gripped him at that moment was the fear for the loss of a human life, that human life was not his own.

As he passed the front door of each crumbling terraced house, he counted off its number in his head. 'Seventy-one, seventy-three, seventy-five . . .' When he reached number 83, he stopped, and rapped confidently on the door.

He had not even seen the guard watching him from the shadows, but now he heard the sound of the man's footsteps and felt the man's strong hand take an iron grip of his shoulder.

'An' where do you think you're goin'?' the man demanded.

'I'm here to see Mr Jones,' the newcomer said.

The guard pulled him closer towards the street light. 'Oh, it's you, Mr White,' he said. 'We wasn't expectin' you.'

'No, I . . . It's Brown, isn't it?'

'That's right,' Brown said, continuing to maintain his firm grip. 'An' we *still* wasn't expectin' you.'

'Something's come up,' the man calling himself White said. 'I need to speak to Mr Jones immediately.'

Brown shook his head doubtfully. 'Mr Jones don't like changes in plans, especially at this stage of the operation. It's not military.'

'It's not exactly military for a sergeant to manhandle an officer, either,' White said coldly.

Brown released his grip as quickly as if he had suddenly realized his hand was on fire.

'Sorry, sir,' he said. 'I didn't mean to—'

'Of course you didn't,' White said. 'And now I'd like to see Mr Jones.'

Brown hesitated for the briefest of seconds, then knocked on the door. When it opened a fraction he said, 'I've got Mr White here, Green. Take him to see Mr Jones right away.'

In every other house in this street, dozens of people would be sleeping, fighting or whoring, but as White followed Green

187

down the corridor, the only sound he could hear in this house was the creak of floorboards beneath his feet.

The room Green took him to was at the end of the corridor. It was unfurnished except for a plain deal table and two chairs. On one of the chairs sat General Harcourt – or Mr Jones as he was to be known for the duration of the operation. He seemed surprised to see his visitor, but after telling Green that he could go, he gestured White to sit down.

'Weren't you taking rather a chance, coming here?' he asked sternly.

'I wasn't followed,' White told him.

'Can you be sure of that?'

'I used to be able to spot a hired assassin in all the crush of a Bombay market. I would have had no difficulty picking out a London copper on my tail.'

Jones nodded. 'You're probably right,' he agreed. 'And I'm sure you have good reasons for running the risk you have. Would you care to tell me what they are?'

White shrugged. 'There was nothing specific. I just wanted to be sure that everything was going according to plan.'

Out of respect for the man he was dealing with, Jones made some attempt to disguise the anger which was welling up inside him.

'Indeed?' he said. 'Well, now you can see that everything's going quite smoothly, I suggest that you leave again as soon as possible.'

White looked around the room. 'Where's the prince?' he asked casually. 'I thought he'd be here.'

'You thought I'd have the little nigger with me? Why? For his excellent company?'

White laughed unconvincingly. 'Of course not. I was thinking more in terms of security.'

'He's secure enough.'

'And still in this house?'

'Why do you ask?'

'Security again. As you know, it will be part of my function to see that he is returned to his father and—'

'Not any more.'

'What does that mean?'

'It means that you will not be involved in that particular phase of the operation.'

'But it was understood from the start that I would be,' White protested.

'And now the orders have been changed.'

'So who will deliver the boy?'

'That is not your concern.'

'Most of the military blunders in our history have been as a result of the right hand not knowing what the left hand was doing,' White said. 'I would have thought that we were professional enough to avoid any such mistake. I would have thought that, given the significant role I have played so far in the operation, I would be entitled to know any details which were of interest to me.'

Jones nodded. 'Very well. We do not need you to participate in the return of the boy because the boy will not be returned.'

'Are you saying—?'

'Why risk any of our men on such a mission, when we no longer have any need to?'

'If the operation is carried out smoothly, there will be no risk at all.'

'You can't be sure of that. Besides, think of the effect on the Maharaja when all he gets back for his hundred and twenty thousand is a head,' Jones said with obvious relish. 'It'll be enough to make him lose his mind.'

'It would be enough to make *anyone* lose his mind.'

'And even if he doesn't quite go crazy, it will certainly make him far too unstable for those meddlers at the India Office to ever think of putting him back on the throne again.'

'The boy is a prince of royal blood!' White protested.

'He's a nigger!' Jones said contemptuously 'Niggers have no value other than the use we choose to make of them, and he can be most useful to us by being dead.'

'And not just a prince, but a child!' White gasped. 'A child!'

'So was the son of that cotton magnate. You raised no objection when we sent his head back to his father in a hatbox.'

'But that was necessary to show that we were serious, and—'

'What are you saying?' Jones asked harshly. 'That you are willing to sacrifice a white child in the interests of necessity, but that a nigger is somehow immune from the same treatment?'

'No, of course not,' White said hastily. He gave Jones a weak smile. 'Got things rather out of proportion, haven't I?'

'So it would seem.'

'Can't apologize enough. Can only put it down to the strain I've been under these last few days.'

'We've all been under strain.'

'That's true enough. But I'm the only one who's actually been on the front line.'

'Can't have been easy for you,' admitted Jones, who, whilst he saw himself as a firm man, also liked to think he was a fair one. 'When you're forced to play as many roles as you have been recently, it must sometimes be difficult to remember who you really are.'

'That's exactly it,' White said gratefully.

'Then let's put this whole conversation behind us. It never happened. And when the accounts of the glorious affair can be safely written up, you'll emerge as the hero you truly have been.'

'That's more than generous,' White said. 'Would you like me to kill the boy myself – as a way of proving my continuing loyalty?'

'That will not be necessary. I may have questioned your judgement for a moment, but my faith in your loyalty has never wavered.'

'Then perhaps I wish to kill him to prove something to myself,' White said. 'I would deem it as a personal favour, General, if mine was the hand which carried out the act.'

'That may not be possible,' Jones told him. 'When the time comes to eliminate the boy, you may be otherwise occupied.'

'In other words, you are not planning to kill him tonight?'

'That is correct.'

White gave Jones a look that could have passed for wholehearted admiration. 'I should have known,' he said. 'Like the brilliant general you are, you're holding the boy in reserve, in case you need him again.'

Jones nodded, perhaps a little complacently. 'It is an unlikely contingency, but I built up my reputation as a military strategist by allowing for unlikely contingencies.'

'So when *do* you plan to decapitate the little nigger?'

'Probably no later than O-ten-hundred hours tomorrow morning,' Jones said. 'By then, our plan should have gained such momentum that any captive would have become no more than a liability.'

'Is it wise to wait so long?' White asked.

Jones chuckled. 'You're a strange cove, all right. One minute you don't want me to kill the brat at all, the next you're pressing me to get it over with as soon as possible.'

White looked a little abashed. 'I'm thinking of security again,' he admitted. 'There isn't much chance that the police will find out where you're holding the prince – Inspector Blackstone is a dunderhead if I ever met one – but what if they did? What if Blackstone himself came here looking for him?'

'Then he'd be as good as dead.'

'Of course he would – if he came alone. But say he didn't come alone. Say he brought half a dozen of his men with him?'

'I have half a dozen of my own men here,' Jones said.

'Really?' White replied. 'I didn't know it was as many as that.'

'Six trained soldiers against six bumbling coppers?' Jones said. 'We'd deal with them in no time at all. And even if Blackstone brought half the Met with him, I don't think there'd be much of a contest, do you?'

'No,' White agreed. 'I don't think there would be.'

191

Thirty-Nine

The soldiers began to assemble on the parade ground at just after dawn. The East Surrey Regiment had been deployed at one end of the field, the Scots Guards at the other. And in between them stood the ranks of native troops. It was as impressive a force as Agra had seen since the days immediately following the Mutiny. It was an army which could sweep away any opposition without even breaking step.

Captain Threlford looked on with growing trepidation. This should never have happened, he thought. He should have been more forceful earlier – should have tried to nip things in the bud while he still had a chance. He turned to his left – towards General Greer, who was mounted on his charger and surveying the whole scene with obvious glee.

Perhaps it was still not too late to stop this farce, Threlford told himself. He marched over to the General, and saluted. 'Are you sure this is wise, sir?' he asked.

'I've never been so sure of anything in my life,' Greer replied.

'But, sir, the intelligence reports—'

'There are times when you sound just like an old woman, Threlford,' the General said.

Threlford gritted his teeth. 'I've been in touch with our people in Chandrapore. Everything's completely quiet there. Nobody's expecting any kind of trouble.'

Greer chuckled. 'That's because they don't know what I know,' he said, patting the pocket which contained his second telegram from General Harrington.

Some of the wagon drivers who cut through Brook Street that early morning might have noticed that all the lights were burning in the most expensive suite in Claridge's Hotel. If they did, they probably thought no more about it than to wonder why the rich – who had neither to collect country milk for King's Cross nor deliver newspapers to Euston – would ever choose to be up and about at such an ungodly hour.

In the suite of rooms itself, the Maharaja, still dressed in his night clothes, was pacing his sitting room under the watchful eye of the captain of his bodyguard.

'A message is delivered in the middle of the night, and no one thinks to detain the messenger!' he said angrily.

'This is England, Your Majesty,' the captain reminded him. 'Such a thing would not be normal.'

'Tell me again about this messenger!' the Maharaja demanded.

The captain suppressed a sigh. 'I have questioned the porter on duty. He says that he does not know the man, and I believe him.'

'And this porter noticed *nothing* about the man?'

'Only that while he was dressed as a civilian, he carried himself like a soldier.'

The Maharaja held up the message, and read it for the fourth or fifth time. 'If what this says is true, then Aggarwal is the basest of traitors,' he said. 'But *is* it true? Would he really have betrayed his lawful master in such a manner? Would he really plot against me?'

'No one can say for certain. But if he is not guilty of the crime of which he stands accused, Your Majesty, then why is he not here to answer those accusations?'

'You are sure that no one has seen or heard of him since he left the hotel with the ransom?'

'Yes, Your Majesty.'

'Then the case is proven. He *has* been conspiring against me. Well, he will pay dearly for it. I will see to it that he suffers in ways which will make death seem like a blessed relief.'

The captain coughed discreetly.

'Yes?' the Maharaja demanded.

'If you will forgive me for saying so, Your Majesty, it is plain that if Aggarwal acted, he did not act alone.'

'That much is obvious.'

'And that most of his co-conspirators are probably still in Chandrapore.'

'That, too, is so apparent that it need hardly be said.'

'Then perhaps, rather than planning what deserved punishments should be meted out on Aggarwal, Your Majesty's time might be better employed in considering how to deal with treachery at home?'

Thousands of miles away from Claridge's, Prince Nagesh was caught up in a state of agitation quite as extreme as that being experienced by his sovereign. He, too, was pacing – though in the open air of the palace gardens, rather than within the confines of a hotel suite. And again like his cousin, he was not alone – for members of the blood royal rarely are – but was accompanied by one of his most trusted followers.'

'Are you sure that what the telegram claims is true?' he demanded. 'Is it certain that this money – this twenty thousand pounds – has been paid into my account?'

'Yes, Your Highness. I have made the bank officials check through the records three times. There can be no doubt about it.'

'But where would a child of the gutter like Aggarwal have ever managed to lay his hands on such a huge amount of money?'

'Perhaps he was working with the kidnappers, and it is his share of the ransom, Your Highness.'

Nagesh showed his contempt for the idea with an imperious wave of his hand. 'Aggarwal is nothing more than a flea who rides on the backs of those greater than himself. He can be useful, I will admit that – but does a flea organize anything as momentous as a kidnapping? Can a flea ever be important enough to his fellow conspirators to be rewarded with *twenty thousand pounds*? Of course he cannot.'

'Of course he cannot,' the courtier agreed dutifully.

'Yet the money must have come from somewhere.' The prince stopped pacing and froze. 'My poisonous cousin!' he said softly, after several seconds had elapsed.

'Your cousin? Is it the Maharaja you are referring to, Your Highness?'

'Of course it is the Maharaja.' Nagesh turned, and looked up at the balcony from which his poisonous cousin had so often gazed down on his subjects. 'Can you not see it? Do you not understand what must have happened? Of course not. You are superior to Aggarwal only by degree, in much the same way as one flea is bigger than another. Only *I* can see it – because I have the heart of a tiger and the mind of a true ruler.'

'It is true that you do indeed have those qualities, Your Highness, but *what* exactly is it that you can see?'

'Aggarwal never sent that money.'

'Did he not?'

'No! Or if he did, it was on the instructions of my cousin.'

'Your cousin wishes to give you twenty thousand pounds?'

'No, you fool! My cousin wishes to see me dead.'

'My poor brain is incapable of following your princely thoughts, Your Highness,' the courtier said. 'If you could make matters a little clearer for me, then perhaps I might be able to—'

'Aggarwal could never organize a kidnapping. That much is clear. But *I* could! And when others learn of the money which has been placed in my account, they will think that is exactly what I did. They will believe that I plotted to snatch my own half-cousin. And when the Maharaja says that I should die for such treachery, even those who have supported me to this point will be forced to agree.' The prince placed his hands on his forehead in a gesture of despair. 'You understand what this means? I am already as good as dead.'

The courtier twitched perceptibly, then gazed into the far distance, towards the road which led out of the state.

'If Your Highness will excuse me now, I have many tasks to complete on your behalf before this day is done,' he said.

'I am *dead*, unless . . . !'

'Unless?' repeated the courtier, abandoning – for the

moment – his plan to flee. 'Unless what, Your Highness?'

'Unless we can advance our own plans a little. We had already intended to seize the throne . . .'

'But only once the Maharaja was dead,' the courtier pointed out. 'Only after Aggarwal had poisoned him.'

'The important point is that I *intended* to take the throne,' the prince said. 'The method by which I planned to accomplish it is of secondary consideration only.'

'Perhaps, but that does not answer the problem of—'

'I cannot have my cousin poisoned, since he is not here. Very well, then, we must choose another way to go about advancing me to my rightful position. Can I rely on the support of the army?'

'Certainly part of it will support you,' the courtier said cautiously.

'The major part?'

'That is possible. We will not know the full extent of your support until you declare yourself.'

'Then that is what I will do.'

'Are you sure, Your Highness?'

'I have three choices,' the prince said. 'The first is stay here, doing nothing, until my cousin decides to murder me. The second is to run away and live the rest of my life in poverty. The third is to stake everything on the success of a sudden revolt. For a man like me – a *prince* like me – that is really no choice at all. I must make my move while I still have some chance of succeeding.'

'I am sure that is a wise decision, as all your decisions are wise, Your Highness,' the courtier said, wondering which of the choices he himself was now faced with was the one he should take.

Forty

Dawn broke to uncover a sky already filled with heavy, menacing clouds. A tram rattled by the corner of Baker Street and Portland Square, packed with workmen from south of the river, taking them to the areas where they toiled for twelve hours a day but still could not afford to live. Half a dozen hansom cabs clip-clopped past the same spot, their passengers mainly pampered late-night revellers returning to their soft feather beds in style. A little further up the street, a pair of beggars, having crawled out of whatever shelter they had found for the hours of darkness, walked slowly towards a stall selling cheap, foul coffee. The city was awakening, but as yet there was no sign of any movement from the second-floor apartment.

Blackstone, standing on the pavement below, nodded to a passing police constable of his acquaintance. There was still time to call for reinforcements, he told himself. He did not *have* to run the risk of dealing with this highly dangerous man alone.

Looking up again, Blackstone saw the blinds of the second-floor apartment being drawn back, and a round-faced servant girl peering out on to the street.

Still time, he repeated silently. Still lots of time.

Yet he knew – as he had known ever since his moment of revelation in the Crown and Anchor – that he would *not* call for support. Wouldn't call for it because support would only guarantee him the capture of his man – and what he wanted most in the world was the rescue of the child.

Ten minutes went by. The front door of the house opened, and Major Walsh stepped out on to the pavement. He could have easily spotted the waiting policeman if he had been looking – but he was not.

Walsh looked rough, Blackstone thought. Yet it was not

the kind of roughness brought on by drinking an excess of alcohol. No, this was entirely different. It was a roughness which came from lying awake, tossing and turning as the questions and doubts raged. It was the roughness of a man who has been forced to wrestle with his own conscience – perhaps, even, with his very soul.

Walsh turned left and began walking up Baker Street towards Marylebone Road. But he did not go far. The public house which lay closest to his apartment had just opened its doors, and the Major, without a moment's hesitation, stepped inside.

Blackstone counted off two minutes in his head, and then followed. Walsh was sitting at a table. He had a large whisky in front of him, and a second glass, now empty, standing next to it. He was not watching the door of the bar, which was what a man in his difficult and dangerous position certainly should have been doing. Instead, he was gazing at a fixed spot on the smoke-stained wall, as if he expected the answer to all his problems to suddenly and miraculously appear there like an image of the Virgin Mary.

Blackstone sat down opposite him, but even then the Major did not notice until the Inspector coughed loudly.

'Wha . . . ?' Walsh began.

'I have a pistol in my jacket pocket, and it's pointing straight at you,' Blackstone said in a low voice. 'If you make even the slightest threatening move, I'll shoot your balls off.'

'You've got it all wrong!' Walsh protested.

'Have I?' Blackstone asked. 'Do you deny that you've played a part in this kidnapping from the very beginning?'

'No, but—'

'It puzzled me how the gang always seemed to be one step ahead of me,' Blackstone said. 'It doesn't puzzle me any longer.'

'I—'

'Let's consider the facts. I go to see Colonel Howarth, and come away with the strong suspicion that he's got something to hide. I tell you of my suspicions – and a few hours later the Colonel is dead. Now how could that have happened? You told me you'd had no contact with him since your time in India, but that was a lie, wasn't it?'

'Yes, it was.'

'You paid a call on him a few weeks ago. You went in the middle of the night, to make sure no one else would see you. But the butler knew *someone* had been, because of the smell of cheap cigars. Or should I say, "cheroots"? *Your* cheroots! You didn't want him to recognize the same smell again. That's why you pretended to misplace your cheroots when you and I visited Amritsar Lodge together.'

'Quite correct,' Walsh agreed.

'Then there was the question of the ransom. The kidnappers asked for a hundred thousand pounds, but they knew Aggarwal had told the Maharaja they wanted more. And how can I be so sure that they knew? Because even before Aggarwal delivered the ransom to them, they had that extra twenty thousand earmarked to stir up mischief in Chandrapore. So *how* did they know? They knew because someone had told them – and that someone could only have been you!'

'It would be foolish of me to deny it,' Walsh said.

'On top of that, we have General Pugh,' Blackstone continued. 'You held his scent under my nose and set me on his trail. That was risky, because once I realized that the scent was *false* – that he was more a hound than a fox – I began to wonder why you'd laid it.'

'I knew I was taking a chance there,' Walsh admitted, 'but I was worried that you were getting too close. I thought that pursuing Pugh might keep you busy for a couple of days – and a couple of days was all we needed.'

'Pugh set me off on a fresh trail, though he didn't even know he was doing it. After he described his visit to Colonel Howarth, I began to wonder why Howarth should have been so pathetically eager to know if Pugh thought a professional secret service was necessary. And there could be only one answer, couldn't there? It was because *necessity* was the only way he could find to justify the kidnappings and murders to himself. The bulk of the money was never intended for Chandrapore, was it? It's to be used to set up your own private secret service!'

'We've needed one for a long time,' Walsh said. 'We've lost thousands of lives through *not* having one.'

'So I'd built up a pretty clear picture of what was going on by this point,' Blackstone continued. 'But the real clincher, if I'd needed one, was the elephant.'

'The elephant?'

'I wondered where the Maharaja got the idea of bringing the elephant to London. I talked to him late last night, and he said it was as the result of a suggestion made by one of his British advisers. You were that adviser! You claimed that if he wished to make an impact in London – if he wanted to make an impression on the Queen – then he'd have to use a little showmanship. But it wasn't *his* show you were planning to stage, was it? It was your own – because you'd already mapped out the little scene between the elephant and the tiger in your mind.'

'And do you know *why* we staged it?' Walsh asked.

'I can guess. You realized that you needed more than just money to run your new secret service. For it to operate successfully, you need some hot-blooded young men who are willing to risk their lives in hostile territory. And what's the best way to attract that kind of man? Launch your enterprise with something brave and daring – something like the spectacular you arranged on Regent Street! The kidnapping was no more or less than the parade which announced that the circus was coming to town and was looking for recruits.'

'You don't need to keep pointing that gun at me,' Walsh said.

'Don't I?'

'No, you don't. I want to help you. I was on my way to Scotland Yard when you caught up with me.'

'You were in this *pub* when I caught up with you'.

'I was only intending to have the one drink.' Walsh glanced down at the empty glass. 'These two drinks,' he corrected himself. 'I needed to give myself a little courage. But I swear to you that I intended to find you immediately after that.'

'Of course you did,' Blackstone agreed. 'And I'm having a secret affair with the Queen.'

'It's true,' Walsh told him. 'I've no faith in a private secret service any more. I really believed it could work – but what happened yesterday has proved to me that it won't.'

'How very convenient for you to have come round to that way of thinking now I've got a gun on you.'

'Listen!' Walsh replied fiercely. 'Listen and learn. The soldier obeys the orders of his officer, the officer obeys the commander, the commander obeys the Viceroy and the Viceroy obeys the government. Sometimes the wrong decisions are taken, but at least there is consultation – and though the government often restrains the Army, the Army has at least the *possibility* of restraining the government. But there will be no one to restrain this new service! No one! It might work, if it were run by a man who was both unerringly wise and unquestionably saintly, but in the whole of history I can think of only one such man – and he was crucified.' The Major paused to light a cheroot with trembling hands. 'It needs a messiah to run it, and since it will never find one, any good it might do will inevitably be accompanied by a much greater harm.'

'A very pretty speech,' Blackstone said, unmoved. 'But in my experience, overnight conversions are a very rare thing. If you're to convince me that yours is genuine, you're going to have to come up with a pretty strong reason for it.'

'The original plan was that, once the operation was over, the young prince would be placed in my custody,' Walsh said.

'And you'd hand him over to the Maharaja?'

'Placed in my custody,' Walsh repeated, evading the question. '*Now* the plan has been changed. *Now* they intend to kill the prince. That cannot be allowed to happen. Someone must rescue him. But such an act cannot be accomplished by an army.'

'Why not?'

'Once his captors know they are under siege, they'll kill the prince.'

'You're sure of that?'

'They planned to do it anyway. And what have they got to lose? If they are captured, they'll be hanged for what they've already done. That is not a soldier's way – and whatever else you might think of them, these men are very good soldiers. They will not allow themselves to be taken – they will go down fighting.'

'You have an alternative plan?'

'The only chance of rescuing the prince alive is to take his captors by surprise. Such a feat can only be accomplished if it is left in the hands of two or three determined men. I've spent a sleepless night wondering whom I should ask to accompany me – whom I could trust on such a delicate and dangerous mission – and, in the end, yours was the only name I could come up with.'

'So you're asking me to risk my life?'

'I'm asking you to do your *duty* – and from what I've seen of you, I believe that if you fail in that, your life would have no purpose anyway.'

'Since the moment we met, you've done nothing but lie to me and try to divert me from my purpose,' Blackstone said. 'Can you give me one good reason why I should start to trust you now?'

'Yes, I believe that I can,' Walsh replied. 'I believe I can give you a very good reason. Put your hands on the table.'

'Why should I do that?'

'Because I wish to perform a demonstration, and I cannot complete it unless you do as I ask.'

He'd be a fool to trust Walsh, Blackstone thought. Yet what alternative did he have? If he arrested the Major now, his superiors would be bound to want to question him. Once they *had* questioned him, they'd undoubtedly order a storming of the place where the prince was being held. And the little boy would die!

Blackstone released his grip on his pistol and placed his hands on the table. 'I'm ready for your demonstration,' he said. 'But I'm not big on palm reading, so if that's what you're planning, you're wasting your time.'

Walsh leant forward slightly, and Blackstone felt something hard suddenly press against his knee.

'That's a gun, isn't it?' the Inspector asked.

'Yes,' Walsh agreed.

Blackstone sighed fatalistically. 'It's a curse,' he said.

'What is?'

'Allowing myself to sometimes believe the best in people. Thinking that they're always capable of changing. Falling for a convincing tale. And you do tell a convincing tale, you know.'

'It took me a long time to realize that courage and honour are not enough,' Walsh said. 'A long time before I came to understand that deviousness is as much a part of a soldier's equipment as his trusty sword. Perhaps I'm the lesser man for having learned it, but it has certainly made me more effective.'

'So what happens now?' Blackstone asked. 'You're not going to shoot me where I sit, are you?'

'No. I'm not going to do that.'

'No, of course you're not. Killing a copper in such a public place would cause too much of a stir at this delicate stage in your operation. So what *does* happen?'

'When I give the command, you will rise from your seat. You will do so slowly, and with no sudden movements. Then you will walk towards the door. I will be right behind you at all times.'

'And let me guess where you'll be taking me,' Blackstone said. 'We'll be going to your headquarters – the place where the head of your operation is based, and where you're holding the prince.'

'Yes.'

'And what will happen when we get there?'

'That,' said Walsh ominously, 'will depend entirely on you.'

Forty-One

A sentry's place was out in the open, Brown thought, as he gazed morosely down the hallway at the inside of the front door. Out in the open – ready and willing to face whatever the enemy chose to throw at him. True, he also made himself a target in such a position. But what of that?

'They also serve who only stand and die!' he said softly to himself.

The crack of a rifle, the dying scream, the last weak battering on the door – these were all alarm signals for his comrades of an enemy attack, and if a man had to lose his life doing his duty, then there were worse ways to go.

Yet though his desire was to be on the outside – dressed in the uniform he had so often risked his life for in the past – he more than willingly obeyed the General's newest order to remain indoors, both because it *was* an order and because he could see the sense in it. This was no normal operation fought in any normal war, he reminded himself. War had not even been *declared*, and it was possible that some of the enemy were still unaware that they were involved in it.

He heard the knock on the front door – two rapid taps, a pause, three slower ones, another pause, and a final dull thud which reminded him of a nail being hammered into a coffin. He wished he had his rifle – a man's weapon, a soldier's weapon – but the General had decreed that on this mission they should all be issued with pistols, and that was what he reached for now.

Brown stepped closer to the front door. 'Who's there?'

'White!'

White? Major Walsh? Why the bloody hell was he back again?

'I'm not sure I can let you in, sir,' Brown said.

'You *have* to let me in. I've got a prisoner with me.'

There shouldn't be prisoners, Brown thought. Not at this stage.

'I'll have to get further instructions,' he said.

'The longer we're here, the more the danger we'll be spotted,' Walsh replied, with an edge of urgency to his voice. 'Do you *want* everything to go wrong at this late stage?'

'No, sir, I—'

'Then open the bloody door!'

Brown slid the catch, then took three steps back, his pistol pointing squarely at any target which might appear in the doorway.

'You can come in now,' he said.

The door opened. A tall, thin man entered first. There was a bruise on his cheek which was already turning purple, and specks of dried blood around the corners of his mouth. Following the stranger was Major Walsh, and Brown could tell by the position of his arm that he was holding a gun in his hand.

Once the two of them were inside the house, Walsh closed the door behind him with the heel of his boot.

'This is Inspector Blackstone of Scotland Yard,' the Major said. 'He's a very dangerous man. I've brought him to see Mr Jones. Keep your weapon trained on him at all times.'

'I'm not sure that Mr Jones will want to—' Brown began.

'Listen to me, my good man,' Blackstone interrupted. 'Major Walsh is a criminal, and you could get into serious trouble for assisting him. My advice to you is to tell him to drop his pistol.'

Brown instinctively squared his shoulders. 'I don't take advice from civilians,' he said contemptuously. He risked a quick glance at Walsh. 'This way, if you please, sir.'

General Harcourt was sitting behind a battered oak desk, smoking a cigar and looking aghast at the new arrivals.

'What's the meaning of this, Walsh?' he barked. 'Don't you realize how dangerous it is to bring this man here?'

Walsh shrugged apologetically. 'I had no choice, General. He tried to arrest me.'

'So why didn't you just kill him?'

'Because if he knew enough to arrest me, there's no telling what else he knows. I thought you might welcome the chance to discover just how much of a danger he is to the operation.'

Somewhat pacified, Harcourt nodded. 'You're quite right,' he agreed. 'Whatever the risk, we must know what the enemy is thinking.' He reached into his desk drawer, pulled out a revolver and pointed it at Blackstone's chest. 'Holster your weapon and search the prisoner, Brown.'

Brown ran his hands expertly up and down Blackstone's body. 'He's clean,' he pronounced.

Harcourt nodded again. 'Good. Now tell us what you know, Inspector.'

'If you think I'm going to say anything to help murderous scum like you, you're mistaken,' Blackstone said.

The General flushed angrily. 'If you were still in the Army, I could have you flogged for speaking to me like that!'

'But I'm not in the Army,' Blackstone countered. 'And thank God for that. I wouldn't want to serve in any army which had men like *you* in charge.'

A sudden look of understanding appeared on the General's face and his anger drained away.

'I see what you're doing,' he said. 'You want to provoke me into killing you now, because you feel – quite rightly – that a quick death would be preferable to what fate actually has in store for you. Well, that is not going to happen, Inspector. First, you tell us what you know, then we kill you.'

'Doesn't it turn your stomach working for trash like this?' Blackstone asked Walsh.

The slap Walsh delivered in response was so hard that it almost knocked Blackstone off his feet.

'Don't you dare refer to a great patriot in such a way!' the Major screamed. 'Don't you dare!'

The General laughed. 'I appreciate your loyalty, Major, but it isn't necessary. We will not play the Inspector's games.

206

Rather we will let him see how he feels after he's played ours for a while.' He turned to Brown. 'I think it's time we all went down to the cellar.'

The steps which led down to the cellar were slippery from the dampness which seeped in through the walls. The air was filled with the dank stink of the Thames and of the sewers which fed into it. At the foot of the steps was a solid iron door, which would have daunted even the sappers of the Royal Engineers.

'The cellar is quite sound-proofed from above,' Harcourt told Blackstone. 'No one will hear you when you scream.'

He knocked on the door. The spy-hole opened first, then there was the sound of heavy bolts been drawn back. The door swung open.

'Inside,' the General ordered Blackstone. 'And you, Brown, can return to your post.'

The cellar was a square room, lit by three oil lamps which filled the atmosphere with eye-stinging fumes. There was a table and chairs at one end of it, and three camp beds at the other. Four soldiers – big, battle-hardened men – stood looking expectantly at the General.

'I've brought you something to keep you amused,' Harcourt said. 'You still have your tools, don't you, Scarlet?'

The man he'd called Scarlet grinned, revealing that his mouth was missing several teeth. 'They're in the canvas bag on the table, sir.'

'Excellent.'

Walsh had been looking desperately around the room. Now he said, 'Where's the prince?'

'The what?' Harcourt asked.

'The . . . the little nigger,' Walsh corrected himself. 'I don't see him.'

'Then you haven't been looking hard enough, have you?' Harcourt asked. 'He's in there.'

He pointed his thumb in the direction of the far wall, at a low arched recess which might once have been a fireplace or perhaps the start of a now-defunct tunnel. Now he knew where to look, Walsh could see what appeared to be a bundle of rags heaped in it.

'He's not . . . dead . . . is he?' the Major asked.

'No, not yet,' Harcourt replied. 'We just keep him there so he won't contaminate the rest of us.' Up until that moment his pistol had pointed squarely at Blackstone, but now he took a step backwards and aimed it at Walsh. 'I think I'm going to have to relieve you of your weapon, Major,' he said. 'Pull it out slowly, with your left hand, and hold it out so that Orange can take it off you.'

'Is this some kind of joke, sir?' Walsh asked.

'I'm afraid not.'

'But what have I done? Why are you deliberately humiliating me in front of the men?'

'I have no choice,' Harcourt replied regretfully. 'I don't know why you're acting so strangely, but I do know that I can't afford to trust you any more.'

'You're making a mistake,' Walsh protested.

'Perhaps I am,' the General agreed. 'And *if* I am, you will be entitled to a full apology in the course of time. In the meantime, Major, I would be happier if Orange took your pistol.'

'As you wish,' Walsh said.

He removed the weapon as he'd been instructed, and held it out to the soldier Harcourt had called Orange. Orange took the weapon, and, at a nod from the General, placed it on the table.

Harcourt holstered his own pistol. 'Now we can begin,' he said. He walked over to the table himself, and sat at its head with Walsh's gun in front of him. 'Now where should Inspector Blackstone sit?' he mused. 'I think, perhaps, at other end of the table might be most appropriate. That way, I can assess his reaction to Scarlet's questions.' He gestured to Blackstone. 'So if you wouldn't mind, Inspector . . . ?'

Blackstone crossed the room and sat in the chair. A sudden change had come over the General, he noted. Harcourt had started to sweat, and his lower lip was beginning to wobble. Some men got into this state at the prospect of sex, but in his case it was the thought of inflicting pain which had driven him into what was almost a trance.

'You may begin, Scarlet,' the General said, with a slight quiver of anticipation in his voice.

Orange and the other two soldiers were standing well back, but keeping a close watch on both Blackstone and Walsh. Scarlet stepped up to the table, opened his canvas bag and took out a coil of thin copper wire.

For tying the hands together, Blackstone thought. No more effective than cord or rope would have been – but one hell of a lot more painful.

Scarlet reached into the bag again, and produced a pair of pliers. He held them up to make sure Blackstone got a good look at them.

'Sergeant Brown is the acknowledged master of extracting information,' Harcourt said, 'but Private Scarlet has been a most promising apprentice.'

Scarlet grinned at the compliment, put down the pliers and picked up the copper wire.

In another few seconds the wire would be wrapped around his wrist and starting to cut its way through to the bone, Blackstone thought. If there was ever a time to make his move, that time was now.

Forty-Two

Under any circumstances, the odds would not have been good, Blackstone thought – but this was just about as bad as it could have been. Harcourt had a pistol sitting just inches in front of him on the table, and could call on the support of four hardened street fighters. And what did he have? One secret weapon – and the element of surprise! No punter in the world would have risked backing him.

Scarlet picked up the copper wire, but made no move to use it. Harcourt had been right about him – he was very good at his job. He knew, as all good torturers did, that there was more to his work than merely inflicting physical pain – that sometimes the *anticipation* of pain could break a man more quickly than any bodily hurt.

'There's . . . there's no need for this,' Blackstone gasped.

Harcourt smiled. 'Isn't there?'

'No need at all. I'll tell you everything you want to know.'

'So you're not quite as tough as you like to pretend, are you?'

Blackstone licked his lips. 'You don't know what it's like. Nobody can until they're sitting where I am.'

'The problem is, you still think there's an easy way out,' Harcourt explained. 'And as long as you think that, you'll hold something back from us.'

'I won't,' Blackstone promised. 'Believe me – please!'

Nothing he could have said would have given Harcourt more satisfaction, and as a man will when he is approaching orgasm, he began to drop his guard.

The General turned to face his henchmen. 'Pathetic, isn't it?' he asked.

He was not the only one to be infected by complacency. Scarlet had allowed himself to get close to his prisoner – far too close. Blackstone lashed out with his right leg, aiming for Scarlet's knee and feeling a satisfactory crunch as the heel of his boot made contact with it.

Scarlet screamed as his leg began to buckle beneath him. Then he was gone – rolling around in agony on the floor.

Harcourt made a grab for the pistol. He had a clean line of fire, and should have used it. But he didn't. He caught a sudden movement in the corner of his eye, and turned just in time to see one of his men double over as Walsh sank his Khyber knife into the soldier's stomach.

The General was distracted for no more than a second, but that was all the time Blackstone needed. Springing from his chair, the Inspector picked up the pliers and smashed them into Harcourt's face with all the force he could muster.

Harcourt's head whipped back. His mouth filled with

blood, and his windpipe sucked in broken teeth. He dropped the gun on to the table, and made a frantic grab for his own throat.

Blackstone reached for the pistol. He almost made it. Then he felt a great weight slam into him, and he was falling forward. He crashed into the table. It groaned and splintered, and then collapsed. Blackstone – and the man on his back – hit the floor with a heavy thud.

The fall drove the wind out of Blackstone's lungs, but there was no time for recovery – no time even to register the pain – before Orange had rolled him over, straddled his chest, and was attempting to choke the life out of him.

The soldier had powerful hands and a lust to destroy. As he squeezed ever harder, dark spots started to appear before Blackstone's eyes.

The longer he allowed this to continue, some small still-functioning corner of the Inspector's brain told him, the weaker he would become. He could already feel his strength ebbing away. Unconsciousness could not be too distant. With his right hand, he groped on the floor and felt his fingers make contact with the pliers.

A little more coughing – a little more gasping for air – and Blackstone had the pliers firmly in his hand. But he couldn't use them as he had used them on Harcourt – not from this position. It wouldn't work. It . . . simply . . . wouldn't work.

The dark spots were coming thicker and faster now, and there were whole moments when Orange's face was no more than a black circle. The Inspector raised his arm a little, and felt a thousand red-hot needles bite their way into it.

How much easier it would be to submit, he thought. To just lie there and allow death to come all the quicker.

He had the pliers open. He aimed them at where he hoped Orange's nose was, and when he closed them again, he felt them clamp on to something solid.

That was good. Very good. If he could only summon up one last reserve of strength . . .

He twisted the pliers. Orange's scream was loud enough

to shatter his eardrums, yet even so, he could still hear the sound of bone groaning and then splintering. Orange's hands went slack. Blackstone gave the pliers a couple of extra twists for good measure, and then pushed the soldier off him.

Orange rolled around the floor, moaning and holding his hands up to protect what little there was left to protect. Harcourt was slumped in his chair, a small waterfall of blood gently trickling down his chin. Scarlet was attempting to rise to his feet, but when the full force of Blackstone's boot struck him squarely in the face, he soon lost interest in any further movement.

Blackstone whirled round to face any fresh enemies – but there were none. Walsh's Khyber knife had done its work, and the other two soldiers lay sprawled on the floor.

The Major himself was bending over the alcove, pulling clear the bundle of rags, and cradling it in his arms.

'Balachandra,' he cooed softly. 'Balachandra, my sweet boy. Are you all right?'

Across the room, the second of the soldiers whom Walsh had stabbed stirred slightly. He was dying, and he knew it. But he was not dead yet, and before he fell into final oblivion he had one last chance to do his duty. Walsh's pistol was lying on the floor. If he could just reach it . . .

Slowly and agonizingly, he forced his hand to crawl towards it.

Blackstone noticed none of the dying soldier's movement. His mind was elsewhere. He knew now why Walsh drank so much! He understood that there had been other motives – aside from the desire to finance a secret service – which had drawn him into the plot! He could see why Walsh had cast aside all his previous loyalties as if they meant nothing to him!

'Speak to me, Balachandra,' Walsh pleaded. 'Say something! Anything!'

'Wal-ish,' the boy said softly and plaintively. 'Wal-ish.'

'Oh, thank God,' the Major gasped, hugging him tightly.

The dying soldier had the gun in his hand. Though it hurt

him more than he could ever have imagined, he wrapped his finger around the trigger, aimed and fired.

The explosion reverberated around the room like the roar of an angry god. Blackstone swung around to meet this new danger. But there *was* no danger any longer – the soldier had given his all to this final act of destruction, and now his throat was filled with the sound of a death rattle.

Walsh stood stiffly for a moment, then gently lowered the boy to the ground. That done, he collapsed in a heap beside him.

Blackstone knelt down beside the fallen Major. 'How bad as it?'

'I'm finished,' Walsh croaked. 'But that doesn't matter as long as the prince is safe.'

'As long as your *son* is safe, you mean,' Blackstone corrected him.

'My mission was to find a wife for the Maharaja,' Walsh said. 'I never intended to fall in love with her, nor she with me. When we learned she was pregnant, I wanted us to run away, but she wouldn't. She said it was her duty to stay and . . .' A cough racked the Major's body, and he spat blood. 'She died,' he gasped. 'Died giving birth to my child. He was all I had left of her.'

'And you hoped that when this was all over, you could finally have him with you.'

'Who has first call on our devotion?' Walsh asked. 'Our country? Or our flesh and blood? I have done many foolish things in my time, but in this, at least, I made the right choice. Whatever they may say later of me, I know I made the right choice.'

'Rest now,' Blackstone urged.

But he was talking to a dead man.

Forty-Three

Blackstone sat on one side of the Metropolitan Commissioner of Police's desk, the Commissioner himself and Sir Horace Fullerton-Smythe of the India Office on the other.

'You are here because Her Majesty's Government, in gratitude for what you have done, has decided to explain to you the probable consequences of your own actions and the actions of others which may follow them,' Fullerton-Smythe said to Blackstone. 'But the privilege of hearing the truth does not carry with it the right to impart that same truth to anyone else, once you have left this office. Do you understand what I'm saying?'

Of course I understand, Blackstone thought. I'm not here because of any service I've done the state – I'm here because the best way to silence a man about one conspiracy is to draw him into another one.

'I asked you if you understood,' Fullerton-Smythe said sharply.

'Yes, sir. I get the picture.'

'Very well, then, let us begin. The story which the newspapers will carry is as follows: there was a revolt in Chandrapore, which was led by Prince Nagesh. The Maharaja, as a loyal subject of the British crown, asked our forces to intervene. In the course of the fighting which followed, Prince Nagesh was killed.'

'Was he?' Blackstone asked.

'He may well have been. If not, that will most certainly be the case by the time the fighting is over.'

'So the Maharaja's back in favour?'

'He was never *out* of favour as far as Her Majesty's Government was concerned. He may have been a little awkward at times – most of these nigger princes are – but

214

we always knew that we could control him. Now, of course, we are doubly sure of that. There is no question but that he owes his throne to us. And he knows that without our help, his son and heir would undoubtedly be dead.'

'So you think he'll behave himself from now on?'

'Undoubtedly. Especially since his son will stay in England in order to continue his education. Our plan is to enrol him in a good private school as soon as possible. From there he will attend Eton, and, in course of time, no doubt will train at the Sandhurst Military Academy.'

'Is that the Maharaja's wish? Or just the British government's?'

'I would not say that the Maharaja is wholly enthusiastic about the scheme, but he certainly sees the necessity of it.'

So the boy would remain a hostage, Blackstone thought, though his captor would now be the British government instead of a group of rogue army officers. Still, if Walsh had knowledge of what went on from beyond the grave, he would no doubt be delighted that his son was to be brought up as an English gentleman.

'Will I be responsible for collecting the additional evidence necessary for the trial of General Harcourt and his men?' he asked.

Fullerton-Smythe looked a little uncomfortable. 'There will be no trial for the common soldiers. Those whom you and Walsh failed to kill at the time have since died of their wounds.'

Have since *died*, anyway, Blackstone thought.

But he felt no pity for them. They had mercilessly butchered one child and one policeman, and would have killed the prince if they'd had the chance.

'What about Harcourt?' he asked. 'Has he "died of his wounds" as well?'

'No.'

'So he *will* be put on trial?'

'Again, no. If he were tried, he would undoubtedly be found guilty and hanged. And we can't have generals being hung in this country, you know.'

Blackstone felt a rage begin to build up inside him.

'Harcourt bears more responsibility than the rest of them combined,' he said. 'I demand that he be made to pay for his crimes.'

'You are not in a position to demand *anything*, Blackstone,' the Commissioner said sternly.

'But you need have no worries on that score,' Fullerton-Smythe said smoothly. 'As part of the deal we have struck with the Maharaja, the General will be seconded to the court of Chandrapore. He will travel back to India on the same ship as the Maharaja's party. It is more than possible that he will contract a fever and die before the ship ever docks. You may rest assured that the illness will be far more punishing than death by hanging could ever have been.'

'And the other officers?'

'Which other officers?'

'Those in India who were part of the plot. What will happen to them?'

'There is no blood on their hands,' Fullerton-Smythe said.

'No blood!'

'At least, not directly. The more senior officers involved will be encouraged to resign their commissions immediately. The more junior officers, seeing the way the wind is blowing, will no doubt soon follow them. And that, I think, concludes our business.'

'Not quite,' Blackstone said. 'I want Walsh to be awarded a posthumous medal.'

'You want *what*?' the Commissioner exploded.

'I want him given a medal,' Blackstone repeated calmly. 'He did some pretty awful things, but as I see it, he paid for his crimes with a hero's death. I think that should be recognized.'

'I'm afraid it won't be possible,' Fullerton-Smythe said.

'Most things are possible if you really put your mind to it, sir,' Blackstone replied. 'For instance, it's possible to use Prince Balachandra as leverage – but only as long as the Maharaja believes the boy to be his natural son.'

'But why *shouldn't* he believe it?' Fullerton-Smythe asked. 'It's the truth, isn't it?'

'Is that a question you really want to ask me, sir?' Blackstone wondered. 'Are you *quite* sure you wouldn't find my answer inconvenient?'

'That sound suspiciously like blackmail,' Fullerton-Smythe said, finally grasping the point.

'I didn't intend it to, sir. I merely meant that if Major Walsh got the medal he deserves, I could finally put him out of my mind.'

Fullerton-Smythe nodded. 'Walsh will get his medal,' he conceded.

'You walk a very fine line, Blackstone,' the Commissioner said, 'and one day you're going to lose your balance.'

'I know, sir,' Blackstone agreed. 'It's a constant source of worry to me.' He turned his attention back to the man from the India Office. 'Could I ask you one more thing before I'm dismissed?'

'What is it?' Fullerton-Smythe asked irritably.

'Bearing in mind that the conspirators felt strongly enough about the need for a military intelligence service to risk – and lose – their own lives in the pursuit of it, might it not be worth the government's while to consider the possibility that we actually *do* need such a service?'

'Now that really *is* out the question,' Fullerton-Smythe said.

'Funnily enough, I thought you'd say that,' Blackstone told him.

Author's Note

It was to be another eleven years before fears of German espionage activity in British naval ports led to the founding of the Secret Service Bureau – the forerunner of the modern intelligence services. Even then, it was established in a half-hearted, amateur manner. Though the bureau, headed by Captain Vernon Kell, did a truly amazing job and was responsible for the arrest of thirty German spies between 1909 and 1914, it only had a staff of ten – and that included the director himself and his secretary.